CW00339036

SIX FEET UNDER

SIX FEET UNDER

Howard Hodgson

The Book Guild Ltd
Sussex, England

This book is a work of fiction. The characters and situations in this story are imaginary. No resemblance is intended between these characters and any real persons, either living or dead.

This book is sold subject to the condition that it shall not, by way of trade or otherwise, be lent, re-sold, hired out, photocopied or held in any retrieval system or otherwise circulated without the publisher's prior consent in any form of binding or cover other than that in which this is published and without a similar condition including this condition being imposed on the subsequent purchaser.

The Book Guild Ltd,
25 High Street,
Lewes, Sussex

First published 2000
© Howard Hodgson 2000

Set in Bembo
Typesetting by IML Typographers, Chester, Cheshire
Printed in Great Britain by
Bookcraft (Bath) Ltd, Avon

A catalogue record for this book is
available from the British Library

ISBN 1 85776 515 X

ACKNOWLEDGEMENT

Endless acknowledgements are a bore for the reader. However, it would be inappropriate not to recognise the selfless contributions of Chris Callaway, Graham Stuart, Eldine Wilson, Moira Spain, Victoria Worgan, Marianne Hodgson, Shirley Woolley, Peggy Vance, Tony Mulliken, Katie Martin-Doyle, Carol Biss and my long suffering and beautiful wife Christine. Thank you.

In addition, I am bound to acknowledge the people of Birmingham, in general, and the folk of funerals, in particular, who during my childhood and early adult life gave me the background which made the writing of *Six Feet Under* possible.

In Memory of Arthur Sloane

White Swans and Silver Geese

And in that minute when you decide to go,
exactly where, only you know,
where to go.
Now I need to know,
or I'll miss you so.

White swans and silver geese,
now where do I find the peace?
White swans and silver geese,
they just gently glide across the sky
and just like life they pass you by.
And I've seen it all before,
couldn't take it anymore.
Don't you go!
Not now,
until I know,
where to go.

Stillion Sloane 1977

THE PROLOGUE

It was Sunday, the second Sunday of December 1979, and the first day of a week that would become famous for its funeral wars. The weather was cold. It had snowed heavily at the turn of the month and it had been cold enough since to freeze the snow in place. The parks, the golf courses, the playing fields and the cemeteries remained white, while along the busy streets and major roads of dirty North Birmingham black slush heaped into frozen gritted pyramids.

The weather was bleak but the economic climate was worse. Birmingham had entered the century as the second city of England, the head of the world's largest empire, and had been famous across the globe as 'the workshop of the world'. In all four corners of the planet one might find guns, jewellery, bicycles, automobiles, production machinery and every kind of component or spare part boasting 'Made in Birmingham'. But the cost of two world wars left Britain vulnerable. Low investment, the distractions of the Swinging Sixties and the trades unions' strong grip had made the economy weak and morale low. 'Unity', the watchword of both Labour and Conservative governments since the war, had meant in reality that for thirty years the private sector had been forced to fight government and unions with one hand tied behind its back. Defunct industries were kept artificially alive and industrial peace was bought at any price, with taxpayers' money. Britain was the sick economic state of Europe, its industry dominated by poor productivity, strikes, demands for tea breaks and higher wages. Competition from Germany, Japan, France and Italy had Britain on the ropes.

On that Sunday in December 1979 the revolution which would turn Britain into one of the most successful economies in Europe over the next two decades had only just begun. Just seven months earlier, in May 1979, Britain had decided to swallow the bitter pill prescribed by Margaret Hilda Thatcher. Like many tough cures things have to get worse before they get better and so far the country – and the industrial West Midlands in particular – had felt pain and little gain. Even Birmingham, dull but steadily successful, was finding it tough. Rising interest rates made business and domestic funding expensive and led to a strong pound, which hurt exports. Thatcher had removed many of the artificial economic supports, but the unions were by no means beaten. Unemployment was rising fast and the inner areas of cities like Birmingham, after years of neglect in favour of commercial and residential developments at cheaper, out-of-town sites, were falling apart, the largely immigrant residents angry and losing hope, especially young Afro-Caribbeans who believed that they had been placed at the back of every queue.

Bad times. At such times communities look to their leaders. But Birmingham was suddenly short of leaders when it needed them.

* * *

John David Edward Martin, OBE, perhaps Birmingham's most famous local government politician since Joseph Chamberlain, was old even beyond his seventy-nine years. Having led the Conservatives in the Town Hall from the end of the Second World War until his seventy-fifth birthday, he was now frail and living by his own request at Old Soldiers' Park, a home for senior citizens. He was tired. Throughout the sixties and seventies he had battled with the Labour governments of Harold Wilson and James Callaghan as they set about robbing Birmingham of its successes to give to Liverpool, safe in the assumption that Birmingham would make it again and that Liverpool would probably lose it again. At seventy-six Councillor Martin had been chosen Lord Mayor of Birmingham and on his retirement he had been awarded the Order of the British Empire. He had left a huge hole behind him. A larger-than-life true blue Brummie hero, he had been adored by the Tories and respected – sometimes even supported – by Labour and the Liberals in his great battles with Westminster in defence of Birmingham.

Councillor Martin, his body and brain worn out, was no more than a forgetful, withered man, struggling to make the lavatory in time. His family, like him, hoped his time would now be short and that, his work done, he may be allowed to fall into everlasting sleep with his dignity intact, leaving a city full of gratitude and with fond memories of a great man.

* * *

In the Intensive Care Unit of the District Hospital lay Charles Nelson Griffiths. He was just fifty-four. Charles Griffiths had arrived in England in early 1952 from Jamaica, with his young wife Ellen and his unmarried elder brother Thomas. Like many of the wave of immigrants from Commonwealth countries who came to Britain in the thirty years after the Second World War, he came in search of work. And he, like others, had looked to the major industrial cities to provide it. He had chosen Birmingham and taken a job at Joseph Lucas in Hockley. His wife had become a nurse at Dudley Road Hospital. Thomas, on the other hand, had found it hard to hold down a job.

In 1952 Charles Nelson Griffiths had been one of a few; by 1962 he had become the leader of many. A senior foreman at Lucas, he had become a staunch member of the West Indian Baptist Church at Lozells and the leader of the West Indian Federation. He had fought against racism and for the interests of his countrymen, but he had also fought against crime and for law and order. He had become one of the most important figures in the communities of Hockley, Handsworth, Lozells, Aston and Winson Green. His fight against drugs had been admired by all except the pushers and those out to buy a short-lived good time. His twenty-five years of hard work for the city had been recognised in 1977, the year of the Queen's Jubilee, when he had been made a Member of the Order of the British Empire. He'd proudly taken his wife to Buckingham Palace for the presentation and had wished his aged parents back in Jamaica could have been there. In 1978, aged just fifty-three, he had been diagnosed with cancer of the stomach. He had undergone several bouts of surgery, the last of which had been on Friday, just two days before that cold Sunday morning. By his bedside in the District Hospital ICU were his wife, sister and sister-in-law. He had no children and his elder brother had not been seen for a week.

* * *

Over in the General Hospital lay Joe Lyons. Joseph Patrick Lyons had been born in Dublin, in 1919. His family had moved to Birmingham in 1930, when he was just eleven, and had settled in Hockley. His father Patrick had worked hard as a self-employed bricklayer. Joseph's memories of his father were of a red-headed man with a white-freckled complexion, ruddy cheeks and thick red moustache matted with snot during the long cold winter, wearing a collarless white shirt, old trousers and boots, a flat cap and an old tweed jacket with leather patches at the elbow. Patrick and his wife had encouraged all eight of their children – three boys and five girls – to work hard at school and to become upright children in the eyes of God. This family of ten had lived in a poor, cramped terraced house – 120 back of 40 Wheeler Street, Hockley – this address describing the nineteenth century mass dwelling architecture of the Industrial Revolution, where houses were built around courtyards that could only be reached from the road by narrow passages. These passages were called 'entries'. Each road would probably have several entries. Therefore, visitors wanting to find 120 should use the entry next to 40. Hence the address 120 back of 40. These houses were so damp that bread left uncovered would be coloured by mildew within the hour. Joseph, the second child and the first boy, had excelled at St Mary's Roman Catholic School, at lessons, sports and the choir. He had been a good and faithful altar boy, and had risen to head boy. With an excellent School Certificate he had gone off to Birmingham University to study engineering, which he had passed with First Class Honours. He had been taken on immediately by a small firm of electrical engineers in Hockley, Birmingham Light Electrical. He had quickly scaled the ranks of the small family business and in 1950 had been made Managing Director, when the only working member of the owning Johnson family retired. By 1960 the company had trebled in size. By 1965 it had grown by a further factor of ten, through a combination of gained market share and acquisition. In 1968, and having grown another tenfold during the previous three years, Birmingham Light had been floated on the London Stock Exchange, under the steady direction of Joseph Lyons. The flotation was a success, and with institutional shareholders to call upon the company expanded with the speed and unstoppable force of a French forest fire fanned by a Mistral.

During Britain's dark days in the 1970s Birmingham Light Electrical had shone out, a beacon of success applauded across the land and a source of pride and hope for the troubled West Midlands. Joseph had been made a Commander of the Order of the British Empire in 1975, for services to British industry, and had won for his company two Queen's Awards for Export in 1976 and 1977. It had been a constant source of sadness for Joseph that neither of his parents lived long enough to see their eldest son become a household name while Richard Branson was still recovering from his time at Stowe School for well-off boys. But perhaps his parents would have been most impressed by the way that Joseph never forgot his roots. He had continued to support the people of Hockley, Aston and Lozells and had taken his place amongst them every Sunday at St Mary's. Then, on the first Thursday of this December, he had been struck down by a heart attack and consequently lay seriously ill in the General Hospital.

On this cold Sunday morning Birmingham really needed these men: the old, irreplaceable politician who guarded the city; the community leader who kept the inner city from tearing itself apart; the commercial giant who had supplied money, jobs and inspiration. All had been vital. All honoured by the Crown. All famous and respected across every division of race, colour and religion. There were no replacements poised to take their places, no inspiring pro-Brummie fighter, no man well-known and respected enough to heal the sores and wounds of the ghettos, no one to show them how to beat the opposition.

Birmingham didn't know these men were so ill, never mind on the brink of oblivion. They knew that Councillor Martin had retired. The local papers had reported Joseph Lyons' heart attack, but the company had played it down in order to protect Birmingham Light's share price. It was generally known that Charles Griffiths was suffering from cancer, but few knew how serious his fight had become and that he may lose that battle within hours.

★ ★ ★

Around nine o'clock in the evening a nurse sat reading Alexandre Dumas' *The Three Musketeers* to John Martin. He'd had a happy day; his younger brother, his wife, two sons and their wives, who lived near Stratford-upon-Avon, had been in to see him. They hadn't planned on seeing Uncle John until Christmas, when he was due to stay with his brother for the festive season, but Matron had phoned and urged a visit, as the doctor had told her that Councillor Martin was fading.

The Councillor was in a gentle mood. He lay in bed, his white hair neatly combed and parted, his moustache well trimmed, his pale red-and-blue-striped pyjamas clean and well pressed, with all the buttons done up. He lay on his back between the newly laundered, crisp linen sheets. His hands rested on the white top sheet. His head was supported by four pillows. His eyes were closed. She read. He listened contentedly to the adventures of Athos, Porthos, Aramis and D'Artagnon. She sat close by, to his left. He took her redundant hand in his and held it. She made no attempt to break the contact. She read to the end of the page. She moved to withdraw her hand in order to turn the page. As she did so his hand dropped back on to the white sheet, lifeless. Old Soldiers' Park had lost its favourite and most famed resident. More importantly, Birmingham had lost one of its greatest sons and revered warriors.

* * *

Charles Griffiths, having shown signs of rallying in the morning, had become very tired during the afternoon. With the heavy sedation necessary to keep the appalling pain at bay, he had drifted in and out of sleep. At nine twenty-five he stirred and looked hard into the eyes of his wife, Ellen, sitting beside his bedside. His gaze was serene, yet distant. He said, 'Ellen, this evening I have seen Heaven. I have seen a brilliant and bright light shining up yonder. I am not afraid to go and I will prepare a home for us until you join me there. Look after Thomas for me, and I will see you in the morning. I love you very much.' The bouncing line on the heart monitor by his bed became a straight line, its blip a constant tone. Ellen cried out. Her sister-in-law Elizabeth rang for a nurse. Her sister Rachel ran into the corridor and called for help. A team came quickly, but he was gone.

* * *

Joseph Lyons had been taken off a life-support machine but remained in Intensive Care. He had that afternoon been visited by his wife, son and daughter, although the rest of his huge family had been told that he wasn't well enough to see them. During the early evening he had complained of further pain in his chest and left arm. Doctors had been called but were unable to prevent a further heart attack. Joe had been put back on the life-support machine and his wife and two adult children had been led from the room, to wait in a nearby private room. His son was silent. His daughter cried quietly. His wife murmured Hail Marys over and over, eventually dropping to her knees and sobbing it out with tears falling onto the seat of a plastic hospital chair. Her son raised her gently. Shortly before ten o'clock the priest arrived. A senior consultant kindly and quietly explained the position, and all returned together to Joe Lyons' bedside. The priest spoke the last rites and Joseph left to meet his maker.

⋆ ⋆ ⋆

In the space of just one hour all three men, of different races and beliefs but alike in their giving goodness, had taken leave of life. The city would awake the following cold morning and feel the loss. There would be memorials, monuments and marks of respect to come. But first would be the funerals, prominent and prestigious affairs, and there would be stiff competition amongst the funeral directors of North Birmingham to secure the jobs.

There were two prominent local contenders: Sloane & Sons Limited (established 1850) and Richards & Gridley Limited (established 1908). Sloane & Sons Ltd was owned and run by Stillion Sloane. At just twenty-nine Stillion didn't look much like a funeral director. He was tall, slim and fair, with blue eyes. Harrow and Oxford educated, with a degree in politics, he had taken over Sloane & Sons on his father's death, in 1977. Stillion's had been an old-fashioned English public school education; as a boy he'd used words like crikey, gosh and jolly, and called his schoolfellows by their surnames. And now, as an adult, his schooling showed; he was sociable and enjoyed team games, but trusted only himself and rarely showed his emotions. He was charming and could be kind, with a well-developed British sense of fair play, but he was also competitive, determined and, occasionally, ruthless.

Politically, he was staunchly Conservative, and had even stood – unsuccessfully – as a local Parliamentary candidate in the two elections of 1974. He had been a devotee of the Tory leader Edward Heath before seeing the Thatcher light in 1975. He had lived through the social revolution heralded by the Beatles and now embraced the Thatcher creed of self-determinism. He was keen to rebuild the family funeral business, which had declined during the years of his father's ailing health, and didn't mind getting his hands dirty in order to re-establish the family's wealth and position at the head of Birmingham society.

He loved cricket; playing cricket, watching cricket, listening to cricket on the radio. He even dreamed of cricket. He was also a Beatles bore. He'd been just thirteen when the Fab Four had made it big, and his obsessive worship of the Four Mop Tops had occasionally raised eyebrows. But he was purely heterosexual. Moreover, he had a huge libido, and he hoped that his marriage to the tall, fair and beautiful Stephanie, when he was just twenty-seven, had put a stop to his indiscriminate sleeping around. They had no children as yet, but Stillion was keen for sons and heirs.

Richards & Gridley Limited was run by Sydney Alfred Gridley. Sydney, now sixty, was a short man, thin and bony. He had black hair, grey at the temples, and a grey and black moustache. His large yellow false teeth were seldom seen, as he rarely smiled and hardly opened his mouth when talking. Many years ago he had affected a clipped manner of speaking, devoid of any Midland twang, his thin, pale lips almost closed. He dressed neatly and precisely. When conducting funerals he favoured a black overcoat and bowler hat, rather than the traditional top hat and tailcoat worn by Stillion. Sydney felt Stillion's garb was ostentatious.

After school – a grammar in Wolverhampton – Sydney had been articled to a firm of solicitors in Willenhall. The Second World War broke out when he was twenty, and he'd spent the war years behind a desk with a Staffordshire regiment. With the coming of peace he'd taken a job in local government. In 1952 he had met Susan Richards, daughter of a Handsworth funeral director, at a dance in West Bromwich. She was ten years his junior. They had become engaged in

1954 and in 1956, in the middle of the Suez crisis, they had married. His father-in-law, while wishing that his only child had married a younger man, nevertheless believed that the precise, cautious, boring Sydney would at least prove a stable partner for his quiet, shy Susan. Moreover, John Richards had to take Sydney to his bosom because he wanted Susan at home. Susan's mother had been killed during a bombing raid in 1942 and John needed Susan to keep house for him. They lived above the shop, and had done since John's father had started the business in 1908. John had no intention of living there alone so there was nothing else for it, Sydney must come and live with them. Sydney would have to join the business. John would teach Sydney the honourable profession and Sydney and Susan could look after him in his frail years.

In 1958 John Richards had given Sydney a twenty per cent stake in Richards & Sons, made him Managing Director and changed the name of the firm to Richards & Gridley. As time went by John Richards moved into the background, content with Sydney's cautious approach to business. John had stood in cold cemeteries all his life and was determined to spend his old age by a coal fire, even in summer.

In January 1961 Sydney and Susan produced their only child, a boy, who was named Marcus after Sydney's aristocratic commanding officer during the war. Sydney loved the associations of the name. No common name for his boy, no Enoch, Ely, John, Bill or Burt for him. Sydney was a snob. He had fought to make his way up. He had worked hard at altering his accent, and at his appearance, dress and manners while an articled solicitor. His marriage to the dull, plain Susan had secured him a place in her family business. Susan, who for Marcus represented solidity, affection, reliability and a wonderful warmth, was for Sydney just a means to an end. Their wretched relationship was a source of great grief to Susan, and one she could only bear because she wanted to give Marcus a stable family life. Sydney felt that Susan's bleak existence was a fair price to pay for her marriage to him, for the son he had given her and for their keep, which had been bought by Sydney's hard graft. He had put up with the whims of his father-in-law and had worked hard, standing at graveside committal services six or seven times a day, five or even six days a week, in the dark, the damp and the cold. When John Richards died, in 1962, Sydney became Chairman as well as Managing Director, and his rise to the head of the firm and family was complete. Head of the household and of the business, he was also a City Councillor (for the Liberals), a Rotarian, a Justice of the Peace and Master of a Lodge of Freemasons. And for seventeen blissful years after John Richards' death he was top funeral dog, the older firm of Sloane & Sons being in the doldrums of Arthur Sloane's illness. Like many small men Sydney revelled in his position and power. He drove a black 1963 Rolls-Royce which he had bought to increase his wedding hire work and to use as a fourth limousine for funerals. Naturally he didn't explain that to his admiring colleagues on the Council or at Rotary.

Sydney believed in class. He liked moving up and believed in keeping the working classes down. But balancing his contempt of the lower classes was no admiration of his social superiors. He hated 'old money'. Everything he had he had earned. He detested the idea of inherited wealth and believed that, given an equal start in life, few such people would succeed. And the thought of failure wiping their self-confident smiles from their pompous faces delighted Sydney. But he wasn't about to throw his lot in with the workers and vote Labour. His father had been a Whig and he was stuck a Liberal, although far from a liberal thinker.

In the early days he had merely disliked his rivals Sloane & Sons. Then, during the years of his ascendance he had pitied them too. But when Stillion had taken over, determined to rebuild the business, Sydney's dislike had turned to hatred, his pity to fear. He wasn't going to be outdone by a flashy public schoolboy who'd never even lived in the community he served. No Johnny-come-lately was going to usurp Sydney's hard-won crown. But it was dangerous to underestimate the brat. Stillion had, after all, made two quickfire acquisitions with money borrowed from the Midland Bank. Richards & Gridley had enough cash in the bank to buy both firms, but Sydney had been frightened to part with it. And Stillion's acquisitions had paid off. And Sydney now suspected that the brat had his eye on Higgins & Co. (established 1918), which was up for sale. Whatever happened, he mustn't be allowed to buy that company. Sydney would have it, and he wasn't going to have to pay too much either, because for many years the respectable Sydney had been having an affair with Joyce Higgins, daughter of the late proprietor. Sydney had married one business and now he expected, by virtue of his affair, to get control of another. Stillion wouldn't get a look in. And Sydney deserved it after all; he'd put up with Joyce's demanding sexual appetite for years, partly out of fear of ending the affair, and partly because he hoped one day to get his hands on her father's business. Now, after all that work and worry he feared that that bloody boy was likely to make a rash offer, and push up the sale price.

Sydney had no interests outside the business. For the last twenty years or so the only time spent away from it had been spent promoting its cause through his public duties or servicing Joyce Higgins while supposedly helping out his father-in-law's friend Albert Higgins with night removals. The two families would assist each other at night and at weekends to avoid having to pay double time to the staff.

So there you have it. Two men with little in common except their chosen career and mutual disdain: Stillion Sloane, the young, self-assured, upper middle-class man, politically Conservative but prepared to be liberal with investment to develop his family firm; and Sydney Gridley, of lower middle-class origin, grammar school educated, politically a Liberal, and yet conservative in his business dealings. Both men, driven by ambition, ego, greed and dislike of the other, were prepared to do whatever was necessary to further their professional interests and beat the other. No doubt when they knew of the events of the evening, both would desperately want to direct these three funerals. Each would seek to control events, with little thought that events may take control of them.

1

Monday

It was eight-fifteen on Monday morning. Stillion Sloane stood at the back of the small Methodist Chapel in Booth Street, Handsworth. The eight o'clock service, the first of several for him to conduct that cold and grey day was well under way. The minister was giving his address when the widow, seated on the front right pew, jumped up and walked with determination back down the aisle towards Stillion.

'Mr Sloane, yaw've brought me on the wrong funeraal,' she whispered in broad Brummie.

'No, I can assure you Mrs Thornhill, I haven't,' whispered Stillion, hoping that no could hear them.

'Oh yes yaw 'ave. The Reverend Jones is up there saying what a good man my 'ubbie was, what a great father and all. Well let moe tell you my 'ubbie was nowt of the sort. He were a drunk who beat me and the babes before pissing in our bed. Yaw've brought me on someone else's funeral.'

Stillion reassured the widow that ministers always said nice things at funerals, and she returned to her seat.

After the service the small congregation moved off to Perry Barr Crem., the first funeral of the day. 'I am the resurrection and the life saith the Lord,' intoned Reverend Jones. The organ droned in the background an ignored comfort to all but Stillion, who could hear in the music a hymned up version of 'Come on baby, light my fire'. Stillion just prayed that there wasn't a musician, or even a Doors fan, in the deceased's family. Michael Russell, the young organist, often played this and other outrageous tunes to relieve the tedium of fifteen cremations a day. Stillion knew he should pull rank and report Michael but he didn't. There was a certain solidarity between the two of them; they were young men in an old man's business, and they both loved rock and roll, the Beatles in particular. Moreover on many occasions Stillion had been asked by families after their service for the name of 'the lovely music played at the crematorium'.

A few miles away Sydney Gridley's first job of the week was a funeral from a West Bromwich council estate. His son Marcus was in the shop, fitting out coffins. An academically bright boy, Marcus was taking a year out before reading architecture at Warwick University. He intended to spend six months travelling the world before he began studying, and was only working with his father in order to save the money to pay for the trip. At just £30.00 a week, plus £5.00 for an out-of-hours removal, the saving was slow, but it was a deal and Marcus didn't argue with father. Particularly as Sydney didn't want the boy to go globe-trotting. Marcus had been left £10,000 by his late grandfather, John Richards, and would have liked some of this cash for his trip. But he didn't dare ask his father for it. And he didn't dare tell his father that he didn't want to go into the family business either. Sydney was proud of having his boy go to university, but wanted him in the business, a source of cheap labour and Sydney's retirement insurance.

Sydney arrived at the council house with a hearse and one limousine to be told by the family, 'Mr Gridley yaw've only brought one car. Wae'be ordered taow. Where's the second car?' The house had no telephone, so Sydney trudged through the snow to the nearest public telephone box to call the office and ask Marcus to bring out the second limousine.

Marcus got the message. He threw on his coat, grabbed a chauffeur's cap, jumped into the limo and raced to the house. In the meantime Sydney had loaded the first limousine and, on seeing Marcus pull into the street with the second, brought the remaining six mourners down the small front garden path. He advanced with his umbrella, selfishly protecting himself from a snow flurry that covered the following mourners. He opened the limo's rear door, but then immediately slammed it shut again. He tapped on the nearside front window. Marcus leant across from his driving position and wound it down.

'Are you trying to put us out of business?' demanded Sydney.

'What?' asked Marcus.

'You heard. There's no back seat.'

Marcus looked back. There was, indeed, no back seat. In his haste to respond to Sydney's call he had failed to notice that the limo's battery had been on charge. The battery on this model was under the back seat which needed to be removed when recharging. Marcus turned back to his father, mouth open in dumbstruck, vacant-eyed panic. Sydney was struggling to control a violent verbal outburst against his son when his squint eyes spotted a short plank sitting on a decorator's scaffold by the house directly opposite.

'Grab that plank,' he spluttered.

'What?' stammered Marcus.

'Grab that plank, you idiot,' spat Sydney.

Marcus ran, sliding and skidding, across the road, over the short grass verge, through the little garden gate, grabbed the plank and made his escape. He flung open the offside limousine door and placed the plank on the two arm rests. Sydney opened the nearside limousine door and showed the first three mourners into the interior, asking them to perch upon the highly placed plank. The remaining three then took the occasional seats.

'Do mind your head as you go, Sir. Do mind your head as you go, Madam,' said Sydney, now regaining his smarmy tone. Once they were all seated he looked into the limousine and smiled. 'All comfortable? Thank you so much,' he concluded before closing the limousine door and striding off towards the front of the hearse so that the cortège could get on its way.

Meanwhile, Stillion Sloane and Walter Warburton, his first limousine driver, returned the bereaved Mrs Thornhill home. Then they made their way back to Sloane House to link up with the loaded hearse for the second funeral, which should leave a house in Kingstanding at ten-thirty for Perry Barr crematorium. Time was short and Stillion knew he would have to make the best use of the ten minutes he would have at Sloane House before leaving again. He picked up the radio telephone microphone and called his administration manager and chief arranger, John Palin.

'Sloane two to Sloane Control, Sloane two to Sloane Control, come in Sloane Control.'

'Sloane Control receiving you,' came the response.

'Hi John, we're ten minutes away. Can you please ask Vicky to line up a cup of coffee and three phone calls, one after the other as I've only got ten minutes. I want Leggett Caskets of Bilston. That's John Leggett the MD. I want James Steele of Steele Taylor and Steele regarding the Higgins acquisition and the cricket commentary on the phone from Australia. Got those? Over.'

'Sloane Control. Will do. Over and standing by,' came back the reply.

As soon as John Palin closed down a woman with a

very strong Brummie accent could be heard. 'Rylawy one, Rylawy one. This is Rylawy base to Rylawy one. Come in Rylawy one." Sloane & Sons shared a wavelength with a television repair company named 'Relay'. There was silence as the mobile driver replied before she continued, 'Thank yaw Rylawy one. Please proceed to 16 High Street Wordsley Staffs, where a Mr Jones is complaining that his knob has dropped off.'

Stillion and Walter stared at each other, then the radio and back to each other in disbelief before bursting into laughter, Stillion grateful that the limo was empty of grieving people at the time.

Minutes later the limousine pulled onto Sloane House's forecourt. The hearse was already standing in the side drive off to the left, loaded and ready to go. Stillion leapt out, dashed through the reception area, across the large hall, up the stairs, along the landing and into his office. He hit the intercom and said, 'Hi Vicky, let's go with the calls.' He took off his tailcoat and warmed his arse by the fire while sipping steaming black coffee as he waited. The phone went. 'It's John Leggett for you, putting you through,' said Victoria before Stillion heard 'John Legget.'

'John, morning. It's Stillion. I'm phoning because Friday's promised delivery of coffins didn't happen. Now I must have the lot today. We are very short of solid raised lid elms, solid panelled oaks, panelled veneered oaks and every type of large coffin or casket. The death rate is going mad. I've got the fridges full, all trolleys taken and God only knows where we are going to put today's scheduled removals after all the weekend's house removals. I can't box up at least ten bodies because we just don't have the coffins to fit out. Now for fuck's sake what's going on?'

'I'm sorry but everyone is busy. We're flat out. This doesn't usually happen until after Christmas but everyone's gone mad.'

'I'm not fucking everyone, John. Now I want to know and I want to know now when I'm going to get my coffins or would you like me to try and explain to my bereaved families that I will have to bury their mothers, fathers, brothers, sisters, husbands or wives in hospital sheets because you can't supply orders that we put in a fortnight ago and should have had but haven't because you have been giving our supplies away to non-clients who have turned to you in desperation because their own supplier can't supply and you try to help them in the hope of winning their business on a permanent basis.'

'That's not true,' insisted John.

'Oh yes it is, and don't give me any more shit you son of a bitch because the same thing happened last year. Now if my coffins are not delivered by midday then I'm coming up there to see you and I promise that you'll never make another bloody stillborn box let alone coffin for us ever again. Is that quite clear?' asked Stillion angrily.

'Quite clear but I can only do half by midday. I

won't be able to get the balance there until four o'clock.'

'That's OK by me, just don't let me down. OK John. Friend or no friend I need those coffins now. See you.' Stillion put the phone down. It rang again almost immediately; Victoria was on the ball.

'James Steele for you.'

'James, why the hell haven't you been back to me about the Higgins deal? You promised me on Thursday to phone me Friday with the appointment time."

'Their solicitor was supposed to come back to me. He didn't. I spoke to him on Thursday and he said he thought the business would probably go to Richards & Gridley as old man Higgins and John Richards had been great friends but that he would indicate to the daughter . . . whatsername?'

'Joyce,' Stillion reminded James.

'Oh yes, Joyce . . . your interest.'

'Indicate my interest! Listen, you bastard, I told you to tell him that we would be prepared to pay a lot for the business and that it must be in his client's interest to hear our offer. Now get back onto him and arrange the bloody appointment now and don't think of doing anything else until you've got it. Because if I have to phone Joyce Higgins myself I shall start to worry what use you are to me in this acquisition campaign at all,' slammed Stillion.

'OK, keep your shirt on,' answered James in his somewhat effeminate fashion.

'Keep my shirt on. I wouldn't dream of taking it, or anything else for that matter, off in your presence,' replied Stillion, who suspected James Steele was queer. 'Phone me later,' he ordered as he put the phone down. Next on came the cricket. England were doing well, mainly thanks to Botham. That was pleasing. At eight minutes past ten he put his tailcoat back on; it was nearly time to go. The phone went again. It was Lottie Wilkes, a friend of his, or more a friend of his wife's. Lottie had been phoning a lot recently. He could tell Victoria didn't approve by the tone of her voice as she announced the call.

'Hi, Lottie, can I phone you back? I've got to dash out on my next funeral.'

'Sorry, I've obviously phoned at a bad time, but I must see you about something important. Could you make the Plough's cocktail bar Wednesday at seven o'clock? You mustn't tell anybody, not even Stephanie; it must be confidential. Please say yes, it's important.'

Stillion thought for a second. He was only going to pop into the cricket club for a drink on Wednesday, as Stephanie wouldn't be back from London until about half past nine. 'OK,' he said, 'I'll see you there. Must dash. Bye.'

Lottie smiled. She knew Stephanie was in London because she had suggested Lottie go with her. Lottie had declined.

Lottie Wilkes was the wife of Harry Wilkes, a scrap

metal dealer and powerful local businessman. Harry, a chunky, fifty-one-year-old, was very strong and quite fit, if a little overweight. He had once been an amateur boxer, and a working life in scrap metal had kept his muscles toned. Harry liked to laugh, tell jokes and be one of the boys. Until, that is, he wanted his own way; then he was the boss. Harry often wanted his own way. No, that was wrong. Harry always wanted his own way. And Harry always got his own way; those who got in Harry's way lost little things, fingers or toes. According to Brummie folklore Harry was an unofficial funeral director, only his clientele were rumoured to be holding up Spaghetti Junction. Such rumours were probably tall stories but Harry did little to deny them because they helped make bullying that bit easier. Harry knew how to be top dog; make people frightened of you and keep them that way. That's what respect was all about; frighten them, make them laugh and show them what you've got. That was the way.

Harry liked clubs, drinking, golf and holidays, and was an authority on all of them. Or that's what people told him. His wife Lottie was Stephanie's best friend. At forty-two Lottie was twice Stephanie's age, yet she looked like Joan Collins at thirty. She didn't get out much, but stayed at home. Harry liked her at home with the kids. She had dinner with him and friends each Saturday night and they watched television with the children on Sunday evenings. Otherwise he went out drinking – and sometimes whoring – with the boys. Lottie, having reached her forties, was keen to build a life of her own before it was too late. In search of a social life away from Harry's common and loud friends she joined the Edgbaston Priory Tennis Club, where she had met Stephanie, their mutual love of designer labels soon drawing them together.

It was ten past ten. Stillion put his top hat on and picked up his leather dress gloves. The phone went again. This time Victoria announced the Reverend Winston Wylde, Jamaican Baptist Minister, good cricketer and loyal friend of Stillion. Winston had been born in Jamaica but came to Britain, to Birmingham, in 1953, aged just six. Under the instruction of his God-fearing Baptist parents he had grown into a truly decent man. As the local Baptist minister his success was stunning; his church, just 500 yards from St John's, Handsworth, could not have been more different, nor his life more different to that of the Church of England minister, Fred Price. Winston's church was newly painted by the army of volunteers that filled it twice every Sunday. Even Father O'Rourke, the local Catholic priest, who did not like West Indians and positively despised Baptists, could not find fault with Winston, though he envied the vitality that engulfed the young minister's church.

''Morning Stillion, it's Winston. Look man, I know you are in a hurry but I thought you should know that Charles Griffiths, the West Indian Federation leader, died yesterday. Is there anything you can do to ensure you arrange the funeral? I want you to have it because you're the only ones who recognise our customs. I will recommend you but the family won't come to see me until after they have been to the hospital, the registrars and the funeral director and you know as I do that the mortuary attendant at the District Hospital is going to recommend Richards & Gridley so he gets his bung.'

'That's unless you'd be willing to accompany the family on their travels in order to assist them. We would be honoured and grateful to conduct such an important and huge funeral.'

'Sure man, and maybe I will if I can. But I don't want nothing for it, OK?' said Winston quickly, for fear of Stillion saying something he didn't have to, never had before and which they would both regret if he did. Stillion took the hint. 'Thanks for the call Winston, speak to you later.'

It was ten-thirteen. Stillion had to go but the phone rang again. This time it was Fred Price, vicar of St John's, Handsworth. 'Stillion, just to let you know that John Martin, the ex-Lord Mayor Councillor, passed away last night, at the Old Soldiers' Park Old People's Home,' he announced and went on to say that the funeral would take place at St John's, where the Councillor had been a church warden many years ago. 'I think his remaining family, who live out near Stratford-upon-Avon, would want you to do the funeral,' he continued in his quiet, well-spoken voice.

'A nephew has phoned to say that they will contact me once they have registered the death. Naturally I will do what I can for you. However, on another matter, which is not really related and which I hate to mention, but St John's is in need of some assistance.'

'What's that, Sir?' asked Stillion trying very hard not to sound rushed as he glanced at his watch – ten-fourteen.

'Well, the stained glass window behind the altar is in need of urgent repair, having been broken by stone-throwing vandals.'

'I am sure Sloane & Sons can take care of the repair for you, Sir. Indeed, we'd be delighted to.'

'Oh, oh thank you so very much,' stammered the embarrassed Church of England minister, hating being reduced to this sort of bribery in order to maintain his crumbling St John's, of which he had once been so proud.

Stillion put down the phone and dashed for the door. He smiled: 'On another unrelated matter, my arse,' he muttered to himself. Without a window repair agreed, there would have been no recommendation.

Victoria was going into his office as he was leaving. 'Stillion, the time. You'll have to dash or you'll be late,' and then at his back as he leapt down the stairs, 'Don't forget that after this funeral and before the next, Father O'Rourke is coming in to bless the new Roman Catholic chapel.'

'OK, see you later,' said a voice fast disappearing through reception.

Meanwhile, the Reverend Fred Price was putting a call in to Sydney Gridley, who was only just back from his first funeral, having run late due to the back seat episode. Reverend Price informed Sydney of the death of the ex-Lord Mayor, then mentioned the stained glass window and a defunct central heating system, which he might have mentioned to Stillion if that young man had not appeared to be in such a hurry. Sydney, like Stillion before him, knew how important it was to arrange this funeral: it would carry a lot of prestige and thus help establish the image of Richards & Gridley as fashionable funeral director for North Birmingham, if not all of the city. It would also put Sloane & Sons in their place and, in particular, that Johnny-come-lately, that upstart, Stillion Sloane. Moreover, it should seal his acquisition of Higgins & Co., and knock Sloane's out of the running.

'So, Father Price. As I see it, you're saying that if we get this altar window of yours repaired and get a contractor to sort out the central heating, you'll get us the Councillor's funeral?'

'Well, I wouldn't put it quite like that,' answered Reverend Price, acutely embarrassed by Sydney's direct approach. He stammered, 'No, now what I am saying is that in gratitude for these two important gifts that you would be so kindly bestowing upon the church, I would consider it proper and indeed my duty to reward you with my only gift available, that of recommending your services. I would be happy to do so but cannot guarantee that the family will heed my advice.'

'Sounds like the same thing to me. Therefore I accept, but I can only deliver if you do. I have to live just like you, you know. Perhaps you will call me later when you have spoken again to the family. Goodbye,' said Sydney and Reverend Price replaced the receiver wondering how such a man became a Justice of the Peace. His next thought appalled him. If he had succeeded in bribing Sydney Gridley JP, Councillor and leading Rotarian, what did that make Reverend Frederick John Price DSO and Master Theologian?

Reverend Fred Price had been vicar of St John's Church, Handsworth for twenty-nine years. His eyes were a dull blue, his hair grey and receding, while his pale face was lined and his nose slightly beaked. This quiet, well-educated man seemed to have the cares of the world placed upon his shoulders. As he got older, Handsworth got rougher and tougher. Lying between wealthy Handsworth Wood and damp, dank and impoverished Hockley Brook, the demolition fever of the early 1960s had seen the area's rows of back to back slum housing pulled down, forcing the wretched residents, known among the lower middle order of Handsworth as the Hockley bog rats, to move away while the hideous sixties tower blocks were built. In their absence immigrant West Indians and Asians took over Handsworth, Lozells and much of Aston. As they came the indigenous English population moved out, leaving behind just the elderly householders who wouldn't or couldn't sell. Fred was trapped there with them as their vicar. The diminishing congregation of the once proud St John's provided ever less money to meet ever greater bills to mend damage caused by increasing assaults by vandals as the first gangs of West Indian and Asian teenagers grew up angry with the poverty of their inner-city lives. Unlike their parents, they had never known conditions in their native lands and therefore could not see Handsworth as a step up. All they saw from their televisions was that they appeared to be amongst the poorest of the land. To Fred, St John's seemed to pay for their frustrations time and time again.

Fred had become a stooped, old and frightened man. He had lost his inner self-esteem while just managing to keep his outer dignity. He was ashamed of himself. He hated the church. He hated the parish. He hated being afraid. He hated being now, in old age, so cowardly. He hated the changes that had stranded him here in Handsworth. He hated himself for hating them and for being a racist. He knew he shouldn't be. He didn't want to be. He prayed not to be. But, to his shame, he was. He hated having to beg for financial support from the Stillions and Sydneys of this world, but he did. He wanted to ask the Bishop to move him to a rural parish in Worcestershire or Warwickshire but he couldn't. If the Bishop were to move him of his own accord then that would be God's will. If he were to ask then it would not be God's will, but a signal of defeat and of a failed life's work.

As Sydney put down the phone to Fred Price he saw Marcus crossing the reception and heading for the stairs that led to their flat. The family was proud to still boast of living 'above the shop'. He called out, 'Marcus, come in. Do you know what I have just been told by Reverend Price of St John's? That Councillor Martin has died!'

'Oh, that's a shame. He's been a big noise in the local Tories as long as I can remember,' replied Marcus.

Sydney, in despair at his son, blasted, 'A shame? A shame! Is that all you can say? Father Price phoned to say that we would be getting the funeral more than likely instead of that public schoolboy twit Sloane. Doesn't that please you?'

'Oh, yes father. I mean, if he's dead then it's good that we get the job.'

'Of course he's dead, you stupid boy. We don't bury living people. If you're going up to the flat don't keep me waiting before the next funeral. Oh, and tell your mother to bring my lunch down to the office later. I must make some calls before going on the first afternoon job. And Marcus, just make sure we have back seats in all the limos, please.'

Marcus nodded and bounded upstairs to the sanctuary of his mother and the flat. It was turning out to be one of those days.

As he left the phone rang again. It was Rory Bruton, mortuary technician at the District Hospital. Rory was a nasty little turd. A militant member of his union and a prominent fighter for the socialist cause, he nevertheless showed considerable aptitude for private enterprise, and made a nice little sum in backhanders from Gridleys in return for recommending their services. When left alone with a bereaved family he asked which funeral director the family would be instructing so that he could speed things up for them by phoning through the measurements. If they replied that they hadn't one in mind, he suggested Richards & Gridley. If they said they were considering another firm, he usually suggested that they had made a good choice but might not be able to get the funeral conducted for days as that firm had just been in that morning and said as much. He then asked if they would like to phone a couple of firms to see how they were fixed. He then phoned Richards & Gridley and made an appointment for the family, giving them directions of how to get there. If the bereaved family answered his question with a positive, 'We always use the Co-op,' or, 'Our family have gone to Sloane & Sons for generations,' he said nothing, wise enough to know that he would be unlikely to be able to change their minds, and that they might report him which could cost him both his job and this lucrative additional income. On the first

Monday of each month Rolley Brown, the Richards & Gridley foreman, brought Rory's dosh to the lounge bar at the Hawthorns, a large pub-cum-restaurant next to the West Bromwich Albion football stadium. Rory got £20.00 per funeral, handed over in a brown paper bag. He always went to the gents and counted the money, checking against the list of names in his little black book, which had itself been double checked against the *Express* and *Star* and *Birmingham Evening Mail* obituary notices. Sydney and Rolley knew better than to cross this nasty little piece of work and always gave him the benefit of the doubt when he claimed a tip for a funeral that would have come to Richards & Gridley anyway.

'Guess what, Guv,' Rory began with his deep Middle England accent, 'Charlie Griffiths, 'ead of the West Indians in Brum 'as kicked it. I've got 'im 'ere in the fridge. The family's due in at two. The nignogs usually prefer Sloanes but I'll see what I can do, all right? No promises mind, but I want double for this 'un. All right?'

'You can have double, certainly, if you get it. Just make sure you get it. It would be a major embarrassment for Sloanes not to have the biggest West Indian funeral ever seen in this city, if not in this country,' mused Sydney.

'I'll call you later with the details,' said Rory, ringing off.

Sydney sat in silence. To get these two funerals

would be two big steps in the relentless march against those pompous and arrogant Sloanes. He had never liked them. The father had been a gentleman, true, but had suffered from a superiority complex. The mother was a haughty battleaxe and the son had inherited the worst aspects of both. He was self-opinionated and inclined to think that he was always right. He was commercially very astute, unusual for a public schoolboy. Sydney disliked commercial aggression that wasn't instigated by himself.

His phone rang again. This time it was Father O'Rourke with the news that Joseph Lyons was dead. Sydney thought, 'Bloody hellfire, not another one.' Joseph Lyons' highly profitable engineering company, Birmingham Light Electrical, was often in the financial pages as market leader. A successful flotation on the London Stock Exchange had seen shares gaining 65 per cent in value in the past year, despite the hardships facing British industry in general and Birmingham in particular.

'Now, it occurs to me Mr Gridley that you may be after wanting to organise this funeral,' said Father O'Rourke in his soft Irish lilt.

'Indeed we would, Father,' replied Sydney, hardly daring to believe his fortune on this happy of happy Monday mornings. He must grasp this funeral as well as the other two. There would never be a better opportunity to show the city what Gridley's could do. The ex-Lord Mayor, the city's most famous business personality and the leader of one of the city's largest ethnic groups. One Church of England, one Roman Catholic and one a Baptist. He only needed a leading Sikh to kick the bucket and he'd have the full set.

'Well, it might just be possible for me to be putting in a good word for you on this one. But, you see, I might be after a little favour in return. I mean, these issues are not connected, you understand.'

'Oh, naturally,' interjected Sydney, wondering what the punchline would be.

'Well, it's only a small thing, really. One of the families in my flock, the O'Briens, wants to send their youngest son, little Stompy, back to the Falls Road to be with his ailing grandfather for Christmas and I've been after saying I would find a sponsor because, to be sure, they haven't a spare farthing to put towards the cost of a ticket. Now, Sydney Gridley, do you think you could find it in your heart to be after helping in this matter?'

'Consider it done, Father,' replied Sydney.

'Oh, to be sure, that's a grand gesture. The family *will* be pleased, and I will see what I can do for you with the Lyons' funeral.' The conversation finished.

Meanwhile, Winston Wylde had phoned the Griffiths family and offered to take them to the hospital, the registrar and then to Sloane & Sons to make the arrangements. This had effectively landed the funeral for Stillion. One-nil to Sloane & Sons.

Reverend Price, on the other hand, had phoned

John Martin's family and put in a good word for Richards & Gridley, as arranged. They thanked him and took the address and directions. They were planning to visit the home where the old man had died, to collect his belongings and the doctor's certificate. They would then register the death and set about making arrangements for the funeral. Fred Price then phoned Sydney to tell him that the Martin family should arrive that afternoon sometime after three. Sydney, not knowing of Winston Wylde's actions, remained confident of getting all three funerals. At midday he phoned Joyce Higgins to boast of his morning's winnings, although he changed the facts to suggest that each family had selected Richards & Gridley on reputation, or because they disliked Sloane & Sons Ltd.

'Aren't you counting your chickens, Sydney darling?' exclaimed Joyce. 'I mean, Daddy used to say if you get a fish on the line pull it in and don't count it until it's on the bank.'

'Maybe you're right but I'd rather be in my seat than that bloody boy's. Fifteen years ago Sloanes would automatically have had all three of those funerals. But not today.' Sydney puffed with pride, forgetting that fifteen years ago neither John Richards nor Arthur Sloane – let alone the Catholic and Anglican priesthoods – would have dreamed of having the conversations that had taken place that morning.

'Talking of "that bloody boy", as you call young Mr Sloane, he wants to see me about buying the business,' said Joyce airily, fully intending to annoy Sydney, while at the same time keeping him on his toes with regard to his own offer.

'You won't see him, naturally,' insisted Sydney.

'And why not?' said Joyce.

'Well, because you are going to sell to me,' answered Sydney.

'Who says, lover? I want the best price. I am only going to get one bite at the cherry and then that's it. Thanks largely to you I'm not married and never likely to be. This is my pension. I am inclined, at the very least, to hear what Sloane has to say,' she said logically. Sensing that Sydney was agitated, Joyce calmed him with, 'Look, darling, naturally I'd prefer to sell to you. We go back a long way. But Daddy would want me to consider all the options. Like the future status of the business and the stature of the buyer, but above all the price. This *is* my future. I'm sure I will sell to you but I just want to know that I am getting a good deal and that's why I will meet with Stillion Sloane.'

'So, you don't trust me. You still don't trust me, after all these years,' whined Sydney.

'No. That's not true. But, after all these years of being your mistress, the bridesmaid and never the bride, I can't afford but to do the best by me.' She concluded, 'As long as you match his or anyone else's price, you know I'll sell to you.'

Sydney pondered as he replaced the receiver that Joyce seemed to have become uncharacteristically greedy, and no doubt if Stillion got involved in attempting to buy her business then he, Sydney, would have to pay more. Nevertheless, if he got these three funerals and matched any offer Stillion might make then she would have little moral option but to sell to him. After all, as she said, they did go back a long way, having been lovers for more than twenty years.

A knock came at Sydney's door. It was his receptionist. A Mr Razek Singh had called to collect his father's ashes. As a Sikh the ashes must be cast on fast flowing water, either back in India or here in England, usually on the River Severn.

'Has he settled the account, and do we have the ashes?' asked Sydney.

'No, in both cases,' replied the girl. 'He hasn't paid the bill yet and we haven't collected the ashes from the crem.'

'Tell him to come back tomorrow. I'll collect them from the crem later today. Oh, and remind him that the bill must be settled before he can have them,' commanded Sydney, adding under his breath to himself, 'Fast flowing water. They'll go on fast flowing water all right, right down the toilet if the bastard doesn't pay.'

Meanwhile, Father O'Rourke had arrived at Sloane House to bless the new Chapel of Rest. Father John O'Rourke, Roman Catholic priest of St Mary's, Hockley, was a big, taciturn man from Southern Ireland. He said little, rather he smiled gently and muttered 'oh yes, oh yes' or 'to be sure' in response to whatever was said to him. He seemed to look beyond you and not really to listen. Was he just vague? Was he bored? Did he secretly despise the British? Perhaps he was an IRA sympathiser? Stillion, who was certain of most things in life, couldn't fathom John O'Rourke at all.

Father O'Rourke's hair was grey with some light brown mixed in, and always cut extremely short – even shaven – at the sides and back. His eyes were blue, small and hidden behind fatty overhanging eyelids and gold-rimmed John Lennon glasses. He was absent minded and prone to forgetting funeral masses, even though he was phoned and written to on several occasions about each one. Sometimes he forgot the holy water, or maybe his committal service book. Indeed, on more than one occasion Stillion had had to supply a cup of water from the cemetery office toilet to be blessed hastily at the graveside, and had lent the forgetful priest a Church of England committal book in order that the dear departed may be dispatched to Heaven with a few remembered words from the Roman Catholic service, a couple of Hail Marys and the balance coming from the *Book of Common Prayer.* In common with many of his profession, Father O'Rourke was partial to a drop of the hard stuff and could more or less rely on getting a year's supply from funeral directors each Christmas. When he ran short, a word or two in the ear of any of them would soon restock the cocktail cabinet in the presbytery drawing room. He also had an eye for the girls but there was no evidence that he had ever strayed from his vows.

Father O'Rourke conducted the short service of blessing of the chapel for Stillion, and at the end presented a small bottle of holy water to place on the altar for the use of bereaved families. Stillion took it, saying, 'Thank you very much, Father. Tell me, where will we go to refill the bottle when the water is used? Should I send someone down to St Mary's for some more?'

'No, no that won't be necessary, to be sure. Fill it from the tap before the existing level falls below this cross on the side of the bottle and then be after giving it a good shake and it will all be holy water.'

Stillion thanked the Father again and escorted him back to a parishioner's car that was waiting for him on the forecourt of Sloane House. As they went, the Father explained to Stillion that he had lost a very important member of his flock. 'Of course, I should be more than happy to say a good word or two on your behalf when it comes to arranging the funeral.' Stillion, like Sydney before him, couldn't believe that another significant Birmingham personality had kicked the bucket over the weekend. Also, like Sydney, Stillion realised the importance of securing this funeral, as Joseph Lyons was not only a very senior member of the Roman Catholic community but also an industrialist of national renown and certainly Birmingham's most famous businessman.

'Stillion, naturally I will be after doing my best for you, you understand, but word has it that the family may be partial to Richards & Gridley. I can but try. However, Sydney Gridley has generously offered to help me with another matter, unrelated you understand. There's a very poor family comes to the church, the O'Briens. The father of the family, Patrick, has a very sick Daddy back on the Falls Road in Belfast and the family was after wanting to send their youngest, little Stompy, back there for Christmas as the old Granddaddy won't be seeing another Christmas after this. But they've no money at all and Mr Gridley has offered to pay for the child to go. Now, you can see how that would present me with a terrible problem, to be sure. You're a good lad and your late Daddy a converted Catholic and all,' O'Rourke gave a most sincerely insincere smile as his voice purred to a timely finish, his point made perfectly.

'Oh, that's no problem Father. I think the whole family should go. I mean, if this will be the Grandfather's last Christmas then he should spend it with all of them. It can't be right for little – Stompy, did you say? – to be parted from the rest of the family at Christmas time either. Sloanes will pay for the whole family,' answered Stillion, displaying diplomatic skills as subtle as those demonstrated by the Father.

'You're a good man, Stillion. I knew I could rely upon you,' said Father O'Rourke, climbing into the parishioner's car. Stillion waved in answer to the smiling and waving Father as the car left the forecourt, and thought to himself, 'Just as well that man chose the Church instead of politics.'

No sooner was the Father back in his presbytery than he phoned Sydney. 'Hello, Mr Gridley, it's Father O'Rourke of St Mary's here. I'm afraid the news is not good. I've just been told by the O'Briens that somehow Mr Sloane has got to hear of their financial problems and has offered to send the whole family to Belfast for Christmas. Now I'm sure you'll be after seeing what sort of a problem that gives me. The Lord does work in mysterious ways sometimes. Young Mr Sloane has been after doing the family such a kindness that I feel . . .'

'I will send the whole family to Northern Ireland and for you a couple of cases of Irish whiskey round to the presbytery this afternoon in thanks for still thinking of us. Can I therefore expect to see you and the Lyons family here at, shall we say, four this afternoon? I'll get one of my senior staff to conduct this afternoon's funerals so that I will be here personally to attend to the arrangements.'

'I'll phone the family directly and will see you this afternoon. The O'Brien family would be after wanting me to thank you for this kind gesture.'

Father O'Rourke phoned the Lyons family and asked the deceased's son, William, if a funeral director had been chosen yet. When he replied no, Father O'Rourke said, 'Oh, to be sure, that's grand because I think the only firm that can be available for Friday's mass is Richards & Gridley.'

'But what about Sloane & Sons?' asked William.

'A fine firm too, not quite as good as when Mr Arthur Sloane was alive, but fine nevertheless. However I saw young Mr Sloane just this morning and they haven't a spare wheel to turn until a week on Thursday,' replied Father O'Rourke, crossing himself at the other end of the phone. The arrangements were made; the Father would get a parishioner to take him to the Lyons' home in Edgbaston, where he would comfort the widow before they went to the hospital, on to the registrars and following the registration of the death, to Richards & Gridley for four o'clock. The score was now Sloane & Sons, one, Richards & Gridley, one.

At about three o'clock the Reverend Winston Wylde arrived at Sloane House with the Griffiths family in tow; the widow Ellen, her sister Rachel, the deceased's sister Elizabeth and his brother, Thomas. All three women took off overcoats to reveal smart black dresses, white cardigans, dark stockings and matching black patent leather shoes and handbags. Like the deceased they were only in their early to middle fifties and all three were both tall and weighty. Thomas could not have been more different from them or his younger brother in either looks or temperament. He was much shorter, and slighter, with a small frame that carried little fat; he seldom ate, but was a heavy drinker, usually of liquor and preferably vodka. He had come to England in the fifties with his younger brother but whereas Charles became a regular at the Baptist church, a good husband and respected worker at Lucas, Thomas never went to church, and never married; he claimed never to see the point, but the reality was probably that his drinking precluded sexual activity. He was a well-known sight at every Caribbean bar or English pub up and down the Lozells Road and although only in his fifties his hair was quite white and his face ravaged, giving him the look of a much older man.

Today, as usual, he was drunk. The others hadn't wanted him to accompany them to make the funeral arrangements, but as Charles' brother, he'd insisted, he had a right to be there. But rights or no rights, he had been warned to behave himself.

As the party walked into the reception area they met Elton Field, the Sloane embalmer, on his way out of the building.

'We've come to see Mr Palin,' announced Winston Wylde. He then proceeded to introduce the family, as he passed Elton the green certificate of burial. Elton didn't need to be told who Charlie Griffiths was. 'Bloody hell,' he thought, 'Charlie Griffiths was no age.' Elton invited them to take a seat, rang the attention bell for them and sat down to wait with them until the receptionist arrived. He noticed that Thomas Griffiths refused to sit down, and stood, swaying from side to side, with a glazed and faraway look in his eyes. 'Blimey,' thought Elton, 'he's had a few.' Elton, like most who lived near the Lozells Road, knew the face if not the name of Thomas Griffiths. He was often to be seen swaying from foot to foot as he wove in and out of the traffic on the Lozells Road, usually with a bottle held aloft in one hand, clearly taking more care to protect the bottle from danger than himself. 'So the kamikaze Lozells Road walker is Charlie Griffiths' brother,' Elton mused to himself.

John Palin's assistant arrived and led the party up the large sweeping staircase which Thomas Griffiths only managed with a lot of help from Reverend Wylde. The assistant sat them in an arrangement room, where they were immediately joined by John Palin himself, who moved smoothly into making the arrangements, capturing all the necessary personal details and requirements by way of sympathetic conversation.

Eventually John retired to his office to speak to Handsworth Cemetery regarding the time of the committal. A true professional, he would never call the cemetery in front of the family, as this might limit his ability to manipulate the times available to suit Sloane's other funerals on the day. To allow a family to dictate the timing of a funeral was a liability, as the service time, however important at the time of arranging, would always pale into insignificance on the day itself, compared to how the funeral itself turned out. And not running to time was disastrous for all concerned. John and Stillion had a motto: 'Give the family the time they want in the arranging room and they won't thank you when it all runs late on the day.' They had devised a method of allowing the bereaved family to select the time they preferred from those available and still to maximise the number of funerals per day while running all funerals on time. For example, if John was with a bereaved family early in the week who were keen for the funeral to be over before the weekend, he would say, 'Now, on which day would you like the funeral to take place, bearing in mind that the hospital will require 48 hours notice to complete the cremation papers and that therefore the first possible day is Friday?'

'Oh, Friday would be fine. We would prefer to have the funeral over before the weekend you see,' was the usual reply.

'I understand. And would you prefer to have the funeral in the morning or the afternoon, or perhaps around midday so that anyone travelling any distance will be able to come and return within normal hours?' John would ask.

'Oh, I think midday would suit us best.'

'I see. Well, naturally we will conduct the funeral at the time you wish but the crematorium can only undertake one committal at a time so, if you'll excuse me a moment, I'll just go and phone them. In the event that they can manage Friday but not midday, would you prefer to go to a day when they can manage midday or accept the closest time to midday on Friday?'

'Oh no, Friday is more important. We'll take the nearest time available.'

John would then disappear and consult his own day book for a time that Stillion and he could work in with the existing funerals before phoning the crematorium. He would then return to the family with the result: 'Well, happily I've been able to reserve a time at the crematorium on Friday but the nearest time to midday is ten-thirty in the morning, if that suits you?' Almost invariably the grateful family would agree that was fine, and how pleased they were to know that the funeral would not be held over until after the week-end.

Stillion and Palin admired each other's professional attention to detail in this, as in all other matters concerning the running of 800 funerals a year. To each family, theirs was the only one that counted. Quite understandably they showed no interest in the other 799. But Stillion and John had to ensure that all 800 – each of which demanded around forty man hours of work and the use of several thousand pounds' worth of equipment – got five-star service.

Having arranged for Charles Griffiths' funeral to take place on Thursday afternoon, John then turned their attention to the casket or coffin. It would probably be a casket. West Indian families preferred burial and usually selected caskets. When Sloane & Sons had moved into Sloane House in 1959, Arthur Sloane had converted the building into a new concept, a funeral home. One of the first of its kind in the land, he had done so in order to supply his growing number of clients with better in-house facilities, such as a service chapel, private Chapels of Rest, a family lounge, a Sikh, Hindu and West Indian wash and dress room (these groups like to prepare and dress their relatives personally) and a selection room. The selection room was used to display coffins and caskets of different materials and prices, so that families could choose what they wanted based on style and price. Their choice would then be confirmed in writing prior to the funeral, along with the disbursement costs. Good and professional. No misunderstandings, and good protection for Sloane & Sons from the rogue clients who existed in far greater numbers than rogue funeral directors.

Stillion's late father had been a great innovator. In the 1950s he had determined that the British way of death – the body staying at home until being removed in its coffin on the day of the funeral – was going to be replaced by the American way of death, involving funeral homes, Chapels of Rest and selection rooms. Sydney Gridley would never listen to any suggestion that he should follow suit, although public demand had forced him to build four private Chapels of Rest at the back of the premises, replacing the tatty, old red velvet curtains which used to be drawn across a corner of the garage next to the mortuary to make a viewing area.

Arthur Sloane had done well until illness overtook him and he, along with the staff, the vehicles and the premises, became a little tired. After his father's death, Stillion had hardly altered his father's concept because he knew the touch of a master. Stillion had, however, perked up the funeral home with smart, white decoration on the outside and extensive refurbishment within. He had fired any staff whom he considered to have taken advantage of his father's illness, and clothed the rest in a new livery. He had acquired a brand new fleet of Fords at an impressive discount, while saving the best of the old vehicles, so that even his B fleet was better than most of the competition. All this had been financed by a combination of better debtor and creditor control, and by impressing the company's bank manager with his youthful drive, determination and enthusiasm.

Palin led the Griffiths family through to the selection room, a large room full of coffins, caskets and cremation urns of all shapes, sizes, colours, woods and even metals. The coffins and caskets were all open to display an assortment of coloured dressing-gowns. John could guess what the Griffiths family were likely to select, from long experience of the consistency with which different social, racial and religious groupings chose. The cheapest range would always be chosen by a middle-class family that already had a second car, home, mortgage and wife, none of which they could really afford along with the school fees and therefore were buggered if their old man's estate was going to be wasted on funeral expenses. Thus they would quickly arrive at the least expensive coffin with the words: 'Well it's only going to be burnt isn't it?'

The next step up would usually be the choice of Sikhs and Hindus. They had no coffin culture; back in India the deceased would be placed on a funeral pyre, with or without a living wife. But it was important to the maintenance of community standing and for business strategy not to be seen to take the cheapest, so they usually went for the second cheapest.

The landed gentry and upper class liked something plain but solid – normally English oak – from the middle-priced selection. Working-class Brummies wanted something to display their love for the departed; a double raised lid elm – called from Aston to Winson Green a 'Sloane Special' – did just that, as well as showing that they had a few bob to spare for a decent send-off. If it was a man's funeral then there was a fair chance that the claret and blue Aston Villa gown would be chosen, and if the committal was a cremation, there may even be a request that the ashes be scattered over the pitch at Villa Park. The Irish Roman Catholic families of Hockley also tended to go for the Sloane Special, only with a crucifix on the lid, and beneath the name and date of death on the breast-plate would be engraved the initials RIP.

Right at the top of the expenditure league table

came the West Indians. Almost without exception they ignored anything coffin shaped and went straight for the top-of-the-range caskets. They would then choose a white interior and for the deceased a white dress shirt, black bow tie, dinner suit and white gloves for a man, or a bride's dress for a woman. At this particular point in British history many more West Indian men died than women; thirty years after the first ship had arrived from the West Indies, the first generation of men were fading, crushed by their physical workload and the unforgiving British climate, and the women had yet to catch up.

Just as John had expected, the Griffiths selected a solid oak casket. John smiled to himself. He liked the West Indian families; they were pleasant, courteous and amusing, and the cash commission he earned from their selections was good.

Thomas Griffiths had not spoken yet, except for the occasional interjection of, 'Jesus be praised, oh yes, Jesus be praised.' He had tottered between the coffins and caskets, quite ignored by the others as widow Ellen selected her man's final mattress. But when they got back into the arrangement room, they realised his seat was empty. His sister Elizabeth retraced their steps to the selection room to collect him. But he was not there. When she returned Palin explained that Thomas could have left the selection room via one of two other doors, and most probably the one leading directly onto the landing, to the gents. If he didn't return directly,

John would go and find him. They proceeded with the arrangements.

But Thomas Griffiths had not gone to the gents. He had somehow managed to fall into an open casket with such force that he had rocked it temporarily on its trestles causing the hinged lid to fall closed. His stupor was such that he was unsure if he was at home asleep, if he had dreamt of going to Sloane House or if he had in fact died, and he lay in his dark encasement attempting to work out which it was. He closed his eyes and drifted off to sleep.

The third door into the selection room then opened and Palin's assistant ushered into the room another family. British Brummie, they were heading straight for the solid raised lid elm with Aston Villa trimmings when the assistant, noticing that a hinged lid on one of the caskets was closed, lifted it up as she passed by. She continued on her way without a glance. The family following stopped and peered into the casket in astonishment. Was this to show what the deceased would look like? Or was this a corpse? Surely not a real dead black man in the selection room? One of their number, a young man, leaned forward. At that moment Thomas Griffiths farted loudly. 'Well fuck me,' said the young man in broad Brummie. A woman with him fainted.

Winston Wylde, the Griffiths women and Palin came running through the other arrangement door to be greeted by smiling, waving, incoherent Thomas, who had been awoken by the commotion and was mighty pleased to discover that he was not dead. He soon changed his mind as his big sister and sisters-in-law hauled him out of the casket and began to beat him severely with their handbags before pulling him back to the arrangement room by the hair. Here a speedy conclusion was made and the Reverend Winston Wylde took the Griffiths family home, where no doubt Thomas would get another pasting.

Having seen the Griffiths safely off the premises John Palin applied himself to calming the other grieving family. Now they knew what had happened they even saw the funny side of it. And they knew Thomas by sight – they too had seen him staggering along the Lozells Road.

Palin returned to his office. At three-fifty he took a call from Gillian Weston, owner and matron of Old Soldiers' Park.

Gillian Weston was in her mid-forties. She was warm, friendly and quite attractive, with very curly brown hair that tumbled down onto her shoulders. Her eyes were brown, laughing and big. Her figure was full but not at all fat. She had been a nurse then married a much older man. After only five years of marriage he had died. Many of her friends joked, although not to her face, that it was probably her keen sex drive that had seen him off. Her late husband had been well insured and left her well off. She used her new wealth to open the Old Soldiers' Park.

Naturally, she knew all the local funeral directors. She found Sydney pompous and cold. She had quite liked old Mr Higgins and was very fond of Joyce, whom she counted as a friend, and in whom she confided many of her flamboyant sexual fantasies. Joyce would listen, and they would giggle together. Gillian never really noticed that Joyce told her nothing, and never grasped that Joyce, if anything, had a stronger sex drive than herself, and she was unaware of Joyce's affair with Sydney.

Gillian also liked Stillion. He was polite, kind and flirtatious. She found him attractive and although she knew he would never love her she fancied he would have her. It had become an ambition of hers to seduce him.

Old Soldiers' Park was Gillian's only real interest, besides fantasy sex. The home was a twenty-four-hour-a-day, 365-days-a-year job. She loved it, and it was her livelihood. Her clients and their families liked this warm and, for her line of business, good woman.

Despite the fact that John Palin was not renowned for his sense of humour she sang down the telephone, 'John Martin's body lies a moldering in my mort,' to the tune of 'John Brown's Body'. John laughed politely, sensing that a funeral might just come his way. 'What can I do for you Gillian?' he enquired.

'Is Stillion still out on funerals?' she asked.

'Yes.'

'Well, tell him to come straight round to see me when he gets back in,' she commanded.

'He should be off by four forty-five,' came back the reply.

'Good, tell him I will expect him by five p.m. Bye.'

At Perry Bar Crem the fifth A-fleet job was coming to a close. Stillion had endured Michael Russell's version of Paul McCartney's 'Carry that Weight' on the eleven o'clock but was not amused to hear him playing 'He ain't Heavy, He's my Brother'. Three in one day was going too far. He determined to speak to the rock-playing organist.

Once the service was underway Michael slipped out of the crem chapel. He always did this so that he might have a quick joint made from the bag of cannabis he kept under the organ and to chat to Stillion, whom he liked.

'Look, Michael, this is getting out of hand,' started Stillion.

'Hey, man. What's the problem? Something not cool?'

'Michael, we're mates, but "Come on Baby, Light my Fire", "Carry that Weight" and "He ain't Heavy, He's my Brother" all in one day is just too much.'

'But it's cool man.'

'Listen, if *anyone* picks up on the chords or the fact that you finish everything with George Harrison's "Something", you will not find anything very cool.'

'What's wrong with "Something"?'

'Michael, how can a song that opens with the words "Something in the way she moves attracts me like no other lover" be appropriate for a dead person enclosed in a box which is just about to be burned?'

'It's a good tune.'

'Fuck that. Look mate. No more. OK?'

'OK, man.'

'You'd better get back in there for the committal music and for God's sake play something...'

' "Something"?'

'No, not "Something", just something normal for a funeral.'

Meanwhile Father O'Rourke had safely delivered the Lyons family to Richards & Gridley while Sydney for his part had dispatched the hard stuff – two cases thereof – to the presbytery. All arrangements had been concluded. At Richards & Gridley there was no fuss. No time wasted with fancy family lounges, selection rooms and the rest. You didn't get told what the price would be unless you asked. It would have been vulgar to talk about money at such a time. Sydney's motto was 'Give 'em what they think they want and charge 'em what you think they can afford.' Families liked to leave it to him, the good and bloody traditional way. That public schoolboy twit would be selling the mourners suits suitable for funerals next. Sydney felt nice and warm about the day, one down and every possibility of two to come.

At around four forty-five Stillion arrived back

chilled to the bone from the fifth funeral. Victoria was telling him he should conduct in an overcoat like the other Sloane staff. He replied that he preferred his tail-coat, it was much smarter. 'Perhaps,' she replied, 'but you're not. You'll end up in bed if you're not careful.'

'Is that a proposition, Vic Vesta?' he joked in an attempt to make her blush, which was really his only office sport.

Victoria Thomas was just twenty. A well-spoken, working-class country girl, she had applied for this job as soon as she had left secretarial college. Stillion had been immediately impressed by her shy but efficient manner and had offered her the job on the spot. Her hair was long, thick, wavy and red. Her skin was white with freckles and her figure trim with small but pert breasts and good legs. Her eyes were dark green. Stillion suspected she was probably a virgin and delighted in saying things to make her blush. His nick-name for her, 'Vic Vesta', alluded to the fact that he suspected that she wore a vest during the long, cold and damp days of winter. Stillion had been known to shout at his staff when the mood took him, but he had never raised his voice to this slender creature, for fear of breaking her. She drove an old white Mini and had a boyfriend who was a farrier in the nearby Clent hills. Victoria admired Stillion and enjoyed working for him. For his part he clearly loved her but wouldn't have dreamt of making sexual advances. As his father had always told him, it was unwise to fuck the payroll.

Palin interrupted their conversation with Gillian Weston's message and before long Stillion was on his way to Old Soldiers' Park, an incongruous sight driving his XJS while still wearing his tailcoat. Once there he was ushered into her office by one of her nurses. As he entered she looked up and smiled. She invited him to sit down. She finished her work on next week's rosta and threw down her pen, pushed her chair back and said, 'You cut a dashing figure in your tailcoat, pretty boy. But don't make a habit of coming here in it; it scares the shit out of my clients and we have enough shit to clear up as it is.'

'I made sure nobody saw me enter,' he assured her.

'Don't you believe it,' she replied. 'And so to business.' This struck Stillion as unusual behaviour for Gillian; she never normally made fun of her guests, nor called them clients and he hadn't heard her so curt before; she was usually soft and kind, with a flirtatious twinkle in her eye.

'So, young lady, what can I do for you?' asked Stillion, turning on the charm with enough genuine warmth to encourage Gillian to believe the 'young lady', despite her 45 years.

'It's not a question of what you can do for me, but what I can do for you. You see, this afternoon the brother and sister-in-law of Councillor Martin came in from Stratford to see me to collect the doctor's certificate. They asked me to confirm some directions that

Reverend Fred Price had given them from the registrars to Richards & Gridley.'

'Jesus,' blurted Stillion, 'I thought he was recommending us.'

'Well, never mind, because I did. You know what I think of Sydney Gridley, so I told them that you were the premier firm in the city and the people who always handle the major occasions. They, living out of town, did not know either of you. So they agreed to go with my recommendation, provided you can meet three conditions. Firstly, the funeral must take place on Thursday. Secondly, you must go yourself to their stately home near Stratford-upon-Avon this evening to arrange the funeral.'

'Well, if the family want a cremation,' interrupted Stillion.

'Which they do,' replied Gillian.

'Then that depends on whether or not you can get me the cremation papers completed by the first and second doctor tomorrow.'

'Which I can,' answered Gillian.

'Well then, the first condition is possible and the second presents no problem. Just give me the address and I had better phone Stephanie to say that I will be late. I need to collect my arrangement case from Sloane House and get changed. It's a good hour to them from here at this time of night. Do you want to tell them I'll be there for seven o'clock,' calculated Stillion.

'No, we had better say eight or eight-thirty; you're forgetting the third condition,' said Gillian.

'Yes I am. What's the third condition?' asked Stillion.

'Well, actually, it isn't their condition, it's mine. Come with me; I want to show you something.'

He followed her to the tiny mortuary. She flung open the door. Stillion saw two feet sticking out from beneath a sheet which was draped over a tatty old mortuary trolley. She pointed in that direction.

'The third condition. This is my body and you want it. Now that's your body,' she said, poking his chest, 'and I want it.'

'Now?'

'Yes, right now,' said Gillian firmly as she turned and beat a path to the small lift. Stillion followed obediently.

They entered the lift. She said nothing but was flushed with excitement. Stillion's head was spinning. He desperately wanted the funeral. He didn't find Gillian unattractive. Indeed no; his old friend Zizi was already pounding against his flies in an attempt to get free and at her. Stillion loved bedding older women. They made much better lovers. Women in uniforms had always excited him particularly. He suspected Gillian would go like a train. But he was very much in love with Stephanie; she was truly beautiful both as a person and to behold. She was his best friend. He might have been a ram before marriage but he had worked hard at being good since. He would hate to hurt Stephanie. His father had always warned him about fucking the payroll, and screwing the owner of the local old people's home in order to secure an important funeral could be described as that. It could also be described as thoroughly depraved and immoral. What would his old friend Winston Wylde think? What would his mother think? Worst of all, what would Steppie think? Where would this all end? A fuck for the ex-Lord Mayor now and just a quick flash of Zizi for poor old Mrs Smith, aged ninety-two, sometime next week? Was he to become a whore?

The lift stopped. She was still smiling. It was the last chance saloon. He must stop now or he would be beyond the point of refusal. To enter the apartment and then refuse would be to insult her desirability and to hurt her. And he was flattered by the flush in her cheeks and the desire clearly visible in her eyes. It was business and pleasure versus honour and love. Stillion was a kind man. He was tough but fair. He had a very British sense of right and wrong. He was, all in all, a good man. She opened the door and stood aside for him to go in. Yes, Stillion was generally a good man. But not just now. He went in.

She led him through to the pleasant but modestly furnished drawing room. She put a standard lamp on next to the TV set. Here on the top floor of an old Victorian house the central heating pump just couldn't get the hot water up for the radiators, so there was a gas fire already on. Stillion noticed it was a very old gas fire, just like those he remembered at prep school in Edgbaston. There was a small bowl of water in front of it. Under the window that looked down over the front drive there was a table. Gillian leaned against it. 'Well, well, Mr Sloane, you are in my parlour. I'm the spider and you are the fly. Would you like a drink before I suck every little drop of protein out of you?'

'I doubt if there's time for a drink and a chat if I am to be in the heart of the Warwickshire countryside by eight,' replied Stillion, taking his tailcoat off and determining in his own mind that he was not prepared to be treated any longer as a little boy in this proposed sex romp.

He advanced towards her. They stood facing each other: he, the taller, faced the window in his immaculate white shirt, Sloane & Sons corporate tie, black waistcoat, pinstriped trousers and black shoes; she, the shorter, faced into the room in her royal blue matron's smock coat with white buttons down the front, navy blue stockings and shoes. He put his hands on her waist and leaned slightly forward and down to nibble gently at her right earlobe. He gently kissed her face across the right cheek over her lips and to her left ear. She moved her hands to the front of his trousers and could feel Zizi, who seemed to be deliciously large and happy to meet her on the other side of the material. Stillion placed her hands back on the table at each side of her. 'Not yet. I will tell you when,' he murmured, as he started to kiss the left side of her neck with his slightly opened mouth, while caressing the right side of her neck with his left hand. He stood up to his usual height and brought both of his hands together in order to undo the first button of her smock coat. He stared into her eyes as his hands moved on to the second and then the third and so on. She was rooted to the spot. Her breathing had become faster and heavier. Electric shocks were shooting from her moist vagina down both legs and they, in turn were turning to jelly. She felt paralysed and blissfully unable to stop his advances. He undid the last button and pushed the smock coat off her shoulders, letting it fall to the floor about her. She was standing in front of him in a white boned bra that cupped her ample breasts, presenting them perfectly. Beneath them and crossing an ageless tummy, undamaged by childbearing, was a white suspender belt worn above surprisingly skimpy white knickers. The white flesh of her full thighs disappeared into her navy blue stockings.

She couldn't move. She didn't speak. His hands moved around her back, his fingers lightly touching her skin, and clicked open the clasp of her bra. He flicked the straps off her shoulders and it fell to the floor between them. Her breasts stood proud, exposed and exquisitely naked before him. Her nipples were erect. Her breathing had now become heavy enough to move her shoulders slightly up and down. He gazed across her naked breasts before fixing back onto her eyes. The boy was transfixing her. This was more than she'd bargained for, but she wouldn't have missed it for the world. She didn't feel sixteen years older. He may be younger but his dominating made age seem irrelevant. And either he was enjoying it or he was the world's most professional whore. Either way she didn't care.

He ran his fingers lightly over her breasts and his palms gently flicked across her nipples. She thought she would explode. Then without losing eye contact he dropped to his knees, his face now directly opposite her slightly gyrating pelvis. His fingers slipped up and under her white knickers by each hip bone and slowly pulled them down. She managed to summon enough strength to step out of them. She was now standing with her hands clutching the table and her back arching towards the window in just her white suspender belt, navy blue stockings and shoes.

She had thrown her head back and in a trance stared at the ceiling. She was standing naked before him. It felt gloriously naughty. Then as his tongue gently explored her clitoris she thought she would burst. He stood up. He lifted her and placed her buttocks on the table. He spread her legs. He undid the front of his trousers to set free a raging Zizi who entered her in a second. He didn't thrust; he allowed Zizi to make circular movements which inspired the most violent multiple orgasm that she had ever experienced. Her groans moved up a gear into yelps of delight. Miss

Angela Blackham, aged ninety and the longest serving resident at Old Soldiers' Park, was watching children's television in her room, next door to Gillian's apartment. The thudding of the table against the window-sill along with Gillian's singing made a noisy symphony; luckily for the lovers' dignity and Miss Blackham's heart, she was stone deaf.

As Gillian came again and again Stillion thought that maybe if he didn't come then it wouldn't count as infidelity. But Zizi was determined to enjoy his holiday and before he could help himself Stillion's arse tightened and he shot into her.

He waited a respectable period of time for her to recover her composure before whispering, 'Miss Weston, I must go if I am not going to let us both down. Please remember to phone the family. I think you were right; eight o'clock will be nearer the mark.' And then he added quietly in her right ear, 'Thank you. I have often wondered what that would be like. I wasn't disappointed and feel exhausted.' She was pleased he had said that; if he hadn't she might have felt exposed, both physically and mentally. Stillion didn't have to dress. He was dressed. He kissed her briefly and lightly on the lips, grabbed his tailcoat and left. It was six-thirty.

He made a whistlestop appearance at Sloane House, collected his arrangement case and changed from his funeral gear into a lounge suit. He asked Victoria to let Stephanie know he would be home late and why, and popped his head around John Palin's door to give him the good news and enquire if the Lyons family had made contact. They hadn't.

Then he was off down the Soho Road and away across the Hockley flyover, through the city and onto the Stratford road. At ten to eight he turned into the long gravel drive of the Martin's sizeable country estate; the drive wandered up a wooded incline before bending to the right and exposing below a magnificent Jacobean mansion. What light there was from the house allowed Stillion a glimpse of formal Elizabethan gardens immediately around the house. This was the sort of place that the young Prince of Wales, Charles Stuart, may have rested in on his flight to the continent following the battle of Worcester. 'Blimey,' thought Stillion as he left the car, 'the Martins must be worth a bob or two.' He knocked at the great front door at eight o'clock precisely.

Councillor Martin's brother and his family were most pleasant. Stillion was offered a dry sherry and then set about the arrangements. The funeral would be on Thursday morning, as requested. He would telephone to confirm the times once he had spoken to the crematorium in the morning. The family felt comfortable with Stillion; it turned out that the Councillor had been a member of the Castle Bromwich Flying Club in the 1920s, as had Stillion's Grandfather. Councillor Martin had been to Harrow, as had Stillion's father and Stillion himself. Stillion didn't strike them as the funeral directing type; they were pleased Gillian Weston had recommended him. What was he like? Well a bit like them really. Top hole, don't you know?

Stillion left just after ten, having spoken to Reverend Price from the house in order to confirm the times at church. He duly made it home for eleven, in time for a late supper and to retire to bed with Stephanie. He didn't feel as guilty as he had expected. He put this down to the fact that he had not sought the encounter but that his actions had been an essential part of a business transaction. He still loved Stephanie as much as ever and he had no desire to be untrue to her again. He was confident that this had been just a one-off that nobody else would know about. Shortly after midnight he and Stephanie were asleep in each other's arms as usual. At the close of play the score was Sloanes, two, Richards & Gridley, one, although neither captain realised that yet.

2

Tuesday

As soon as Sydney arrived in his office from the flat upstairs he made straight for the telephone. He rang Rory Bruton. 'What happened to the Griffiths family? They were supposed to come in here yesterday afternoon on your recommendation.'

'I couldn't say a word. They brought Reverend Wylde. Wiv 'im in the room it would've been more than my job's wurf to say a word,' whined the crooked little National Health worker. 'Any road, it's too late now. They've gone to Sloanes.'

'How the hell do you know that?' interrupted Sydney.

'That bloody John Palin has already been on the blower this mornin' for the measurements.'

Sydney, without a further word, slammed down the receiver, only to pick it up again immediately to call Reverend Fred Price. 'Good morning Father Price, it's Sydney Gridley here. I thought I ought to phone you as I haven't heard from the Martin family yet,' he said politely, for although he had a tiny inkling that he may have lost this funeral too, he mustn't lose his temper with a member of the clergy for the future's sake.

'No, and nor will you either, I'm afraid,' came back the response. Sydney's heart plummetted as Reverend Price went on, 'I did recommend you and they told me they were going to contact you, so you can imagine my surprise when Stillion Sloane phoned me at around ten last night from their house to confirm the time at church on Thursday. After the service we've got some awful trek out into darkest Warwickshire to some hardly-used crematorium.' By stressing the long and monotonous journey, Fred Price hoped to make Sydney feel grateful that he was not conducting the funeral and thereby to allay his anger. But both men knew how important this funeral was to Richards & Gridley and they ended the difficult conversation without Price having to explain how he had failed and before Sydney informed the Father that he, his congregation and the whole bloody Church of England could whistle for the stained glass window and central heating repairs as far as he was concerned. As Reverend Price put the phone down the financial implications were on his mind. Obviously, Sydney wouldn't lift a finger to help St John's at that moment. Stillion had promised to repair the stained glass window and Fred hoped that Stillion would know nothing of his recommending Richards & Gridley. Of course, Stillion had worked out what Freddie Price was up to, thanks to what he had been told by Gillian Weston. However, he was becoming far too shrewd to risk damaging his developing relationship with the old man by refusing to pay for a stained glass window repair. What's more, the occasional stained glass window repair was a lot safer way of securing the odd funeral than sex sessions with randy matrons, which could bring down his marriage.

Sydney, for his part, didn't know whether to vomit with disappointment or to scream out aloud with anger. In the event he did neither. He had just managed to retreat from the conversation with Fred Price without a loss of too much dignity and now he had to keep a clear head in the face of such a hammer blow. He kept telling himself that at least he had got the large Lyons' funeral, but a little voice inside him told him that, although that was a good high-profile funeral to have, it was not quite in the same league as a famous ex-Lord Mayor. The Martin funeral was a small-scale state funeral for Birmingham. He had boasted to other benchers and to his chums at Rotary that Richards & Gridley were *the* Birmingham funeral company nowadays due to his high standing in the community and the fact that young Sloane wasn't fit to wear his daddy's tailcoat. How they would laugh at him now. Sure, the Lyons' funeral was a feather in the cap, but a feather that few would notice by comparison to Stillion Sloane's two feathers.

What a bloody disaster. How had that bloody boy managed it? The ex-Lord Mayor's funeral would attract the present Lord Mayor, the Corporation, Birmingham society, the national Conservative hierarchy, the press and perhaps even the television. All of this could not but help Sloane's position; even Joyce Higgins could be influenced by these events. Sydney felt he couldn't be sure of her just now. Maybe she was just trying to raise the stakes with him. Or maybe she really had meant a lot of what she had said yesterday.

Sydney just wished that Stillion would cock up both funerals, but he knew he wouldn't. He knew Stillion would grab the opportunity with two grateful hands. He hated to admit it but rumour had it that Sloane was a good funeral director and, although Sydney would conduct the funerals differently himself, perhaps with less pomp, nevertheless there wasn't a chance that the boy would slip up.

A chance? Why leave it to chance for them to go wrong? Why not just ensure that they went wrong? He had never had such an unthinkable thought before, let alone allowed it to settle. But these were desperate times. If the bloody upper-class, self-righteous Sloanes were to be stopped, then Stillion Sloane had to be stopped before the city fell for his shallow charm. He, Sydney, had had Sloanes on the run before Stillion had got his feet under Arthur's desk. But with Sloane & Sons making acquisitions, doing up Sloane House, buying new fleets, threatening to outbid him for Higgins & Co. and now getting two out of three of these high-profile funerals, Sydney felt the tide was turning against him. He felt old. And that bloody boy was young. He hated him. By God he hated him. He hated every bloody thing that the spoilt, public school twit and his wretched family stood for. No, he was not going to leave it to chance. If Stillion wanted centre stage then let him have centre bloody stage and may he die of shame as his two big funerals collapsed around him.

He called the garage on the intercom. He asked for Rolley Brown and requested his presence. Rolley, the hearse driver and garage foreman, had been with Richards & Gridley since 1928. He had started in the coffin shop, progressed to the stables and then, when horse power gave way to motorised hearses and limousines in the 1940s, to the garage. He lived with his wife in a small flat above the garage. They had had several children there, but they'd long since grown up and flown the nest. Born Robert, his name changed to Rolley probably because of his great size, although nobody could really remember. He was certainly very fat, no doubt due to the quantities of fried food and beer that he consumed; indeed he, his clothes, his equally fat wife and his tiny flat all smelled of beer mixed with stale fried bread, with a heady dose of body odour.

Rolley was a rogue. He lived by begging, borrowing and stealing, but he never got caught. Sydney had inherited him with the business but had never got rid of him. Why, nobody knew, not even Sydney. Maybe it was because he was a well-known character in the community. Maybe because, rogue as he was, he was liked by most, including ministers and matrons. Maybe because he had made it clear to Sydney whom he could bribe and whom he couldn't, and even took the money round for Sydney. Or maybe because Rolley was cheap – in exchange for no rent for that disgusting little flat, Sydney paid him very little. It was for this reason that Rolley could justify in his own mind fiddling petrol for his car from the company's pump; unlike Lawrence Kemp, his opposite number over at Sloanes, he never got caught.

Rolley was interested in horse racing and making little earners on the side. Saturday afternoon was his favourite time; the television turned to BBC1's *Grandstand*, bets already placed, a pint of Ansell's mild in one hand, a Park Drive in the other and the missus out, either at her sister's or buying his tea. He could then watch the racing, pick his nose and flick it anywhere he wanted without fear of nagging.

Rolley Brown would help Sydney with this little destruction job. Only the two of them must ever know. That was no problem. It had been just the two of them at this dirty little coalface ever since Sydney had taken the reins from John Richards. Certainly neither Susan nor Marcus must know. Both had a strong sense of right and wrong; indeed it was their sense of right and wrong that allowed Sydney to control them. He knew that neither really liked him but they believed it was only right to love, honour and obey one's husband and father. But they might have less respect if they knew just a quarter of what Rolley and he got up to.

Money to local solicitors, doctors, matrons and mortuary porters had played perhaps a bigger part in the build-up of the business than recommendations or even the death rate itself. Richards & Gridley weren't bad funeral directors, but Sydney did like to ensure that, for a few pieces of eight, business was herded his way and nothing was therefore left to chance.

Rolley arrived at the door of Sydney's office. 'Come in, Rolley. I need to ask your help with a thought I've had. Shut the door and take a seat.' Rolley obeyed. 'You see,' continued Sydney through tight thin lips, looking straight into Rolley's pokey blubber-surrounded eyes, 'we haven't got either the Griffiths funeral or, more importantly, the Martin funeral. Worse, both families have decided to engage the services of Sloane & Sons Ltd. Now I don't know about you but I happen to think that that is a shame for us. And it might be a shame for them, if that bloody public school twit was to cock up the funerals.'

'Yeah, but he won't, will he?' interrupted Rolley.

'He just might if you were to help him,' answered Sydney.

'Well, how would I do that?' asked Rolley.

'I don't know, and that's why I'm asking you. You've always been so good at this sort of thing.'

Sydney was not known for paying compliments; some days even the expression 'good morning' could not be forced through those thin lips. He really wanted Rolley's help.

It worked. 'Elton Field,' said Rolley.

'What?' asked Sydney.

'Elton Field. He's the Sloane embalmer. He bets on the nags, he's in debt and he steals. I had him steal some coffin handles from the Sloane fitting shop last winter when we ran out.'

'Well, OK, but why him? I mean, what can he do for us?' enquired Sydney.

'Well, guv, it strikes me that we are powerless to fuck up those funerals from here. I mean what opportunity do we have? None. Whereas a man on the inside can really screw things up and it'll appear so realistic because it will be them doing the fuck ups.'

'Brilliant,' pondered Sydney, 'bloody brilliant. How much will it cost?'

'Oh, it'll cost. We'll have to make it worth his while. There'll be big risks involved for him. But he must only be paid for success. That's our insurance,' added Rolley thoughtfully.

'Yes, pay only after the event. And warn him of the dangers of talking to anyone about this. See him for a drink tonight. Will £500.00 per funeral do the trick?'

'Should be about right,' replied Rolley.

'OK, it's ten-seventeen. We have to be at the first house at ten-thirty. We'd better go. Phone him from

West Brom Crem to fix up the meeting. Keep me informed,' finished Sydney. Rolley put on his chauffeur's cap and helped Sydney into his heavy black overcoat with black velvet collar. Sydney, with black bowler perched on the top of his head and the day's fees, gratuities, certificates and accounts in hand, turned his office light off and walked into the garage to leave on the first funeral confident that the bloody public school twit would live to regret having arranged those two funerals. Sydney felt a lot better than he did an hour ago. The events of the week just may work out in his favour after all.

As Sydney and Rolley drove out of the garage, Mr Razek Singh called to settle his account. But he couldn't collect his father's ashes, because with all the excitement Sydney had forgotten to collect them from the crematorium. Mr Singh was not at all pleased, and said he would return tomorrow.

Elton Field was the embalmer and an occasional limousine driver at Sloanes. His full name was Elton John Field. He'd been christened John Field, but had in his teens adopted the additional first name because he thought it would be cool to announce his name as Elton John. He thought it would win him favour with the girls. It didn't. Elton was not cool in the least; at the age of twenty-six he was small, slight and shifty looking. Educated at a secondary modern in Aston, he had left school with just one O Level, in Religious Knowledge. After several small jobs he decided to become an embalmer, becoming apprenticed to the Birmingham Cooperative Funeral Division and studying at night school. He had been taken on by Stillion's father in 1973.

There was something slightly untrustworthy about Elton but nothing had ever been proved. Neither Stillion nor Mary Sloane, Stillion's mother, had ever really liked him but he appeared to work hard and was always very polite. Perhaps too polite; he was humble to the point of reminding Stillion of Dickens' Uriah Heap. But funeral staff were hard to find in 1979, despite rising dole queues. And trained embalmers were even harder to find, so Stillion pushed unkind thoughts of Elton to the back of his mind and put up with his constant playing of Elton John tapes while he worked.

Both Sloanes and Richards & Gridley had a busy, hectic and cold day, typical of those when there were many funerals to conduct, bodies to move and embalm, coffins to fit and cars to wash. So it was two tired and thoroughly chilled men who gratefully grabbed the table by the blazing fire at the Builders' Arms at seven forty-five that evening. Elton would usually have been sinking into a hot bath in his Lozells council flat, before tucking into a pie and chips while reading the *Sporting Life*, but Rolley's promise of a substantial amount of extra cash had lured him away from home on this freezing night.

Where they were sitting was not only pleasantly

warm but also confidential. To their right was the large fireplace and to their left a wall. The nearest table was six or seven feet away, on the other side of the passage to the gents. As he put two pints of Ansell's Mild on the little table, Rolley opened the business discussion with, 'Are you sure you didn't tell anyone anything? About seeing me? Or money? Nothing?'

'I'm sure,' replied a fascinated Elton.

'Good. Now, how would you like to earn yourself five hundred extra notes this week?'

'Great. 'Course I would. What've I gotta do?'

'Nothing too difficult, sunshine. I'll tell you just now but first I must know before you decide whether to do it or not I have your word that this is just between you and me, OK?'

'Bent, is it?' asked Elton.

'You'll never fuckin' find out if I don't get your word on it now,' replied Rolley angrily.

'OK, OK, keep your hair on, mate. I was only asking,' said Elton.

'Your word,' repeated Rolley sternly.

'You have it. OK?' replied Elton.

'Say the words,' continued Rolley.

'You have my word.'

'Good. Now, I want you to screw up both the Martin and the Griffiths funerals. You see, we feel we should be conducting those funerals. Somehow they ended up with you lot.'

'That's because we're a better firm than you, firstly.

Secondly, you must be fuckin' mad. Five hundred nicker only. My bookie wants eight hundred notes, like, tomorrow. No way mate. Five hundred nicker's no good to me. I could end up in big shit with no job and the bookie still wanting to use my balls in his fuckin' pinball machine. No mate. No. Anyway, how the fuck do I fuck up a funeral mate, just tell me that?' Elton's voice squeaked out in excited Brummie, rising in tone and octaves.

'Keep your voice down for fuck's sake, you stupid bastard,' growled the lumpen Rolley nervously before continuing himself in a whisper. 'Look, there are hundreds of ways to cock up a funeral for fuck's sake.'

'Yes and no doubt you know them all but we don't cock up funerals,' interjected Elton, pleased with himself.

'Don't get clever with me or I'll throw your fuckin' glasses in the fire you four-eyed little git. And what's with all the loyalty bit anyway? Don't give me that shit. Remember the handles last winter. You sold your soul for twenty notes that night.'

'Yeah, well, that was different. A few free handles to you, so what?'

'It was stealing mate, that's what, and you stole and took money for it. So that's what. How do you do cock ups? Well crash the hearse. Run down the fuckin' vicar. Send the wrong bleeding coffin on the funeral. Put the wrong breastplate on. Make a limousine break down or even go to the wrong cemetery, take your pick,' Rolley told Elton.

'Yes, but I can't influence a lot of those things. Stillion has so many checks and double checks that anything I did before the funeral would get discovered. And on the funeral Stillion is the conductor and Lawrence Kemp drives the hearse. They're always in control. Anyway, the bung isn't enough, so forget it.'

'Look, I'll get you a grand for the two, but I want a ten per cent kick back for talking Gridley into it. That leaves you with eight hundred notes to give your bookie and a hundred left over for Christmas,' said Rolley, having just offered what Sydney had told him to offer in the first place and carving himself out a hundred notes in the process. 'Now, I can't do better than that; all your debts paid and cash in hand for a couple of mistakes. I don't care how you fuck 'em up, just fuck 'em up, that's all up to you. Just do it and then keep your trap shut.'

'I want half in advance,' answered Elton.

'Get lost mate. I'll get you half now. You pay the cash to your bookie and you don't deliver, I can't get the cash back. What do I tell Mr Gridley? Be realistic. You get it all the day after you deliver. I can't do better than that, mate.'

Elton thought. He looked away and stared into the fire. It could be done. He could think of better and less obvious ways of doing it than those suggested by the fat lump Rolley. The money would be great. His bookie was making his life hell with phone calls to both work and home. It was getting to a point where violence couldn't be ruled out. He hadn't got the money for the rent, housekeeping or electric final notice, let alone Christmas presents for the kids, who also badly needed clothes, as did the missus. He knew his wages, over-time and night removal money would do if it hadn't been feeding the bookie as well as his family. It would be a risk, but so too was not paying the bookie. Indeed Stillion was less likely, being a gent and all, to snap his legs than was the bookie. And with nine hundred notes, his salary and the Christmas bonus all coming in before the holiday, Christmas might not be so bad after all.

His mind made up, he turned back to Rolley; 'OK, its a deal. But I want my money before the weekend and if I get sacked I want a job with you lot or some part-time work until I get sorted out.'

'I'm sure Mr Gridley will be happy with these terms,' responded Rolley.

'Shouldn't you ask him?' enquired Elton.

'No need. But if there is a problem with any of it I'll phone you at home tonight. If you don't hear from me it's OK and therefore just get on with it.'

They finished their Mild and went their separate ways. Judas had been bought. Elton phoned his bookie to buy time until the weekend. Rolley phoned his boss. All four retired for the night happy with their deals. Three slept well; Elton lay awake plotting the fall of Sloanes. Cock-ups seemed so easy when they just happened but inventing them was bloody hard. Perhaps even an art form.

3

Wednesday

As Elton stepped from his front door into a typically bleak, damp and foggy Birmingham December morning, the winter dawn was shedding its first grey light on the Dickensian horrors of the surrounding Lozells slums and, in the distance, the depressing 1960s tower blocks of Hockley.

He had formulated his plan overnight and now set about his tasks of destruction, motivated by the thought of enough money to cure his problems and maybe a little bit more besides for a little flutter. Like most of those with his illness Elton hadn't learnt that the little flutter he longed for would sooner or later bring him full circle to where he stood on that cold morning – in debt and with a price on his legs.

Quite uncharacteristically, he arrived at work very early and got on with as much embalming and presentation work as he could. A large number of bodies were awaiting collection from various hospitals, and Lawrence Kemp had set off in the ambulance at the crack of dawn to battle through the rush hour traffic and gather as many as he could before the first A-fleet funeral left Sloane House at ten-fifteen. After that Lawrence would be out with the A-fleet for the rest of the day, and the remaining removals would have to be done by a fireman from the local station's blue watch who helped out occasionally when off duty, for a fee of £1.00 per hospital removal and £2.00 for driving or bearing on a funeral. Like most funeral directors, Sloanes had a full-time permanent staff, but when the death rate rocketed in the winter they had a supply of firemen, policemen and ambulancemen who helped out for cash in hand.

At nine-twenty Elton wandered out of his embalming theatre and into the coffin-fitting shop next door, where Walter Warburton was working frantically. Walter was down for four A-fleet jobs today, and also had to finish at least six coffins and two caskets by the end of the day. He wanted to get as much done as possible now because he knew that after the last funeral he would have to spray, sponge, spray and leather his limo, clean the carpets, the mats, the interior and panel windows, the back door chrome strips, check the backs of the wing mirrors and black the tyres. It was Sloanes' rule that all vehicles were washed and covered every evening, so that they only had to be dusted off in the morning before the first funeral of the day. This would mean at least an hour of finger-numbing work in a cold garage, with the water freezing on the limo before he could leather it off. He would then have to study tomorrow's garage orders to see which funerals he was on, and which coffins needed fitting out for Friday. The last thing he wanted, after all that, was to have to come back into the fitting shop. So he'd been in since six. It wasn't always this frantic. There were only so many people going to die, but the bastards didn't die at a nice steady rate through the year, or during working hours.

Walter Warburton was the lead A-fleet limousine driver. He was only twenty-seven but his prematurely grey hair and moustache gave him an appearance well beyond his years. At the age of sixteen he had left his West Bromwich comprehensive to become a car mechanic, but an engine falling on his right hand had put a stop to that and he'd then become a driver for a firm of local funeral directors, which Stillion had bought earlier that year.

Walter was always worried. He expected the worst, a negative attitude that may have been born out of his support for lost causes such as West Bromwich Albion, which had just failed to win the 1979 league championship, and the Labour Party, which had just begun eighteen years in opposition. He munched crisps and chocolate in huge quantities but never seemed to put on weight, which led to him being ribbed by the other chauffeurs about the amount he must shit. He still lived with his parents and, almost devoid of ambition was one of the last generation of the working class who aspired to be just like their dad – with a flat cap, raincoat and a whippet.

'Hi Walter,' said Elton, as he entered the fitting shop.

'No, I can't come and give you a lift. I'm far too busy. You'll have to wait until one of the others comes back in,' replied Walter, without looking up from the engraving machine. He knew Elton only came in when he wanted help.

'No, I've got as far as I can go until Lawrence brings in more bodies, so I thought I'd come in and start off one or two coffins for you while I'm waiting,' answered Elton, to Walter's disbelief.

'Blimey, mate. You serious? You feeling all right. You're not coming down wit' somethin', is ye?'

'Well, if that's 'ow you feel,' said Elton, looking down at the ground like a hurt little boy, a pose he had evolved to deal with the frequent bollockings he got from Stillion.

'No, no, I'm only joking. 'Course I'd like an 'and,' said Walter, now looking up and smiling.

'Look, I'll put the handles on these coffins for you. You do the plates and then you can fit out the interiors in between funerals. Okay, mate?' suggested Elton.

'Cheers mate,' answered a pleasantly surprised Walter. Getting all the handles on before going out on the first job was a bonus. Elton set to work on the coffin destined to take ex-Lord Mayor Councillor Martin.

* * *

After the first A-fleet job Elton returned to the mortuary. He wasn't driving on the next three funerals; his place had been taken by a part-timer, to enable him to prepare all the bodies for Thursday's jobs and to deliver some outstanding cremation papers.

He made an excellent job of Messrs Griffiths and Martin; there may be trouble ahead but nobody was going to be able to fault him on his embalming. That would have pointed a finger straight at him. And in any case, his professional pride as a member of the British Institute of Embalmers – the only exam, with the exception of that O Level in Religious Knowledge, that he had ever passed – forbade him to cock up. When the Griffiths female relations (with, traditionally, the exception of the widow) arrived at three o'clock to wash and prepare the body, they would find a clean and impeccably embalmed Charles Nelson Griffiths waiting to be dressed in white vest, pants, dress shirt, black dress suit, tie, socks, shoes, handkerchief and gloves. The Martin family were not expected to come to Sloane House to view but if they had they would have found the ex-Lord Mayor Councillor well embalmed, smart and clean-shaven except for his famous white moustache and white hair, which had been washed, dried and parted in exactly the same way as had been seen in every official photograph for the last fifty years.

When he was satisfied with his efforts Elton picked up the intercom to John Palin. 'Look, John, I've finished today's bodies. I'll need a lift up to the chapels later, before I go on the Griffiths take-home, but I'll take the Martin B, C and F papers over to Ebbwell Crem now; they 'ave to be there before two. I've got to be quick but do you want me to recce the route and mark up a map for tomorrow's funeral? If the Griffiths family arrive before I get back then just show 'em into the wash and dress room. He and the casket are already up there and I'll help 'em put him in it when I get back.'

'Good,' replied Palin, 'that sounds good. The papers are up here, completed and ready to go, and I've got a map of South Birmingham and Warwickshire that Mr Sloane wants marking up with the best route from the Town Hall onwards. And by the way, you couldn't fetch one out of Dudley Road for me on the way could you?'

'John, mate, I'm really racin' as it is and that's out of my way by at least twenty minutes.'

'OK, OK, I was only asking.' John didn't drive and was sensitive to the jokes that he knew went on behind his back about his sense of direction and time when it came to removals. In point of fact he'd now become quite good at timing funerals; Stillion had made him a chart of directions to crems and cems and listed the length of time that each of the various denominations took over their services, so he could normally work it out. Anything unusual, like a trip to Ebbwell Crem, he'd ask Stillion. It usually worked well, and it was only occasionally that a Palin timing error screwed up the garage orders.

Elton collected Councillor Martin's cremation papers from John's office and set off in the firm's white transit van. Watching him go, John, like Walter, couldn't quite get over how organised and helpful Elton was being.

Meanwhile, Stillion, Lawrence Kemp and the rest of the A-fleet team were conducting a funeral for a Sikh family living in a terraced house in a small cul-de-sac just off West Bromwich High Street. It being a Sikh funeral, the cul-de-sac was packed with old vans and four Corporation double-decker buses hired for the occasion. As was usual among Sikh families the coffin had been taken home earlier in the day so that the family, friends, friends of friends, professional mourners and wailers could pay their last, and loudest, respects. There were now what seemed like several hundred Indian men and women noisily seething in and around the house.

The cortège stopped in the High Street. Stillion got out of the hearse and set about guiding both limousine and hearse backwards into the cul-de-sac, so they were facing in the right direction when it came to leave for the crem. A large number of people and several vans had to be moved away from the front of the house, but Stillion had expected this and had allowed enough time to do so with polite charm. As he was guiding the hearse into position he became aware of a change in the din outside the house, and looked up. To his horror he saw the lidless coffin being passed, hand by hand, out of the door and towards the hearse, over the heads of the assembled company. The elderly Sikh gentleman bouncing around in his coffin looked very smart in his grey suit, white shirt, blue tie and white turban, but while parading the deceased through the streets was of course quite usual in the Middle East or Indian sub-continent, it was not at all the done thing in Middle England. Stillion, with the help of Lawrence Kemp, managed somehow to guide the coffin back, overhead and hand by hand, through the front door, into the front room and back down onto the trestles from whence it had come.

The wailing was immense. There was a wailing record on the gramophone in the back room, and in the front room professional wailing women half lay on the floor, banging their heads against the coffin and screaming. And now that the men, having paid their respects, were gathering in the street, it was the turn of the women, who had until now been squeezed in large numbers into the back room, kitchen and small back garden. They began to file through the front room, past the coffin and out into the street, wailing and crying and beating their faces with their fists.

The coffin lid was now in place and Stillion stood to attention by the foot end, Lawrence at the head end. The eldest son and therefore chief mourner stood behind the coffin, in front of the fireplace. The women passed. The wailers wailed and the women passed. With veils over their heads, blanket-patterned overcoats and sari trousers, the women passed. Six minutes passed. Still the women passed. Stillion glanced at Lawrence and then his watch. He knew that there had been a lot of women in the rear of the house, but not this many, surely? He stepped forward and joined the procession of women, through the front door, down the side of the house to the kitchen door, through the kitchen and back into the front room.

Such were the similarities in the women's dress and height that neither he nor Lawrence had noticed their passing for a second or even a third time. The very next woman to come through the door of the front room was quietly and gently escorted by Stillion through the front door, out into the street and onto a Corporation bus. The other women followed. They filled two of the buses, and the men filled the other two and most of the vans. Stillion returned to the front room. The wailing record was still bashing out the wailers' top ten but the house was now empty save for the eldest son, five or so of his brothers, who would bear the coffin with him, and Lawrence Kemp.

Stillion had not seen any floral tributes. There didn't have to be floral tributes, but he felt he should ask if there were, in case they'd been put upstairs to preserve them from the wailing stampede. 'Excuse me, Sir. Do you have any family flowers that you would like placed on the coffin?' he enquired.

'Oh, family flowers. Oh, I see, yes, of course, family flowers,' replied the eldest son, looking nervous and embarrassed that he had forgotten something important. He looked around him and, suddenly announcing 'Yes, we do,' he grabbed a plastic pot containing one large plastic daisy from the centre of the mantelpiece and slammed it down on the coffin lid.

Lawrence looked at Stillion. Stillion glared back with a look that said, 'Act normally, or I'll kill you.' Lawrence attached the coffin wire from the head moulding, over the plastic pot, and secured it on the foot moulding, so that the floral tribute stayed in place. The sons then carried the coffin to the hearse, and were led to the limousine driven by Walter Warburton. Lawrence Kemp got behind the wheel of the hearse while Stillion took up his position in front of it, ready to walk the cortège down the cul-de-sac and left into West Bromwich High Street. They were still in good time for four o'clock at the West Brom Crem.

Stillion marched gracefully. Behind him there came a hearse, a limousine, four Corporation buses and many transit vans. People stopped and stared. They always did. It was a funeral. No, it was a big funeral. But, wait a minute. What was that on the coffin? A large plastic daisy in a plastic pot, looking for all the world just like Weed, friend of Bill & Ben, the Flowerpot Men. The great West Bromwich public could not conceal its mirth.

* * *

Elsewhere, Elton had driven hard and happily. The traffic wasn't too heavy so he'd made it back to Sloane House for three o'clock, in time to help the Griffiths female relations with the wash and dress before taking Charles Nelson Griffiths home for four-thirty. As was usual with his countrymen, the senior West Indian would 'lie in state' between now and the funeral, with the lid of the casket open, and be visited by family, friends and associates from all over the country, while the customary Jim Reeves' 'Distant Drums' played in the background. Lawrence Kemp had returned from the Sikh funeral at four-twelve, they had loaded by four-fifteen and arrived at the Griffiths' establishment, on the borders of Handsworth and Lozells, bang on time. Just like the boss planned.

Lawrence Kemp and Elton walked down the short driveway of the neat, white, semi-detached house to the small enclosed porch. Lawrence rang the bell and when the widow opened the door they stepped inside. She showed them into the lounge. The three-piece suite had already been pushed back against the walls. She would have her husband rested there, she said, pointing with her right hand to a spot between the doorway to the hall and the sliding double doors that led to the dining room. This would allow folk to enter from the hall and, having paid their last respects, pass on into the dining room where drinks would be laid out on the table. From the dining room the mourners could then move through into the kitchen and thus back into the hall. Excellent; no traffic jams.

In fact there wasn't anywhere else the casket could go. Charles Nelson Griffiths was a big man and big men need big caskets, and the post-war semi wasn't spacious. Having placed the trestles as requested, Lawrence and Elton returned to the hearse to carry the great West Indian home. There should have been four of them on this job, but two late funerals meant they had to manage on their own. They had done so often enough before, and even preferred not to have others getting in the way if space was tight. Lawrence took the head end and walked backwards, drawing the casket out of the hearse. Elton waited until the foot end appeared and slid his fingers underneath the casket. Now it was his turn to walk backwards, slowly, towards the front door, while Lawrence, who could see where Elton was going, issued quiet instructions.

The casket only just made it through the front door, with less than an inch to spare on either side. Elton then put the foot end on the ground and held it steady while Lawrence, purple in the face, lifted the other end above his head and swung it towards the lounge door. Inside the casket, Charles Griffiths slid down, knees buckling, and only the firmly screwed-on lid prevented him from departing the casket altogether and landing on Elton. Walking backwards into the lounge, Lawrence lowered the casket to waist height. Elton picked up the foot end and they manoeuvred the unwieldy weight towards the waiting trestles. It occurred to Elton that he could cause trouble here and now simply by dropping his end of the casket. But he decided against it. There was still plenty of time to put the damage right, and no point in incurring the wrath of Stillion for no more than a minor hitch. No, he had a much better plan.

Lawrence and Elton unscrewed the lid and straightened up the late Charles Griffiths. Once everything was ready Lawrence went in search of Ellen Griffiths and found her in the dining room, along with the rest of the family. He ushered them all into the lounge. Charles Nelson Griffiths was resplendent – a Martin Luther King for Birmingham – and the widow seemed pleased and grateful. Thomas, the deceased's bibulous brother, turned unsteadily to Lawrence, saying, 'You done good job, man. Lemme give you a drink.' Kemp would have dearly loved to accept, but it was expressly against Sloane rules. Just one drink and the men arrived at the next funeral smelling of booze, and after four or five funerals a day many of the drivers would have failed a Breathalyser test. But it was hard, because there was always booze at funerals. Indeed, it was of no surprise to Stillion that funeral directors were second only to doctors as a profession beset by drink problems. It wasn't being surrounded by the bereaved that caused them to drink, it was being surrounded by drink itself.

'No, thank you very much, I'm driving,' replied

Lawrence sadly. He didn't dare accept with Elton there. He didn't entirely trust Elton Field.

Lawrence and Elton took their leave of the Griffiths family. As Lawrence retreated towards the front door Elton turned back to the lounge. Handing Thomas Griffiths a white envelope he said quietly, 'Mr Stillion Sloane has asked me to give you this. Good evening.' And with that he turned away and walked briskly to catch up with Kemp in the drive. The two were soon on their way back to Sloane House, Lawrence to wash the hearse, and Elton to get all tomorrow's funerals into the designated Chapels of Rest before viewing started at six.

Meanwhile, over at Richards & Gridley's, Mr Razek Singh called again to collect his father's ashes, but Sydney was out and no one was able to find them.

⋆ ⋆ ⋆

Stephanie Sloane often went to London on a Wednesday. Sometimes she went with a friend, such as Lottie Wilkes, and sometimes on her own. Either way she would spend the morning in New Bond Street, then get a taxi to Knightsbridge, lunch in Beauchamp Place and while away the afternoon in Harrods and Harvey Nichols before having her long and beautiful hair washed at a salon in Motcomb Street. She usually returned on the six forty-five from Euston, dined on the train and arrived home at about nine. On

Stephanie's London days Stillion either dined with his mother over in Streetly or with friends at a restaurant, in the city centre or perhaps in Harborne or in Edgbaston itself. On this particular Wednesday, Stillion had agreed to meet Lottie Wilkes in the cocktail bar of the Plough & Harrow at seven o'clock. He didn't know the reason for the meeting because Lottie hadn't said. She had only said that it was important and that, for some reason, nobody must know.

Stillion had been very busy at work and hadn't got back to the office from the last job until four forty-five. By the time he'd checked off that day's garage orders, gone through those for the next day (a most important day) with Lawrence Kemp, gone over the day book and new arrangements with John Palin and checked all the Chapels of Rest with the night staff, it was five past seven before he finally drove his XJS away from Sloane House.

'It was twenty years ago today, Sergeant Pepper told the band to play...' Stillion cranked up the volume and put his foot down. The slightest traffic delay annoyed him, and he was already late. He reached the Plough & Harrow at seven-twenty.

But there was no sign of Lottie in the cocktail bar. He took a seat anyway; she could be late herself, or she might be in the ladies. If she wasn't there in five minutes he'd ask a waiter if she'd been in. For some reason he was beginning to feel guilty just being here. It hadn't occurred to him before, but he realised he was feeling coy about asking the waiter if Mrs Wilkes had been waiting for him. The Plough & Harrow was popular with many of Stillion's friends and acquaintances and he knew most of the waiters; they could easily jump to the wrong conclusion. Jesus; what if they were jumping to the right conclusion? But he knew how dangerous that would be. Lottie's husband was the biggest gangster thug in town, with a small private army rumoured to have buried offenders under Spaghetti Junction. And if Steppie was ever to find out, her beautiful, pure and loving heart would be shattered. It was that that really scared him. Standing up to Harry Wilkes and his thugs might be considered honourable, heroic even, but there was nothing heroic about an affair with your wife's best friend.

Most men would have given their right arm for a wife like Stephanie. Before his marriage Stillion had had a lot of difficulty controlling his penis, but he'd been a saint since. Well, except for Monday evening. That encounter with Gillian Weston had proved that he could slip backwards all too easily. It mustn't happen again. Stillion was appalled that he was even considering it, tonight, no more than forty-eight hours later and with no business motive to justify his incontinence. He decided to leave. But then he pulled himself up short. Who said sex had anything to do with this meeting? Had she? No. It was purely his imagination. 'Well, you big-headed git, she probably wants to ask your advice about something. She probably doesn't even find you vaguely attractive,' he thought.

A waiter approached with a silver tray on which was a white envelope. Stillion thanked the waiter and opened the envelope. Inside, written on paper headed with the Plough & Harrow logo, was a simple message: 'I'm in room 129. Come quickly it's important. Luv Lottie'. Wondering what kind of trouble Lottie must be in to behave in such a clandestine fashion Stillion made his way to the hotel's bedroom wing. As he arrived at room 129 the door opened. Lottie poked her head out and looked left and then right down the corridor before asking if he'd been seen.

'No, I don't believe so,' answered a bewildered Stillion. 'What's all this . . .'

'Come in. Quick,' Lottie interrupted him, taking hold of his arm and pulling him through the door. 'Take a seat,' she commanded, and Stillion slumped back into the one big easy chair in the room. On the table next to the chair was an ice bucket with an opened bottle of champagne protruding from the top. Lottie poured a glass for Stillion before sitting on the bed opposite him with the glass she'd clearly already been drinking from in her left hand.

She smiled. Her black eyes twinkled, her black hair shone and she crossed her long, brown, shapely legs before she began, 'We haven't known each other very long. I only met Stephanie at the tennis club last spring and I didn't get to meet you until June or July. But I feel like I've known you a long time. So I've decided to confide in you and tell you what I need because I'm sure you'll understand and will want to help me.'

'Of course, if I can I will,' interjected Stillion, wondering where she was leading.

'Well,' said Lottie, leaning forward and lowering her voice. She cut a good figure sitting there in a short pale green suit. Stillion noticed that she wasn't wearing stockings, despite the time of year. 'Well,' she repeated, 'I have decided that I lead a terrible, useless and boring life. My kids don't need me anymore. Harry needs me but for all the wrong reasons and I can't stand another bloody Saturday night with all his uncouth friends and their even worse wives.' She put down her glass and began unbuttoning her top. 'So, I've decided to have an affair with you.' She pushed the jacket off her shoulders and down onto the bed, and leaned back with her arms outstretched behind her. Her upper body was now clad only in a long silk scarf, which ran round the back of her neck and over each breast before running to the centre of her back where the ends were tied. The scarf was floral and transparent and hardly concealed the fact that Lottie was in remarkably good shape for a woman of forty-two with two teenage children. Stillion was mesmerised. Lottie sat up straight and untied the scarf, so that the ends flopped into her lap. Stillion's head was desperately searching for ways to say no to Lottie without getting on the wrong side of her and thus making a mess of this already potentially dangerous situation, but Zizi was on heat and raring to go. Lottie then leaned forward and dropped to her knees between Stillion's open legs. He caught glimpses of naked breast as she undid his jacket, his tie, his shirt and pushed her hands inside and over his chest. His hands remained rigid against the arm rests.

'What about Harry? What about Stephanie?' he asked, weakly. 'I mean, do you think we ought to be doing . . .'

'This?' Lottie finished his sentence. 'Of course not. Are you frightened to, because of Harry?' Her tone was mocking.

'I'm not frightened of Harry.' Stillion was defensive.

'Oh, is it me you're frightened of?' She was taunting him.

'Of course I'm not frightened of you.' Stillion wanted to say that she should stop, that he was a happily married man, but before he could get the words out she had run her hands over the front of his trousers and discovered for herself the certain proof that whatever he may say, he couldn't help but want her.

Lottie took confidence from his erection. She knew that however much he might want to reject her advances, he wouldn't. She took his hands in hers and pulled him up from the chair. 'Your mind may say no, young man, but your body says yes,' she said, removing his jacket, his shoes and socks, and undoing his trousers, which fell to the floor. She pushed him gently back on to the bed, then stood momentarily to allow her loosened skirt to fall to the ground. She knelt over him as he lay there, motionless, in opened white shirt and boxers. She whisked the scarf away and threw it to the floor, leaving herself naked, but for a pair of small black knickers, and with her well-shaped breasts looking down at Stillion, the nipples fully projected with excitement. 'Don't love me, sex me,' she said, as she pushed his shirt off his shoulders before taking the top of his white boxers and easing them down over his fierce erection, to his knees and off. She looked long and hard at his penis, her black eyes glinting with delight; Lottie had married Harry very young, and before she'd had much experience of the male body. And Stillion was so young and ribby that the size of his engine had surprised her. She took it in her hands and was pleased to observe from his reactions that he found the sensation overwhelming. She felt a great sense of power.

Lottie was keen to show that, while she might not be as young or as beautiful as Stephanie, she was a true giver in bed. She lowered her head and licked his purple helmet with her extended tongue before going fully down on him. Stillion still lay immobile, as if not moving would absolve him from all guilt of infidelity. But he knew that unfaithful was unfaithful and just lying still made him no less guilty. The desires of his body were fast eclipsing those of his mind. And he didn't want that. Moreover, Lottie would think him an incompetent lover and, whatever his misgivings about the situation, his arrogance and pride in his cocksmanship would not allow that. So he took her head in his hands and gently pulled her up the bed before rolling her onto her back. He kissed her neck, her shoulders, her breasts, her nipples and on down over her stomach. He removed her knickers with his toe while looking straight into her eyes, before burying his head in her shaved pubic area and darting his tongue between her legs and around her clitoris. Her hands clenched the cover of the bed and her back arched so high that her buttocks left the mattress. Her toes curled down and she thrust her vagina towards him. He entered her in the missionary position before rolling onto his back, leaving her kneeling astride him. They now began to show off, and several positions later they left the bed for the table, the window-sill and the sideboard. Lottie was getting wilder and wilder; she had become a river of excitement and a volcano of orgasm. She was exhausted and had to ask for a rest. The two of them lay back on the bed, side by side. His erection was still huge and throbbing. She was disappointed.

'You haven't come.'

'I daren't, in case I couldn't keep up with you.'

'Well, I want to see you come now.' She raised her moist body, with soaked hair and red finger marks on her buttocks, and knelt between his legs. She took his thick long engine in her left hand and gently tickled his balls with her other hand. She watched his eyes to see them glaze over as his whole body went rigid. His mind spun, his legs went limp and a rushing express train arrived from far away to explode hot steaming cream over his chest. The orgasm was long, painful and draining. It was delightful. But guilt, shame and horror crowded in at once, and Stillion was grimly reminded that an erect prick knows no morality

He didn't care about Harry, or Lottie's kids. He cared about two things: firstly, he had cheated on his wife a second time in three days; secondly, he now believed what he had long suspected, that despite his desire to love and cherish Steppie, forsaking all others, he could only love and cherish her while continuing to fuck all others. He was, he felt, a whore. He was born a whore. He'd had dirty dreams at five. At the age of eight he'd befriended the family housekeeper so that he could visit her room and watch her change, avid for a glimpse of breast and perhaps even pubic hair. When he had stayed with his two girl cousins during the school holidays they would climb into his bed and strip him. He would let the older one measure his erect penis while the younger one watched. Indeed, it was they who had induced his first trickle of transparent treacle. By his teens he was having several women a week, and often more than one at a time.

He was a sexaholic. He couldn't help himself. He had desperately wanted to be different after marriage. He didn't want to find women so easily attractive. But he did. And all too often for his own good, they were easily attracted to him. It seemed to him that when this happened, chemistry just took over. He really loved Stephanie, had made his marriage vows and for some time he had managed well. He wanted more than anything to love Steppie and to build up Sloane & Sons into a commercial success, so that his wife and any children would be secure. Now, like a dry alcoholic having just one drink, he was back on the booze. Now that the evil thrust of Zizi had left him he realised, like a sober drunk, how this sort of behaviour could put everything in jeopardy.

His friends thought he was very lucky, with a beautiful wife and always easy to pull a bit on the side if he wanted. But he knew differently. He knew that Stephanie had waited her chance, had let him sow his wild oats. He knew that Stephanie had turned down his first proposal because she couldn't believe he could ever be with just one woman. He had taken the pledge, and she had promised him it would be all over if he broke it. He had kept it until this very week and now his inability to resist the pleasures of the flesh had led him to break his promise twice in three days.

Stillion was careful not to let his mood show as he and Lottie showered and dressed. Despite the fact that she had made all the running, he knew that if she were to feel rejected now she may become vengeful. Kindly and gently he said they should think hard before doing this again, out of respect for their partners and her children.

'But I need to talk to you. We must be able to talk,' Lottie demanded.

'Oh, I'm sure, if we control ourselves then we could do that. There is no reason why we can't be friends.' Stillion knew that a slow and gentle reverse was the best way out of this cul-de-sac.

'Absolutely,' smiled Lottie, safe in the knowledge that all she had to do was get her hands on his penis and he would do as he was told. He was a forceful young man when dressed, but just a little lamb once his trousers were down.

'Together they took the lift down to the hotel reception, where she settled her bill with cash given to her by Stillion. He walked straight to his car and drove the short distance home. It was ten twenty-five. Stephanie was already at home and greeted him with a smile and a kiss.

'Gosh, darling, you look shattered.' Stillion's heart sank. 'Is it still very busy at work? You'd better get to bed, with both of those monster funerals to conduct tomorrow.' He breathed again but felt like a shit. Stephanie launched happily into an account of her day in London, while Stillion washed his hands and cleaned his teeth, looking all the while for any of those tell-tale signs that amateur lovers often overlook.

At ten forty-five the telephone rang. It was James Steele, Stillion's solicitor, with the news that he'd managed to get an appointment for Stillion to see Joyce Higgins at her place on Friday at six o'clock.

4

Thursday

Sydney Gridley and Rolley Brown rose on Thursday morning with great expectations. They could hardly wait to hear news of disasters occurring over at Sloane & Sons. Stillion, on the other hand, oblivious to their plotting, was looking forward to conducting the two funerals back to back. Yes, he was nervous – they were big occasions after all – but he knew he was a fine funeral director at the head of a well-trained team.

The ex-Lord Mayor's funeral started well. The cortège left Sloane House on time, with Stillion walking ahead of the procession along the length of the Soho Road. The A and B fleets had been combined to ensure that the floral hearse, the main hearse and the five limousines all matched. It was cold, but the sun shone and the vehicles sparkled. Once at the church the liveried bearers, the ex-Lord Mayor borne in state upon their shoulders, glided behind a resplendent Stillion as he strutted the slow march behind the stooping, haunted Reverend Price. There were no mistakes on the service sheets, the imported choir sang powerfully, and even the congregation acquitted themselves, in particular with 'Land of Hope and Glory' which at the end of the service boomed out in full nasal Brummie through the doors and into the churchyard as the shouldered coffin made its way back out of the church. Stillion walked the cortège away from the church towards the Hockley flyover, where he stood to one side, placed his top hat on his head and flicked up his tailcoat ends into one hand. As the hearse glided past he opened the door with his free hand and slipped into the passenger seat with the consummate ease of a true professional. Things were going well.

They arrived at the Town Hall bang on time. Flags flew at half mast and hundreds of Corporation employees lined the street, hatless and with heads bowed. The cortège paused for two minutes. Stillion could hear the bustle of the city in the distance but the top ends of New Street and Colmore Row – closed to traffic today – effected a near-silence in respect for old Johnnie Martin. Bystanders sensed the occasion and stood still. Only the occasional child spoke. One yelled 'There's a dead 'un for the angels if it ain't all bunk.' When two minutes were up the cortège moved off, and with a speed set at twenty miles an hour it snaked its way out of the city, into the suburbs and out into open countryside.

Stillion and Lawrence were constant companions in the hearse. They were the two solemn stars of a rolling roadshow that progressed through the streets of North

Birmingham as often as five times a day, five, sometimes six days a week. Onlookers saw their sober gazes fixed silently ahead, but in the cab Stillion gave commands and passed comments on the outside world out of the corners of his mouth. 'Put her on twenty I said bloody twenty Lawrence. Look out, watch the old lady stepping off the pavement. Shit, madam, there's plenty of room for you on the lower deck if you like. Left Lawrence. I said left. Lawrence, for fuck's sake go left here. Steady. Steady now. I said steady. Hold her back. I said hold her back. we haven't got the private cars round the corner yet. Hold her. Hold her. Okay, return to twenty. Oh shit, watch that bicycle. Lawrence, the bloody bicycle on my side. Okay, well done. Keep her on twenty. Shit, a fucking pig car's got between the second and third limos. Shut off all speed and make the ignorant sod think about what he's done. The pigs aren't the boys they were in my father's day. Okay, that's it. Well done. Green light ahead. Slow now, the whole cortège can't make it on this green. Steady. Slow. Hold her back. Let it change to red.' Occasionally Lawrence would grunt, in acknowledgement of a command or a driving error of his own, or comment on the quality of the beer at a pub the cortège passed. Lawrence was an expert on pubs and beers.

Lawrence Kemp, at fifty-six, was almost a cameo of a Middle England undertaker. He wasn't tall but he was solidly built. His receding black hair, greying at the temples, was greased back with Brylcreem. His unappealing bloodhound jowls and red, ulcerated alcoholic's nose belied a kindly, if somewhat lazy, nature. He'd left his Dudley state school at fourteen been apprenticed as a coffin maker to the Birmingham Cooperative Funeral Division. He'd worked his way up to Funeral Conductor, and left the Co-op in 1960 to set up his own business, which had been surprisingly successful. In 1978 Lawrence's firm had become Stillion's first acquisition, and keeping Kemp on as principal A-fleet hearse driver and garage foreman had been a condition of sale. Kemp found himself having to work really hard for the first time, which he didn't enjoy, but he could nevertheless be relied to work like a Trojan when the body count stacked up. Stillion and Lawrence came from very different worlds and didn't always see eye to eye, but there was a strong mutual respect. Both knew what they didn't like about the other and found more to like than dislike, which was just as well as they spent most of their working lives side by side in the front of the hearse.

Stillion had Elton's map on his knee and began to refer to it once they passed the boundaries of the Birmingham A–Z. Stillion gave instructions based on the route that Elton had marked in red. 'Go round the next bend, which is a gentle right, before forking left into a small lane which we will follow for a mile straight into the crematorium,' he concluded. The lane was narrow and seemed too small to be leading to a crematorium, but Elton had been out here to recce the route, so it must be right. But when the lane petered out into a gravel drive leading to a large house, Stillion's heart sank. Worse, according to a large sign by the gate, the house was some sort of institute for the mentally ill. And there was nowhere to turn round but its large front lawn, where several people, who Stillion assumed to be residents, were disporting themselves under the watchful eyes of a few uniformed staff.

'Fuck me,' whispered a horrified Lawrence. 'What are we going to do?'

'Just keep calm and turn round,' ordered Stillion, in the most controlled voice he could muster. As the hearses and limousines began to make three-point turns on the lawn of the house the staff began to protest, while an exercising inmate walked right up to one of the limousines and leered through the window, waving and shouting that the Queen had come to see them.

Eventually the hearses and limousines, and some of the private cars, were turned. But the cortège couldn't get out because many private cars were still stuck in the lane, facing the wrong way and unable to make their way into the grounds to turn around. Bedlam in bedlam. Stillion was forced to leave the lead hearse and guide a number of private cars backwards down the lane, through a gate and into a field in order that the cortège could retreat back to the main road. Warmer temperatures here, some twenty miles south of

Birmingham, had thawed the ground and in the field some of the cars became stuck in soft ground. Their mud-spattered drivers and passengers could only stand in impotent dismay. Tempers became frayed. One smart Edgbaston couple abandoned their hopelessly stuck Jaguar and started to walk back to the gate in the hope of getting a lift to the crematorium. As they picked their way gingerly across the mud another turning car managed to get some traction and began to move slowly towards the gate, engine revving. As it moved it splattered the couple from head to toe. The woman screamed, her husband yelled out, 'Stop that. I say, stop, you dirty bastard.' The offending driver poked his head out of his window and replied, in broad Brummie, 'Dirty bastard? You can talk mate. You and your missus is covered in shit,' before continuing on his way to the gate. The outraged pedestrian attempted to run to catch the car, and was lunging for the boot when the car pulled into the lane. He fell headlong in the mud.

Another well-attired woman had left her car and walked a few paces, into deep mud. The sludge filled her shoes and crept up past her ankles. She pulled out her right foot; it was shoeless. After a few minutes of burying her hands into the black mud in an attempt to find it, it appeared that her shoe had sunk without trace. She now noticed that her white fox fur coat was trailing in the mud. She attacked the mud in a fury.

Stillion climbed back into the hearse, his face white

with shock, his brain numb. He knew he mustn't panic, nor must he yet give a thought to what had happened. He must just get the show back on the road and find the crematorium. He furiously studied the map. The crematorium was marked, in tiny print, down a lane adjacent to the one Elton had marked out for him in red. Elton had clearly made a careless mistake.

'The silly fucker has marked up the wrong bloody lane. Go back to the main road, turn left, and then it's first left again. The crematorium is actually marked on the map, as is that nut house,' said Stillion. 'Have we got all the private cars?'

Lawrence looked in his wing mirror, 'I can't see the end of the line, but we seem to have most of 'em.'

The crematorium was indeed only a mile away, and despite the unplanned tour of bedlam the muddy fleet rolled up the crematorium drive on time. Stillion had never had a cock-up like this. Why did it have to be on an ex-Lord Mayor's funeral? He was shocked, embarrassed and ashamed, but he kept going. The Reverend Price and Sloane's staff were dazed by the events, but the bearers managed to shoulder the coffin into the crematorium, although their minds were still back at the mental institute. Nevertheless, they placed the coffin on the catafalque in the usual foot first position. It had to be moved forward slightly, so that the curtains could close round it, and as the right head bearer applied pressure to his handle, as fitted by Elton, it came clean off in his hand with such a force that his fist, still holding the handle, hit the right foot bearer a great left hook to the jaw and sent him flying off the raised catafalque surround and crashing into scores of vases full of flowers below. The poor man struggled to his feet, flowers in his hair and soaked to the skin. The stunned congregation didn't know whether to laugh or cry. The crematorium organist had no such problem. His giggles were quite audible and his shoulders heaved visibly as he struggled to regain control.

* * *

After the committal service Stillion took the Martin family home. He offered his profuse apologies to the Councillor's stony-faced brother and assured him that, naturally, he would not be submitting an account for either his charges or the disbursements. At this the brother's attitude softened slightly and Stillion took his leave as quickly as might be perceived to be decent.

He travelled home in the lead limousine which as usual was driven by Walter Warburton, the two hearses having left the crematorium to go directly back to Sloane House. As Walter drove, Stillion could only wonder if the press had got hold of the story. The Central Television crew had only bothered to go to the church, but they may have heard of the fiasco some other way. Stillion thought on the morning's events. He could believe that Elton Field was lazy enough or simple enough to cock up the map. Indeed, he was surprised that John had sent Elton in the first place. From Stillion's point of view Elton was really only useful as an embalmer. But the handle must be down to Walter, which he found hard to comprehend. Walter was a hard working, dour, honest and reliable Middle England worker, if a little cynical at times. Walter didn't make mistakes. Stillion felt he had to speak. 'Walter, how the fuck did you forget the screws in the head right handle? I mean, you never make mistakes like.'

'I just don't know, Mr Stillion,' replied a subdued and hesitant Walter.

Once back at Sloane House Stillion marshalled the A-fleet staff. He had just enough time to say, 'Look lads, we have another big funeral this afternoon. We must do it with our usual efficiency. We must concentrate on it and not be distracted by the events of this morning. There is no time for inquests until after the Griffiths funeral. Now, you've all got your garage orders and you all know what to do.' They took up their positions on the forecourt and the procession pulled out for the Griffiths' house.

When they arrived they found the Reverend Winston Wylde waiting for them outside.

'Stillion, how could you?' he asked.

'How could I what?', replied Stillion, bemused.

'You know Thomas has a drink problem.'

'What?'

'You know what.'

'No I don't.'

'So you didn't send him a credit for a case of vodka at the off-licence on Lozells Road?'

'No, I did not.'

'Well, he says you did and he and some mates are three sheets to the wind in there and the family are none too pleased with you.'

'Shit.'

* * *

Inside the Griffiths' house it was packed. Winston, Stillion and his staff had to get inside to talk to the family in order to arrange the flowers, discuss the seating plan for the limousines, close the casket, say a couple of prayers and generally get the show on the road in an orderly fashion. But, typically with a West Indian funeral, and especially for such an important one, the house was heaving. People crowded into every room, upstairs and down. Jim Reeves could be heard above the din, and occasionally the record jumped as the multitude jogged the gramophone. Winston took the lead and the others followed, Stillion with one hand raised high in the air holding his top hat, protecting it from the crowd. It took several minutes for them to move through the small hall and into the lounge, where the family were waiting by the casket. As they fought their way through a large middle-aged West Indian man stepped out in front of Stillion. Very steadily he introduced himself as a cousin of Charles Griffiths, and one of a large contingent of the family living in Clapham, South London, which had come up to Birmingham for the occasion. It was quite clear that he was very, very angry.

'What yo' done, mon? Why give 'im all this booze?' he challenged Stillion.

'I can assure you, Sir, I don't know what you are talking about.'

'Your mon gave me the credit, mon,' interjected Thomas, who had appeared in the midst of the family group, glaze-eyed.

'Yo' shut up. Yo' drunk, mon,' said the angry cousin. Thomas squeezed his way out of the group, pushing one large lady who fell towards the casket, which rocked on its trestles. The cousin from Clapham leaned forward to restrain Thomas, who looked suddenly frightened. Half in fear and half in drunken anger he took a swing at his cousin, but he missed and hit Stillion full in the mouth. It was quite a blow. Stillion would have gone down but the sheer number of people in the room kept him upright. He just rocked.

One large West Indian woman took a swing at Thomas with her shiny black handbag, possibly in the belief that brute force was the best way to deal with drunks. She too missed, and hit one of Thomas' drunken friends standing just behind him, who responded by lashing out with fists and feet. Within seconds punches were being exchanged all over the place as the Clapham mob thought they were being attacked by their relatives from Brum.

The fight spread like wildfire through the lounge, into the dining room, the kitchen, back into the hall and up the stairs. Lawrence leaned towards Walter. 'I wouldn't have missed that for the world,' he whispered, still grinning from the sight of Stillion taking a whack. Walter, seeing that they were penned in by a writhing mass of pumping fists and the occasional flying potted plant, wasn't so sure.

In the end it was Winston Wylde who managed to regain control, his arms held high above his head and his fine singing voice booming out, 'Enough. Enough.' As the hubbub subsided he rebuked the assembled company for their behaviour, a disgrace to their family, their race and faith, and worse, a slight to the memory of the great man they were all here to honour this day.

* * *

More than a thousand people were crowded into the church; many had to stand and some could only listen from the porch. Thomas needed restraining twice, once when he left his seat and offered the excellent female choir a swig from a new bottle of vodka, and again when he attempted to give his own eulogy to his dead brother during Winston's sermon. But the girls had had enough; his sister and sister-in-law frogmarched him out of the church and, once outside, gave him a good handbagging and threw his vodka bottle over the church wall into an adjoining garden. Winston's great voice, boosted by the PA system, drowned the cries. Eventually the service concluded with the choir and congregation belting out 'When the Roll is Called Up Yonder' as the mourners filed past the open casket to pay their last respects to the great man before the lid was replaced for the last time.

In late December gloom the cortège glided on time into Handsworth cemetery. The close family gathered round the graveside, surrounded by mourners for several hundred yards. It was getting dark as Winston commenced the committal. 'In the midst of life we are in . . .' His voice trailed away. He couldn't believe what he saw. Thomas Griffiths was pouring the contents of yet another vodka bottle so that it cascaded down into the grave, drenching the widow's flowers and thundering on the casket lid. 'Let's give my brother one last drink' he chanted. His sister and sister-in-law both made a move to grab the bottle. Thomas saw them coming and flicked the alcohol, like holy water, in their direction. They screamed, and in an attempt to save themselves from being splashed with vodka stumbled backwards, both falling off the green matted boards and against the mourners massed behind them, who in turn fell against those standing behind them. They went down like dominoes.

The cousin from Clapham approached Thomas in a

rage. Thomas drew the bottle tight against his chest, saying, 'This is mine.' The Londoner made a lunge for him. 'Okay, mon, you've asked for this,' he yelled and jumped across the open grave. As he landed Thomas swung his left fist, still holding the bottle, and scored a direct hit to his cousin's chest. He wobbled for a second, fell backwards and down into the grave. It was a family grave, dug deep enough to take four coffins, and it was a long way down. As the dazed man lay on his back on top of the casket Thomas rained vodka down on him, laughing so hard that he could hardly get out the words, 'Have a little drink, mon.'

The Griffiths women were now back on their feet, and it was all that Stillion and Winston could do to keep them from getting their hands on Thomas. Lawrence led the drunk away to wait in the lead limousine. Stillion knew that he must rescue the vodka-soaked Londoner immediately; West Indians always filled in the grave themselves, and so the support planking around the grave had already been removed. The sides could give way at any moment under all this strain, and Mr Angry from Clapham could be buried alive. Stillion climbed the long way down into the grave and tried to raise the stunned man, no easy feat as he must have weighed at least fifteen stone. Having got him on his feet Stillion got him to hold his arms up high, so that Walter and various cemetery staff, lying flat on their chests at the graveside, could reach down and grab his hands, and haul him, with some difficulty, to safety.

The sides of the grave started to crumble. For some reason Stillion wasn't scared. He got a thrill from danger, similar to the thrill he got from sex. He was also glad to have had the opportunity to save Charles Griffiths' cousin; it was clear that the family still believed that Stillion was responsible for supplying Thomas with a case of vodka, and this might just deflect some of their anger.

Stillion was pulled clear from the collapsing grave and the committal service began again. When it was over the men filled in the grave while the women sang hymns, Elizabeth shouting out each line in advance for the benefit of the many who didn't have hymn books. It was dark when they finished. Stillion said goodbye to Winston before Lawrence took the Minister home in the hearse.

'I know absolutely nothing about this case of vodka, Winston, I promise you. Nothing at all.'

'Sure, mon, I believe you, but if I were you I'd try to find out who did, 'cause the family is mighty mad with whoever did and at this very moment, mon, they think that's you.' The hearse disappeared into the night.

Stillion remained with the limousines and eventually took Ellen Griffiths and her direct family home. As he took his leave of her she said to him, 'Maybe you did fine. Reverend Wylde did fine. But my husband has been disgraced. His funeral will be remembered for all the things that went wrong – a fight in the house, a comedy in the church and a fiasco by the grave, and that is not how it should be. You say you didn't give Thomas the credit, but he said someone from your firm did. Who was that, is what I want to know?' Stillion assured her that he wouldn't rest until he had found out, and left.

He climbed into the waiting limo outside. 'Walter, go back via Lozells Road. I want to stop at the off-licence.'

At the off-licence he could make no progress with the Asian woman on the till, but a younger woman, whom he took to be her daughter, appeared from the stock room. Yes, she had taken cash payment yesterday evening for a case of vodka to be collected this morning, which it duly had been. Could she describe the person who had given her the money, Stillion asked. Yes, she could, and went on to give an accurate description of Elton John Field – the fair hair, the thick glasses and the spots would have been enough, but she also remembered that he had been wearing clothes like those that Stillion had on, his funeral gear. Stillion thanked her and returned to the limo. 'Home, Walter, and don't spare the pissing horses. Please come and see me when the limos are finished.'

* * *

At about the same time Mr Razek Singh was paying his now nightly call to Richards & Gridley. He was informed by the luckless receptionist that unfortunately Mr Gridley had not had a chance to collect the ashes yet, but that he would do so tomorrow.

'Now look here. This is absolutely very bloody disgraceful. I am very, very unhappy man. You tell Mr Gridley this is not very British gentleman behaviour. You tell him he must put totally right tomorrow or I will be seeing my MP or the person at the DHSS office or both.'

The receptionist was tempted to give him one of the hundreds of old jars of ashes that had never been collected, and was only prevented from doing so by the fact that she couldn't then give him the correct crematorium certificate.

* * *

Stillion got back to his office. What a day. He threw his top hat to the floor and kicked it, then relented and put it carefully away, along with his tailcoat. After all, they would both have to be used again tomorrow. Then he sank into his comfortable executive chair and summoned John Palin. He gave John an account of his disastrous day, beginning with Elton's cock-up with the route, and told him of the overwhelming evidence that Elton had given Thomas Griffiths a credit note for a case of vodka from the off-licence in Lozells.

'Well,' said Palin, 'it makes you think.'

'What, John,' said Stillion, 'makes you think what?'

'Well, that maybe Elton isn't just having a bad day.

That handle that came off this morning, Elton put that on.'

'Whaaaat,' roared Stillion in disbelief.

'Yes. Walter told me between the funerals that when you got around to bollocking him about it he would have to tell you the truth. That Elton offered to help him out yesterday morning and put the handles on for him. And he offered to take the papers to Ebbwell Crem and mark out the route. And just now Lawrence told me that Elton must have not touched the handle when he helped him load up the Martin box this morning. Look, Stillion. I can't prove it and I don't know why he would want to, but I think Mr Field has fucked up both these funerals on purpose.'

'So do I. Get me Elton up here, John, now.'

Elton duly appeared, accompanied by Palin. Stillion invited them to sit down. He stood up, and stared down at Elton. Elton looked down at the ground. Stillion knew that Elton was guilty. Elton knew that Stillion knew that he was guilty. In silence he concentrated on the pattern of the carpet. Maybe Stillion wouldn't be able to prove premeditation and would be forced to accept that the events of the day were just accidents. But he knew that was impossible. Elton wished he'd never got involved; his plans had looked so securely secret before he carried them out, but now his guilt seemed all too clear.

Quietly and calmly, Stillion began to recount the day's events. Elton stared at the carpet. Stillion expressed his inability to believe that these events were unfortunate coincidences. Elton stared at the carpet. Stillion leaned over him menacingly and demanded an answer. Elton stared at the carpet and wished he'd joined a trades union after all. 'Okay, Elton,' said Stillion, 'if that's the way you want it. John, could you get the police up here and the young girl from the off-licence on the phone.' John rose and moved towards the door.

'Wait. Okay, please wait a minute,' said Elton, who had gone quite pale.

Stillion held up his arm and John stopped. Stillion hadn't really thought the police could charge Elton with anything, but he'd counted on the fact that Elton didn't know that.

'Okay, Elton baby, start spitting it out now, and I want the whole fucking story.' Elton told them the story and, with a bit more pushing from Stillion, he told them the whole fucking story. Money and all. Stillion listened in disbelief. That bastard old man Sydney had been determined to damage Sloane & Sons' reputation and ruin Stillion's chance of buying Higgins & Co. or, for that matter, any other firm within fifty miles. He was very, very angry. It was all he could do to stop himself from physically assaulting Elton.

'Why the fuck shouldn't I thrash you within an inch of your life, you little shit?' the ex-public school prefect screamed at the little fag who still stared at the carpet, head bowed. 'How are you going to make this up to me, you bloody little toerag?'

'I'm sorry.'

'Sorry! Sorry! Oh, that's rich. Did you hear that John? The little fucker is sorry. Perhaps I should explain to Joyce Higgins that we didn't really fuck up two huge funerals today, but that you and Sydney destroyed them and now it's okay because you're fucking sorry. No, I'm sorry Elton, that's just not good enough. What you've fucked up is fucked up and can't be unfucked up. We won those two prestige funerals. The eyes of the city were on us and thanks to you our chance is gone and Richards & Gridley, who didn't get either, are the only beneficiaries. I should kill you. Yes. I should fucking strangle you now with my bare hands.'

Out of the corner of his downcast eye Elton could see that John looked worried. This made him very nervous. He understood that the business was Stillion's life, and that thanks to his actions Stillion saw the future as unimaginably bleak. He also knew that Stillion was famous for his temper. If he didn't stop looking at the carpet and start coming up with ideas that might calm Stillion, he was unlikely to get out of the room in one piece. For the first time he raised his head.

'Look, Boss,' Elton peered up at Stillion through his gold-rimmed thick jam jar specs. 'Look, don't get mad.'

'Don't get fucking mad, why you little . . .'

'No, hear me out. Don't get mad, get even. I mean, if Richards & Gridley screw up tomorrow you'll 've paid Sydney back and maybe not all will be lost with Miss Higgins. She can't say she won't sell to you because we screwed up if they screw up too. And tomorrow's mass is almost as big as the ex-Lord Mayor's funeral and a lot of the same people will be at it.'

'I have never even considered that sort of behaviour, let alone been involved,' moralised Stillion.

'Sure,' said Elton, 'but nobody thinks Sydney has either. They think he's a solid JP. Now, thanks to me, they might think that you are incompetent, and the fastest way to help this city forget that is to give them a Richards & Gridley balls-up to think on.' Elton's Brummie voice sang out. He was warming to his argument and gaining confidence from the fact that Stillion hadn't hit him yet.

'Oh, really, and how do you propose to wreck Sydney's mass tomorrow?' asked Stillion.

'Leave it to me. The least you know the better. Then you're evens with Sydney Gridley and you and me is quits too. I know I'll have to go but no violence and with a reference. Deal?'

'How will you do it?' asked Stillion, who couldn't help but find the idea seductive.

'I'll go to Mr Gridley and tell him you sacked me after today's fuck ups. I'll say you think they're just fuck ups and I'll get him to pay me the money and give me some work to tide me over.'

'All of which you're going to give us so that we can split it fifty/fifty between Reverend Wylde and Reverend Price.'

'But...' interjected Elton.

'No buts, Elton.' Stillion was uncomfortably aware that he was sinking to Sydney's level, and by giving away Elton's fee he hoped to buy his own conscience.

Palin spoke, slowly and deliberately. 'How will you do it, Elton? And rest assured, if you involve Mr Stillion, me or anyone in this company, or if you double-cross us, then perhaps I'll recommend that Mr Stillion introduce you to his friend Harry Wilkes. We all know what that can mean.'

'No, that won't be necessary Mr Palin, I can assure you. I wish I had never got into this mess and I'm sorry, really sorry, really.'

'Well, it's a bit late to be sorry now,' said Stillion.

'I know but I'll make it right tomorrow, boss.'

'Like Mr Palin said Elton, how?'

'You just be outside their premises at eight-forty tomorrow morning and you'll see."

'Why eight-forty?' asked Palin.

'That's when the cortège leaves.'

'Surely the coffin will be in church overnight?' said Stillion.

'No, the family will visit tonight at the Richards' chapel and will be in church tomorrow when the coffin arrives for the nine-fifteen mass. I'll see you outside Mr Gridley's place tomorrow. Can I go now? I gotta phone Rolley Brown. I won't let you down, promise. Just give me this chance.'

'Okay. But just one question. Why didn't you just give Thomas Griffiths the cash, or even just buy him the booze? Why the credit?' asked Stillion, who couldn't see why Elton had done something so easily detectable.

'I couldn't think of a way of getting the vodka to him without being caught, and I thought he might lose the cash before he had a chance to buy any booze,' replied Elton.

'Okay, fuck off now and don't even think of letting us down.' Stillion didn't think for a moment of the poor family whose bereavement would be compounded by tomorrow's sabotaged funeral. All he could think of was saving the Higgins deal and getting back at Sydney. Joyce hadn't called to cancel their appointment, so maybe, just maybe, at the end of this dreadful day, all was not lost after all. And tomorrow would be a disastrous day for Sydney Gridley.

* * *

Lottie had spent a quiet day at home, looking at *Vogue*, *Cosmopolitan* and holiday magazines over endless cups of coffee. She tried to concentrate, but her thoughts kept drifting back to Stillion. That felt good, warm and exciting, the way she used to feel as a young girl when she'd had a crush on a boy. She couldn't decide if she was in love with Stillion or the idea of being in love with him, but she did know that her feelings were developing in her mind to be more than lust.

As morning became afternoon she began to feel disappointed. She had expected Stillion to phone. He may have said that they shouldn't do that again, but she hadn't believed him. His body had said something quite different. But now she felt rejected. Naturally she had no idea that Stillion had been going to hell and back while she decided whether or not to go to Mauritius for Easter. She poured herself another cup of coffee and turned her thoughts to dinner. Whatever they would have, it must be low in calories; she had to keep herself trim for Stillion, who was years younger than her and probably not used to bedding older women. Little did she know.

* * *

Sydney had heard the good news from Rolley. He could hardly contain his pleasure. What a wonderful day; Stillion undone in front of the city fathers and the West Indian community both in one day. Marvellous, bloody marvellous, and it was he who'd thought of it and had it bloody well executed. He was in a good mood.

Marcus, passing his father's office on the way

upstairs to the family flat, caught sight of Sydney relaxed deep into his chair, his feet on the desk and a large scotch and water in his hand. Marcus couldn't believe his eyes. His father never slouched, never put his feet up and a drink in the office was quite unthinkable. If he hadn't seen it with his own eyes he wouldn't have believed it. Seeing his usually tight-lipped father looking almost light-hearted, Marcus wondered if this might be a good time to broach the subject of his future.

Sydney and Marcus had different views about Marcus' future. Naturally, Sydney was proud to have a boy going to university; he would have hated to have to tell his chums on the bench or at Rotary that his boy hadn't made the grade. But that was it: get a degree, yes; use it, no. He wanted Marcus running the business with him. It was only right that he should give back to the business that had provided him with his private education. Father to son, that's what a family business was about, and what Sydney had never had. He'd had to marry a family business and had worked hard for it ever since. He'd been given a twenty per cent share – no more than he'd deserved – and had gone on to strengthen the business and increase family respectability by becoming a Councillor, Rotarian and JP. He'd looked after his father-in-law in old age and sent his only son to a good public school. Now Marcus wanted to gallivant off around the world instead of going straight to university and, what's more, Sydney suspected that the boy harboured ambitions as an architect, rather than a funeral director.

And he was right. Marcus, although grateful for the sacrifices his father had made on his behalf, wanted nothing to do with the business. He couldn't bear dead bodies and didn't like seeing people upset, so a career as an embalmer, spent more with the dead than the living, or as a funeral director, dealing with bereaved families, could not have been less appealing. He didn't want to hurt his father but couldn't help feeling that it was not his fault that Sydney had chosen to be a funeral director. There was no animosity between them. Sydney loved his son, in his own way. He didn't understand him and didn't know how to talk to him. Marcus, for his part, had always been a bit frightened of his father. He did love him, in a distant and respectful way, but was uncomfortably aware that if Sydney had not been his father he probably wouldn't like him much.

Marcus knocked lightly on the open door and went in. Sydney's office had changed little in seventy years. It was where Sydney worked and where he warmed his arse between funerals. Clients never came here, so there was no reason to spend money on it on their account. He was a working funeral director, not an oil tycoon like J.R. Ewing from that telly programme, *Dallas*. If Stillion needed to play the tycoon, let him. Let him have a plush office, drive a Jag, live in the posh part of town. Yes, let the little Johnny-come-lately make a noise. Nobody would be taken in. Sydney was the professional, the traditionalist. The state of his office was evidence of that, as was living above the shop. The Richards family had lived in the apartment above the office since 1908, and John Richards had decreed that Sydney should live there after his marriage. Sydney had since taken some pride from the fact that he lived with the business, a twenty-four hour a day servant of the community, while the Sloanes lived in the posh suburbs of Edgbaston and Streetly, and commuted into these poorer areas of town in their flash Jags.

'Hi, Dad. Everything okay?' Marcus said as he entered. Sydney reacted as if he had been caught enjoying a dirty magazine; he took his feet hurriedly off the desk and swung round in his chair, spilling his scotch and water on his right hand. He shook his hand and then dabbed at it with his handkerchief. 'And why shouldn't it be?' he said defensively.

'Oh, no reason. I just thought I'd pop in to say hello. I must go and change – I'm off to the cricket club for a drink.' Marcus was already feeling that he'd made a mistake coming in. But Sydney then seemed to relax, smiled and said, 'Good. Good. Sit down a minute. Like a drink?' Bloody hell fire, thought Marcus. He hesitated; he hated scotch but was aware that such an opportunity might not present itself again for months. 'Yes, just a small one, thank you.'

Sydney opened the desk drawer and pulled out a

bottle of Johnnie Walker and a glass. He poured a small measure into the glass and added ample water from the jug on his desk. 'Here,' he said, thrusting the glass towards Marcus. 'I think, Marcus, that you and I, as the men of the household, should take a few minutes to look at future plans.' Marcus was speechless. His father had offered him a drink, had just referred to him as a man rather than a boy and wanted to talk about the future. Bloody hell fire.

'You see, I never wanted you to have this year out. But I have agreed. I think it a waste of time and money. But your mother says you are only young once and that I shouldn't expect you to lose your youth just because the war took mine away. So, go and see the world and come home and get your degree. But then, Marcus, you must come to help me in the business. I want your word on that. I am close – and this must remain between the two of us – I am close to clinching a deal with Higgins & Co., and expect to have Joyce Higgins' decision by the weekend. There's no one else in the running since that bloody boy cocked up his two big funerals today.'

'Cocked up his funerals? What do you mean, Dad?'

'Cocked them up, both in one day. I knew that arrogant little sod would get his comeuppance.'

'Poor Stillion, Dad. I mean, you've always said, "There but for the grace of God" ,' said Marcus, genuinely sorry. Marcus wouldn't wish ill to anyone and certainly not Stillion; the two of them shared a passion for cricket, played in the same team and often socialised after matches. He didn't share these facts with his father.

'Poor Stillion! Poor Stillion, my arse! He's not a funeral director. He's a jumped-up failed Tory candidate and tonight Sloanes are the laughing stock of the profession in this city. And you'd do well to listen to me about the future rather than feeling sorry for young Mr Sloane. With Higgins coming on board, plus the fact that I expect to build the business from Sloane & Sons' losses, we'll have a lot more to do. I know you won't be joining me for another four, or perhaps five, years. I know that. But after that I want your word that you'll take up your rightful position in the business. This is a family business. Your Great-grandfather started it, your Grandfather and I have continued it and you will become its custodian for your children. This business has put the shoes on your feet, the shirt on your back and the food in your mouth. Your Grandfather looked after your mother and I in turn looked after him. Your mother and I have looked after you and soon it will be time for you to take your turn. I don't want to be standing around in cold cemeteries when I'm seventy. As it is I'll be over sixty-five before you join me. So I want your word on this, now. Good health.' Sydney raised his glass to his son. There was a silence 'Well?' said Sydney, 'come on, boy, give me your word.'

'I c-c-can't, Father,' stammered Marcus.

'Can't! Can't!' roared Sydney, exhibiting an unusual degree of emotion.

'No, Father. I'm sorry, but I can't,' began Marcus more steadily, having found courage from somewhere. 'I can't give you my word because I don't think I will be joining you, then or ever. You see, I hate the business. I'm so sorry to disappoint you, but I never want to come into it.'

'The Lord giveth and the Lord taketh away,' said Sydney, cryptically. 'Listen, boy, you have until Monday morning to change your bloody mind or out you go with last week's money. And you can leave the company car behind as you won't be needing that either.'

'But what about the ten thousand pounds Grandpa gave you for me?'

'There's nothing in writing. Anyway, he asked me to give it to you when I considered you were ready and clearly you are not.'

'But it was for me at eighteen.' Marcus was horrified at how badly wrong this conversation was going.

'Where does it say that?' asked his father, sarcastically. The combination of the drink, to which he was not used, and the impertinence of the usually controllable Marcus kept Sydney's adrenalin pumping. He now sensed that Marcus was retreating, which was just as well as he had got himself into a position from which he couldn't retreat without a great loss of face.

'But Grandpa was mother's father, not yours. I'm going to ask her.'

'You can ask who the hell you like, boy. I am the master of this house and this business. Now get out and don't talk to me again until you are ready to apologise for your impertinence this evening, have come to your senses and can give me your word.'

Marcus obediently got up and left. What a disaster. He climbed the stairs to the apartment. Should he tell his mother? Should he apologise, forget about his own plans and throw himself on his father's mercy? He hated that idea but he also hated the idea of being cast out without a penny. He remembered he'd left the keys to the apartment in his car. He went back downstairs to fetch them. He approached his father's open door shyly, hoping to pass it without a further broadside. His father was on the phone to Joyce Higgins. Marcus knew he shouldn't have listened but he couldn't help it. One sentence caught his attention. The conversation went on for some time, and Marcus quietly sat on the bottom stair, just out of sight, and listened to every word.

5

Friday

The temperature plummeted over night, bringing a return of snow, ice and biting cold. Stillion rose at six. He had slept well and therefore was horrified, on waking, to realise that life was the real nightmare. His promising future had certainly changed, if not in the twinkling of an eye, then from Monday morning onwards. The young, squeaky clean ex-public schoolboy, business whizz-kid and funeral director of the future had encouraged a man of the cloth to secure a funeral on his behalf. He had seduced the matron of a local nursing home to gain another. He had started a dangerous sexual liaison which he really didn't want and hadn't had the moral fibre to resist. He had then watched two prestigious funerals blow up in his face and was now getting up at six in the morning not to make amends but to get even by sabotaging the work of his arch rival.

Stillion had arranged for Graham Stone, the B-fleet conductor, to cover for him on the first funeral of the day. He dressed in a smart suit, put his pinstripes in the car for later and left to keep the appointment he had made with Elton Field.

By seven-thirty Elton was at his new place of employment. When he saw Rolley he asked for his money. 'Later,' said Rolley. Elton insisted, 'Now, or I blow it. For fuck's sake Rolley, a deal's a fucking deal.'

'Wait here. I'll have to see Sydney.' He came back just before seven fifty-five with the loot, having already broken out his little earner on the way back from Sydney's office. 'There's your money. Now we're all even and neither Mr Gridley nor me want to talk about this again. Is that clear?'

'Clear,' agreed Elton.

'You're to drive the second limousine, CEA, over there in the far corner. A copy of the garage orders is on the wall in the canteen.'

'Is that my copy?' asked Elton.

'No it fucking isn't. It's for all of us.'

'I see, it's just that at Sloanes we all had a copy to take on the funerals with us.'

'Well you bloody don't here. And another thing, you work for Richards & Gridley now and if I were you I'd shut it about poncy Sloanes. What happens there is of no fucking interest to us all right kid?'

'Sure,' droned Elton drearily.

'Start up and dust off your limo and I'll introduce you to the others. All right?'

'Okay,' sighed Elton over his shoulder as he walked across the garage towards CEA. CEA, the first part of the car's registration number, was used to identify it from the other, identical, limos. Elton removed the dust-sheet and rubbed down the limo. He looked at his watch. It was now eight-twenty. He started the engine and jammed the automatic choke on full by revving the engine, thus flooding the engine and soaking the plugs. The engine cut out. Elton pretended to turn it off and then joined the other drivers in the canteen, a small room off the garage with a gas ring, a kettle, a bottle of sterilised milk on a table covered with old newspapers and surrounded by an assortment of six or so broken-backed chairs. On the walls were ranged hundreds of photographs of semi-clad or naked women, clearly ripped from girlie magazines. An old foil takeaway carton in the middle of the table acted as an ashtray, used by this last generation of untipped Park Drive or Woodbine smokers, who dragged on their fags in between swigs of hot and strong, three-sugar sweet tea.

'So thou hast left those ponces for us has thee?' wheezed one old chauffeur.

'Yeah,' said Elton, with a smile.

He looked around him. He was glad he wasn't going to be working there permanently like they thought. He'd had to do what he'd done yesterday, for the money, but he'd liked working for Sloane & Sons. The hearses, the limos, the livery and even the staff were in better nick there than here. Sydney Gridley was living in the past, kidding himself. He might call himself a 'professional traditionalist', but that just meant not replacing vehicles and letting the livery get threadbare. Elton, always criticised by Stillion for not being smart enough, smiled to himself as he realised he was the smartest in this tiny, smoke-filled room.

Rolley Brown, whose great bulk and ill-fitting shirt and suit ranked him among the scruffiest, gulped down the last of his mug of tea, saying, 'All right, let's be having you. Load up time.' This was the signal to fetch Joseph Lyons' coffin from the Catholic viewing chapel, screw the lid down and load it into the hearse. This done, Rolley Brown got into the hearse. Elton and the first limousine driver took up their positions in their respective vehicles and the fourth bearer climbed into the front passenger seat alongside Elton. It was now eight thirty-five. Rolley was about to pip the horn to let Sydney and Marcus know all was ready, when Elton came running up to him.

'My fucking limo won't start.'

'You what?'

'You heard. My fucking limo won't start.'

'Oh shit! What is it?'

'Don't know, but I can smell petrol.'

'Oh, for fuck's sake, you bloody well flooded it, you bloody fool.'

'What?'

'Never mind. Get out of the road. I'll sort it out. Quick lads, open the fucking bonnet.'

All hands gathered round as Rolley leaned his great bulk under the bonnet and into the engine to remove the plugs. All hands that is except Elton. Elton slipped away around the back of the hearse and out of the garage into the street. It was exactly eight-forty when he crossed the street and approached a man in a double-breasted overcoat and brown wide-brimmed fedora, standing with his back to the Richards & Gridley premises.

'Here's a little something for you sir,' muttered Elton, shoving the coffin backstop from the hearse into the man's hand. The man didn't turn round. Elton slipped away and was soon standing at the back of the gathering watching Rolley drying the plugs.

'What on earth's going on?' Sydney's clipped voice was suddenly there, and all turned as one to see him crossing the garage towards them. 'We're going to be late.'

'Elton's not used to the automatic choke and the engine flooded, Mr Gridley, but it's okay now I've dried the plugs,' said Rolley calmly.

'Well, let's bloody get going,' Sydney demanded.

'Certainly, Sir,' the drivers chorused, taking up their positions. Elton's engine started first time.

'Where's young Mr Marcus?' asked Rolley.

'He'll do hospital removals today instead of coming with us. We've got Elton, so there's enough of us.'

'But he hates removals,' said Rolley, getting his bulk behind the wheel of the hearse.

'Precisely,' said Sydney, dryly. 'Now, let's go.'

Rolley pulled forward gently to the kerb edge and

waited for a couple of cars to pass. The street was busy with people on their way to work. The old café across the road was full of construction workers swigging hot tea and revelling in the last few moments of inside warmth.

Sydney commanded, 'Push out. Push out, or we'll be late at church.'

Rolley judged that he could pull out if he was quick. He put his foot on the accelerator and swung out across the road and to the right, passing in front of the café. As he did so Sydney noticed a man in a smart coat standing with his back to the road. He couldn't see his face. Yes he could, reflected in the café window. It was Stillion Sloane, and in his hand he held what looked like a hearse backstop. He twirled it around like a football rattle. It all clicked into place in Sydney's mind. 'Stop,' he screamed. But it was too late. There was a terrible smashing of glass followed by the sound of wood meeting tarmac head on. Punters in the café sat and stared, open mouthed, mugs in hand. Two elderly ladies sat chatting in the window; one, with her back to events, babbled on while her friend stared over her shoulder, unable to believe what she saw. The chatterer finished her tale and looked into her friend's astonished face. 'It weren't that bloody amazing,' she concluded.

Sydney and Rolley jumped out of the hearse, ran to the rear and looked in horror at the damaged coffin lying in the road. There they were joined by the others. 'Pick it up as if there's nothing in it,' whispered Sydney. Lifting a damaged coffin containing a fifteen-stone man from a busy roadway as a crowd gathered wasn't easy; making it appear as if the coffin was empty was impossible. Even Sydney, who was never known to help the bearers, lent a hand in getting it back into the hearse. Then he looked around for Stillion, but Stillion had vanished.

The hearse was reversed back into the garage. A hammer and pins were produced and the lid and base mouldings, which had sprung free on impact, were banged back into place. The deck was swept to clear the broken glass and any remaining jagged pieces left between the rubber grips in the back tailgate were removed. A sidestop was brought in as an improvised backstop, and at last Richards & Gridley were ready for the off again. But by now it was five past nine and even if the cortège broke through the rush hour traffic at an undignified speed it would still be late at church.

The hearse and two limousines left the garage at speed, crossing as one to the far side of the road before pulling hard right. All three moved off down the High Street, to the ironic cheers of the few left in the café who'd witnessed the earlier debacle. The hearse wove in and out of the traffic as if it was going through the chicane at Monaco, and the limos strove hard to keep up. Sydney wondered how Stillion had come to have the backstop. He could, of course, have come into the garage and just taken it. But Sydney thought that that was fairly unlikely, as Stillion wouldn't have been able to guarantee easy access. He wouldn't have been able to predict when there might be a distraction like that limo that wouldn't start. Hang on a minute. Who'd had problems with their vehicle? None other than that little ex-Sloane shit Elton. And Sydney knew what foul play Elton was capable of; only yesterday he'd been doing dirty deeds for Sydney himself, and had been well paid for them too.

Sydney knew he must get to the bottom of this, but that it must wait until later. For now he must concentrate on getting this funeral back on schedule. The only way to do that would be to shorten the service a little, and Sydney knew he'd have to have a silver tongue in his mouth when asking Father O'Rourke if he would oblige. It wasn't going to be easy. O'Rourke was quite a showman. He was at his happiest when centre stage, cassock on, declaiming the mass – preferably in the forbidden Latin – before a large congregation. And as this funeral was certainly the most important to be held at St Mary's for several years Father O'Rourke was doubtless looking forward to being the centre of attention for a few minutes. And Sydney was sure he would be reluctant to shorten the service to suit them when it was their fault that it had started late.

'Can't you go any faster?' yelped the distressed Sydney.

'I'm doing me best, guv,' replied Rolley, who had also been reflecting on the events of this morning.

'You know, guv, I know I bloody put that fucking backstop in. I know I did. I mean, I never forgot that these fifty years here. It's like taking a fucking pee, you don't just forget to do it. And, anyway, we ain't bloody found the fucking thing,' he said, puzzled.

'I know where it is, or rather, where I last saw it,' said Sydney in a quiet, distant voice.

'What d'you mean, guv?'

'I mean I saw that bloody boy with it in his hand.'

'You mean young Mr Marcus?'

'No, of course I don't you fool! I mean bloody Stillion Sloane.'

'Stillion Sloane in our bloody garage? Well, bugger me 'til Friday.'

'No, not in the garage but standing arrogantly in the street twirling it about in his bloody hand.'

'Well I never. I never saw 'im.'

'Well I did, which is why I shouted 'stop', but it was too late. Now, it occurs to me that either Stillion took it or he was given it while all that commotion was going on with the flooded engine. That was all very convenient, wasn't it?'

'You mean it was down to that little bleeder Elton?'

'Precisely. I think we can safely assume that he caused the diversion on purpose, having been put up to it by Mr Sloane. Perhaps you would be good enough to recover my money from Mr Field while the service is on. Make sure he knows that I'm very unhappy with him, won't you Rolley?'

'Wouldn't it be better later at the garage?'

'No, now, before he loses or spends it,' said Sydney firmly.

The hearse and limousines came to rest outside St Mary's. It was nine thirty-two. They were seventeen minutes late and would be at least twenty-five minutes late by the time the service began. The bearers prepared the wheel bier as Sydney slipped, silent and unnoticed by the packed congregation, down a side aisle towards Father O'Rourke's little room. He knocked and entered.

'Holy Mary, Mother of God, Sydney, what time are you after calling this? We're going to be starting twenty-five minutes late. All the altar boys and the choir are out of school and the headmistress will be after having my guts for garters. The church is full o' people and this is my chance to redeem their souls. The family must be worried sick. And don't you dare be after asking me to cut the service down, because I won't. And I don't care even if you think it's going to screw up all the Anglican, Methodist, Sikh, Hindu or any other funerals you may be after having today. Now is that quite clear Sydney? Okay, you can wheel in the box.'

Sydney departed, not having uttered a word. He returned swiftly down the side aisle, looking straight ahead of him; he was now facing the congregation and, sick with embarrassment at being so late, had no wish to make eye contact with anybody. This was such a big funeral, and many of his friends from Rotary, the bench and the Council were here in the church. Instead of witnessing his hour of glory as master of ceremonies they were watching some kind of funeral sitcom. He dreaded the jokes that would follow. He hated Stillion for doing this to him. It didn't occur to him that he'd started this dangerous professional tit-for-tat.

Back at the door of the church the coffin was on the wheel bier and the four bearers had a handle each. Rolley looked very worried. 'Boss, we have a problem. There's a hole in the head end of the coffin.'

'Oh bloody hell. Put the pall on.'

'But Father O'Rourke won't have palls in St Mary's.'

'I don't care, put it on.'

'Well, we can't 'cos I sent it to the dry cleaners. I knew we wouldn't be needing it today.'

'Oh God,' said Sydney, through his tight, thin lips. 'What're we going to do? I said what're we going to do?' Sydney appeared to be crumbling; blind panic had set in behind his solemn face, and he seemed almost paralysed with fear. Rolley found the solution. He pulled a piece of chewing gum from his mouth, rolled it into a ball like putty and pushed it into the hole in the end of the coffin. He flattened it out to sit flush with the wood. It looked awful, and Sydney would normally have exploded at such a silly idea. But this time he didn't have a better one nor the time to think of one.

The coffin proceeded into church at nine forty-one, twenty-six minutes late, with broken moulding pinned together and a hole in the end bunged with chewing gum. Richards & Gridley had let the city's leading industrialist down badly, and the evidence was there on the wheel bier before the altar for all to see.

Sidney bowed to the altar and retreated back up the main aisle. It was a long and lonely walk. The bearers had had an easier time of it by slipping down each of the side aisles. Once outside Sydney put his bowler on and wandered a little way up the road to regain his composure.

It was a cold morning and two of the bearers got in the front of one of the limos, turning on the engine in order to keep warm. Rolley suggested that he and Elton go round the back of the church for a fag.

'Fancy a Park Drive, Elton?'

'Sure, why not mate?'

They strolled down the narrow side path. Once out of sight of the road Rolley pulled out his packet of cigarettes. 'Here,' Rolley said, thrusting the packet towards Elton. As Elton reached for one he was overwhelmed by a sickening pain that shot through his balls, up his arse, through his stomach, and hit him in the roof of the mouth. Rolley had kneed him viciously in his genitalia. He couldn't breathe, he couldn't see, he couldn't think; he wasn't sure he could live. He fell back against the church wall. Rolley reached into Elton's pockets and found the cash easily.

'You're not having this, you little shit. Not after this morning, you little toerag.'

'Leave me alone you bastard,' cried Elton, almost fainting. 'I dun nuthin'.'

'You dun nuthin'. Oh, you dun nuthin'.' Rolley grabbed a handful of Elton's greasy blond hair and pulled it backwards, smacking his head hard against the church wall. 'We know what you dun mate. No you ain't having the money and you ain't squealing to a soul, 'cos you've done all the damage. We'll just deny it all. All the fuck ups – bloody vandalism and criminal damage more like – will be down to you, either accidentally or on purpose. It's all you. No other fucker's dun a thing mate. Nobody here or at Sloanes would ever admit any involvement. You're the only little shit with dirt on your hands. Now, like I said, we don't talk about it again, okay?' Elton didn't reply. 'Okay, I said?' repeated Rolley with menace in his voice.

Elton nodded. Rolley may have been sixty-seven, and Elton just twenty-six, but Rolley was seventeen stone to Elton's ten. And Rolley remained strong, Elton a coward. Rolley smiled, 'That's the way, mate. Oh, and at the end of the day, when you've finished leathering the limo, just fuck off. It wouldn't be safe to be around us. You see, we don't like toerags like you. Okay? Better get back to the others, yeah?' Rolley led the way. Elton, white as a sheet and feeling faint, staggered behind him.

'There you go, boss,' Rolley slipped the cash to Sydney.

'Bloody hell, he looks like he's seen a ghost Rolley.'

'Maybe he has guv. His own.'

Sydney and the bearers waited the few minutes for the service to finish then they retraced their steps through the church towards the damaged box. They faced the altar, bowed and turned the coffin so that they could carry it back up aisle foot first, behind Father O'Rourke. Sydney stepped to one side to let the coffin pass before conducting the mourners in leaving their pews, starting with the direct family, who were seated on the front right pew.

As Sydney processed up the aisle behind the coffin he hoped that his body blocked the family's view of the head end and of the hole bunged with chewing gum. He then noticed that Elton Field was not processing as a professional pall bearer should. Indeed, his gait was anything but right. A bearer should walk upright and in step with the other bearers, one hand lightly on the coffin handle, the other by his side; Elton was gripping the handle, stumbling. Occasionally he rested his other hand on the coffin lid to steady himself. He looked ill, and the congregation was beginning to notice. 'Here comes another crisis,' Sydney thought to himself. But Elton made it back to the hearse, although he struggled to lift his share of the coffin off the wheel bier and into the vehicle.

Now that the service was over Sydney had to ensure

that Father O'Rourke didn't disappear into the presbytery for bacon and eggs, but rather that he was safely seated in the front seat of the lead limousine, committal service book and holy water in hand. It was then time for the cortège to move off, and Sydney, in his black coat and bowler hat, walked ahead of the hearse a short way down the road. Sydney only ever took a few steps in front of the cortège, unlike Stillion who favoured the full pomp and ceremony of a Victorian funeral; precision timing, top hats, tailcoats and a walking pace – particularly for working-class funerals – as far as time would allow. Stillion believed that a funeral should be a splendid occasion, whilst Sydney followed the 1950s fashion for sombre but discreet direction and dismissed Stillion's style as ostentatious exhibitionism. But then Sydney, a short thin little man in his early sixties, cut a poor figure when compared to the far younger, taller and better-looking Stillion, and perhaps felt it would be foolish to compete.

Sydney then climbed into the hearse and the long cortège of hearse, two limousines and scores of expensive private cars set off through the back streets of Hockley towards Lozells and then on to Witton Cemetery, where they should already have been.

Sydney had hardly shut the hearse door before he asked Rolley, 'What the hell have you done to him?'

'Done to who?'

'Done to Field, of course. He looks ill. That's the last thing I want after everything else this morning.'

'Well, he weren't gonna give the lolly back just like that you know,' said Rolley defensively.

'Well, we should've done it later.'

'But you said now.'

'Okay. Okay, concentrate on your speed. Hold twenty miles per hour and then twenty-five once you're on the Birchfield underpass.'

Two cars back, Elton was sweating. He kept going hot and then cold. He felt sick and dizzy. It was all he could do to drive. 'You okay, son?' asked the elderly fourth bearer, riding shotgun beside him. Elton nodded. He didn't dare reply for fear of being sick. He opened the window a little, then more, then fully, despite it being a bitterly cold day with overnight snow on the ground and an easterly bite in the air. He hoped the cold air would revive him, but it didn't. He wasn't sure if it was the knee in the balls or the bash to the back of the head that was to blame. He started to make circular movements with his head and groaned quietly. 'You okay son?' asked the elderly bearer once more; the first time he was just being polite, but now he was concerned. 'No,' groaned Elton, 'I'm . . .' At that moment the welling inside him finally exploded and he just managed to get his head sufficiently far to the right so that the torrent of vomit, when it came, was directed out of the window. Twenty-five miles an hour was sufficiently fast to carry the stream away, pebble dashing the offside of the limo and depositing Elton's breakfast – cereal, mixed grill and tea – through the slightly open rear window and over the mourners inside. Some even reached the windscreen of the private Rolls-Royce behind, whose driver, finding himself suddenly unable to see, slammed on his brakes. Rolls-Royces are well engineered and, if commanded to stop suddenly, do just that. And this one did just that, and a little too quickly for the driver of the BMW behind it. Crash! Crash. Crash. Crash. One by one the private cars ran into the car in front.

The hearse and the first limousine moved on ahead, oblivious to these events. So was Elton, who felt suddenly much better, and the poor family in the rear of his limousine, who were far too distracted by being splattered in puke to care about anything. Sydney should have been looking in the rear view mirror from time to time, like all good funeral directors, and if he had he would have noticed that all the private cars had disappeared from sight. But he was altogether too preoccupied with the events of the morning, and he didn't. Nor did Rolley, who was starting to worry about being late for the Sikh take-home he was down to do at eleven-fifteen.

It was eleven o'clock when the hearse and two limousines pulled through the gates of Witton Cemetery. They stopped outside the lodge to collect Tom, the foreman.

'Where you been?' Tom demanded. 'You're half an hour late. Good job you're committal only. The eleven o'clock Sloane job has just gone up the drive to the chapel.' As Sydney followed him out of the lodge he noticed there were no private cars behind the limos. From where he stood he couldn't see the splattered vomit on the second limo, but he could see that the mourners from this car were behaving very oddly. What were they doing? All six of them had climbed out of the vehicle and were wiping themselves and their clothes with tissues and hankies. Sydney approached them. 'Everything all right?' he asked, and without waiting for a reply continued, 'Could we take our seats, please? The cortège is about to move on.'

'No, everything is not all right. And we will only be able to get back in that car when it's been cleaned up,' said one of the men, removing bits of bacon from his trousers.

'I beg your pardon,' said Sydney, dumbfounded. He was in a daze; he had never had a funeral like this, except in his wildest nightmares, but he suspected he was not going to wake up from this one.

'Your chauffeur has been car sick, and a lot of it managed to find us.'

'Oh, dear I am so sorry.' Sydney spoke quite sincerely, but in such an expressionless voice that the words might have been spoken by a robot. He found himself unable to deal with the situation and began to walk towards the hearse, passing the first limousine. As he did so the front passenger window was lowered and Father O'Rourke's voice whispered, 'So what's the hold up now?'

'The second limo driver's been car sick, Father,' answered Sydney, and carried on walking. Father O'Rourke turned to the first limo driver and said in an even quieter whisper, lest the bereaved family sitting patiently on the other side of the glass partition could hear, 'So, Sydney Gridley JP stands for Sydney Gridley Just Puke.'

By this time the mourners in the second limo had clearly decided they could live with their improvised clean up and climbed back into the vehicle. At the same moment the group were joined by the puke-stained Roller with a dented boot, and the other crumpled cars. The cortège set off again, following the foreman's old council Escort van up the hill towards Stillion and his staff, who were waiting outside the chapel while their own service was in progress. Sydney wanted to die; he stared straight ahead, not wanting to make eye contact with Stillion. But as the Richards & Gridley cortège turned left at the chapel the full effect of the puke pebble-dashing was exposed to the Sloane contingent.

Stillion was astounded more than pleased. He had left Richards & Gridley's premises and gone back to Sloane House to change in time for this, the second A-fleet funeral of the day. He hadn't expected to see Sydney's lot. He had expected them to run a little late, following Elton's little wheeze with the backstop, but they'd been due at ten-thirty for a committal only, and now it was ten past eleven, the cortège had only just arrived and some of it was splattered with sick.

The Gridley cortège proceeded on past the chapel and took the top main drive before turning into the narrow path on the right that led to the re-opened grave. This path descended the hill that looked out over the M6 and across to the impressive Villa Park stadium. The gradient was very steep and the icy paths were covered by an overnight fall of snow, making them treacherously slippery. 'Second gear and very slowly Rolley,' warned Sydney.

By now Elton was beginning to recover and sickness was giving way to anger. He'd made a deal; okay, so it was with bad people and not a good thing to do, but it was a deal. He'd delivered. And now they'd taken the money back and given him a beating. He'd lost his job, lost his grand, kept his debts, kept the bookies' threats and gained a beating! He couldn't even squeal, because all fingers pointed to him. It wouldn't be any good asking Mr Stillion for help; he probably loathed him even more than this lot, and they loathed him so much they'd beaten him so hard he'd nearly fainted at the wheel. Hang on, that was it. Nearly fainted at the wheel. Of course, nearly fainted at the wheel. Don't get angry, get even. Nearly fainted at the wheel. Well, perhaps he'd faint at the wheel. It would be an accident. Rolley Brown and Mr Gridley could hardly say that it wasn't an accident because they'd beaten him up and taken the grand back and they would never wish to risk opening that can of worms. So at least to the outside world they would have to agree Elton, probably as a result of food poisoning, had become ill and lost control of the vehicle.

As the cortège turned right into the narrow, steep path Elton was thinking, 'Get even. Get even.' Up ahead the hearse came to rest on the steepest part of the hill, just before the small road forked. Gingerly, Sydney Gridley and Rolley Brown clambered out onto the steep, icy road. Tom had left the council van on the main drive and was walking down towards the grave. The lead limousine driver parked and stepped out onto the snow-covered grass verge and headed towards the rear of the hearse. Father O'Rourke, who hated the cold, especially without a drop of the hard stuff to warm him, sat in the limousine waiting for one of the Gridley staff to open the door for him. This was Elton's moment. Don't get mad, get even. Elton groaned and slumped forwards over the steering-wheel in a semblance of a faint. His foot hit the accelerator and the limo began to gather speed. 'Steady, son,' yelled the elderly fourth bearer, but to no avail. Elton's limo crunched into the back of limo number one, stationed at the start of the steep descent. Number two limo, with Elton, the fourth bearer and the puke-splattered mourners, came to a halt. Not so number one which, shunted in the back, took off down the slope like a toboggan on the Cresta Run, with Father O'Rourke and six of the mourners on board. A few seconds later it smacked into the back of the hearse with such violence that the hearse took off with just the deceased on board. By some divine guidance it took the path to the right as it sped downhill. Gridley, Brown, Tom the foreman, the gravedigger and the first limo driver could only stand and watch, wide-eyed and open-mouthed. Their horrified attention was then wrenched away from the hearse by the predicament of the first limo. Engine off, handbrake and wheel lock on, the first limo, having shunted the hearse, had gathered pace. At first it moved off down the left-hand road, but then its fixed steering position pulled it away from the roadway, up the left verge and on down the hill, leaving a trail of flattened gravestones in its wake. Father O'Rourke leaned across from the passenger side and grabbed the wheel. He couldn't drive and didn't understand why his pulling on it had no effect. The women in the back were screaming, the men 'for Christ saking'. All were bobbing up to the roof and down again as the limousine rode over gravestone after gravestone.

Tom, the grave digger and the first limousine driver scrambled down the hill after the runaway limo, while Sydney remained frozen to the spot in disbelief. Rolley started off down the right path after the hearse, but didn't get far; he lost his footing on the ice and fell, a five-foot, seven-inch, seventeen-stone ball, and bounced down the hill in the same direction as the hearse. Sydney switched his astounded gaze back to the first limousine, which had now come to rest against a large Victorian monument that, having stood the test of time, wasn't going to be moved by a 1970 Daimler limousine. Then he looked up the hill, where scores of people were climbing out of private cars and the puke-splattered second limousine and were clambering down the hill, clinging as they went to any gravestones still standing. He could just make out amongst them the elderly fourth bearer, who had also got out of the second limousine, and was shouting down the hill to him, 'It's Elton, sir, he's fainted, sir.' Sydney didn't make any acknowledgement that he'd heard, but just turned back to look down and to the right to where the hearse had left the path and smashed into the outer cemetery wall, having taken out at least ten gravestones in its way. Then he gazed to the left, to the trail of destruction left by the first limousine, which would probably be a write off. He looked back up the hill to the second limousine, with its smashed-in front, broken radiator and smatterings of puke, inside and out. He had three more funerals scheduled for later that day, many more for next week and no presumable vehicles. It was now twenty-five past eleven and the coffin was way down the hill, far from the grave. For the first time since he had married the business, Sydney wanted a divorce.

By now the puke-splattered relatives had caught up with the shaken and stirred ones. They clung on to each other and made their way back up towards the grave, assisted by Tom and Sydney's staff. They looked more like survivors of a rail accident or motorway pile-up than the mourners at the funeral of a major industrialist. Joseph Lyons' son, with one arm round his mother and holding his sister by the hand, approached Sydney. He could hardly contain his rage, and was only just able to spit out the words, 'Gridley, you seem intent on burying most of our family today. What's the matter, business not good enough for you?' Sydney was appalled, and all the more mortified because these comments were made within earshot of several of his fellow benchers and Rotarians.

Tom meantime had collected the coffin in the back of his old council van and returned it to the graveside, with a bruised Rolley beside him in the front passenger seat. Father O'Rourke, though badly shaken, completed the committal service after which the principal twelve mourners, still in a state of shock, arranged lifts back to the Lyons' house in the various crumpled private cars. The Gridley fleet was abandoned in the cemetery to be rescued later in the day by the local British Leyland dealer. A taxi took the battered Richards & Gridley staff back to base, except for Elton Field who was abandoned, like the vehicles, in the cemetery. A telephone call had secured the loan of a hearse and two limousines from the Co-op for the rest of the day, and even next week, at a price, and so the remaining three funerals of the day were undertaken, albeit extremely late.

⋆ ⋆ ⋆

Stillion's third funeral of the day had taken him back to Perry Barr Crem. The events of the week had wiped any memory of his little chat with Michael Russell about the music from his mind, and it was clear that Michael had forgotten, too. With pupils fully dilated the stoned organist was now punching out an accurate and undisguised rendition of Arthur Brown's 'Fire.'

* * *

At the end of the day a tired, broken and visibly aged Sydney took a phone call. It was a friend. 'I say, Sydney, are you okay? I heard about today. Well, I mean, I would wouldn't I?'

'Would you?' asked Sydney, wearily.

'Oh yes, rather. It's all over town. Rum lot you funeral directors. I mean, you trying to bump off half the mourners at old Joe Lyons' funeral and Stillion Sloane caught with his trousers down in the Plough & Harrow on Wednesday night. No bloody morals, you lot.'

'What did you say?' demanded Sydney, suddenly interested.

'No bloody morals, you lot,' repeated his friend, affably.

'No, before that, about that bloody boy?'

'Which bloody boy?'

'Stillion Sloane.'

'Oh, that. Well, young Mr Sloane was seen by

Johnnie Hunt from Evergreens, the solicitors. You know Johnnie Hunt, loves hunting and . . .'

'Yes, yes, go on,' interrupted an impatient Sydney.

'Well, Johnnie Hunt was taking supper with friends at the Plough and went for a pee. He's always had a bit of weak bladder you know.'

'Really?' interjected Sydney with irony.

'Yes. Well, anyway, as he's on his way back to the table he notices Stillion Sloane and Lottie Wilkes coming out of the lift.'

'Well?'

'Well, that's it. Coming out of the lift at the Plough can only mean one thing and that's bed. They've only got bedrooms upstairs, you know. I mean, she's a looker all right but nearly old enough to be his mother. And him playing away when he has that pretty young slip of a girl to go home to. Dangerous game, too, don't you know? I mean, what if Harry Wilkes was to find out.'

Sydney couldn't wait to finish the conversation. He made his excuses and hung up. 'Well, well,' he thought, 'I've got you, bloody Stillion Sloane, I've got you.' If he'd loathed Stillion Sloane on Monday and detested him by Wednesday, it was nothing compared to the indescribable feelings towards him that Sydney had developed following Joseph Lyons' funeral. In three hours that morning Stillion had wrecked both Sydney's reputation and his fleet. Sydney didn't for a moment consider that it was he who had started this war and that the greater part of his troubles that day had been a direct result of his order to Rolley to beat up Elton Field. He saw it as all the fault of Stillion Sloane, and now there was a chance to strike back and cause Sloane damage and pain. Sydney knew that his next action was unlikely to help him beat Stillion to the purchase of Joyce Higgins' business, and conceded to himself that today's events wouldn't have done him much good in that direction either. And revenge wouldn't take away the nightmarish memories of the day, which were bound to haunt him, both in his own dreams and in the taunts of his fellow Rotarians, his peers on the bench and in the Council chamber, never mind those of his fellow funeral directors. But his action, with any luck, would cause Stillion Sloane both physical pain and mental stress. He picked up the telephone and dialled Lottie's husband.

'Good evening. Could I speak to Mr Harry Wilkes please? Thank you. Mr Wilkes. This is Sydney Gridley. A word in your ear . . .'

* * *

As Sydney made his call to Harry Wilkes, Stillion having enjoyed a calm and trouble-free day, was about to drive over to Higgins & Co. to keep his six o'clock meeting with Joyce. He had heard about the catastrophic events at Sydney's big Lyons funeral and had been rather shocked by the extent of the destruction.

He had only expected Elton Field to play the one prank, and was somewhat confused as to how all the other disasters had come about. But as far as his own business was concerned, he was feeling a little better. John Palin had arranged seven funerals today; two were for West Indian clients and one was for a member of Fred Price's congregation, so it appeared that his reputation was not irretrievably damaged, nor had his business collapsed as he had feared. There had thankfully been no mention of the ex-Lord Mayor's funeral in either the *Birmingham Post* or the *Evening Mail* and he felt he could breathe again. And he'd better be on good form if he was going to talk Joyce Higgins into selling to him rather than to Sydney Gridley, even given Sydney's disastrous day. Stillion only knew Joyce slightly – he had danced with her once at the Birmingham Funeral Directors' Guild Ball – and he knew that Sydney knew her well, and suspected they were fairly close friends. He turned into the Higgins' car park, locked the car and rang the front doorbell. The old pensioner who showed families into the viewing chapels in the evenings answered the door with a very funereal, 'Good evening. Do come in.', Then, after a pause, 'You wish to see . . . ?'

'Miss Higgins, please,' answered Stillion, politely. The old boy referred to his viewing list and looked perplexed. 'No, no. I want to see Miss Joyce Higgins, the owner of the business,' said Stillion slowly and more loudly, suspecting that the stooping white-haired old man might be a bit deaf.

'Very good. Please take a seat, Sir.' Stillion took a seat in the hallway while the old man, having asked his name, went upstairs to the offices. He returned a few minutes later. 'She won't keep you waiting long, Sir. She knows you're here. She's just finishing a phone call.'

Upstairs Joyce was talking to her lover and Stillion's rival for her business, Sydney. 'Not a good day for you, darling. What a mess. Everyone's talking about it. And all of this following young Mr Sloane's mistakes of yesterday. Perhaps I shouldn't sell to either of you.'

'Listen, you know perfectly well these things happen. We haven't put a foot wrong in seventy years and you also bloody well know that you're going to sell to one of us and it had better be me. For Christ's sake, woman, I've been sharing your bed for nearly a quarter of a century. You can't sell to him.'

'Can't I? Actually, I can sell to whomsoever I choose.'

'Okay, okay, of course you can. I'm not saying you can't.'

'Yes you are.'

'No, I promise you. I'm not. Just make it me. Please, Joyce. Look, whatever he offers you, I'll add twenty-thousand to it, guaranteed. You mustn't let me down on this.'

'I could just make his offer up and then get you to add twenty grand to that.'

'No, you wouldn't do that. I'll pay you the best price and therefore there's no conflict. You'd rather sell to me. Our firms, our families, and most important of all you and me, go back a long way. I'll give you the best price. Promise me it's a deal.'

'Sydney, he's downstairs waiting. I must go.'

'Promise me. We mean a lot to each other. This means a lot to me and when it's done and we are one firm I can easily see a lot more of you. Now, promise me.'

'Okay, I promise, but I must go.'

'Look at that bloody boy's pretty face one last time and don't be tempted, old girl, by his tarting. Perhaps he won't quite look the same next time you see him.'

'Why? I suppose you're going to give him a good thrashing are you?' laughed Joyce.

'No, but I know a man who is. That public schoolboy prostitute has been fooling with the Wilkes woman.'

'Lottie Wilkes! But she's nearly my age.'

'Well, he was seen leaving the Plough with her and I let that slip to that thug husband of hers.'

'Did you, darling? Well done. I'll phone you later.' Joyce put down the receiver amused by the end of the conversation. She didn't believe for a minute that Sydney would have lowered himself to speak to Harry Wilkes. Sure, he hated Stillion enough, but Sydney was a Justice of the Peace and a sensible man. JPs who'd worked so hard to get where they were today didn't talk to the Harry Wilkes' of this world. It was just too easy to get caught up in his mob-type behaviour and lose everything. But she did believe what he'd said about Lottie Wilkes and Stillion. She knew how Stillion had secured the ex-Lord Mayor's funeral. How did she know? She knew because Gillian Weston had told her. Gillian Weston told her everything and they had giggled uproariously over every detail of Gillian's Monday afternoon romp when they had met for lunch on Wednesday. Joyce had been probably going to grant Stillion an audience anyway, but the exciting tale of Gillian's several orgasms had prompted her to call her solicitors that afternoon with the instruction to contact Stillion's solicitors with a time and place for their meeting. And now she'd learned that he'd been servicing Lottie Wilkes too. Well, well! What a naughty boy.

Joyce didn't like Stillion Sloane. He was too self-assured and, she suspected, big headed for her liking. Moreover, her father, in common with John Richards and Sydney Gridley, had never liked the haughty Sloanes or their superior attitude. On the other hand she did find Stillion extremely attractive and very sexy. How delicious. She was in the perfect position to exploit his desire to buy her business. To punish him on behalf of womankind made every part of her sadistic body tingle with excitement. She glanced in the mirror, tidied her hair with her hands and began to descend the stairs to keep her appointment, her juices already flowing.

* * *

Throughout his telephone conversation with Joyce, Sydney had been completely unaware of a presence close by. It was Marcus. Marcus had had an awful day. His father had subjected him to hours of driving in the ambulance to hospitals and old people's homes, collecting the bodies for next week's funerals. Sydney knew he hated it, and was punishing him for their conversation of the previous evening. Marcus didn't want to be kicked out of home without a penny, but he really couldn't face life either as a funeral director or working with his father. The conversation between Sydney and Joyce that he had overheard yesterday evening had worried him, for his mother's sake. It seemed that, not only had Sydney treated Marcus' timid mother as a half-witted housekeeper, addressing her merely with orders and edicts, but he had been having an affair with Joyce Higgins as well.

Marcus suspected that, to avoid detection, his father telephoned Joyce from his private line in the office after close of business, so Marcus had crept silently down from the flat in the hope of gaining more information. The conversation he had overheard tonight had shocked him far more than the one he'd heard yesterday. From it he deduced not only that he was right about an affair between his father and Joyce Higgins, but also that it had been going on for years. Maybe it had started before he was born, and perhaps even before his parents were married. His poor mother. And something else the conversation he'd just overheard had revealed was that, probably as a result of the day's dreadful events, his father's loathing for Stillion had become an insane hatred, and Marcus knew that Sydney's ringing Harry Wilkes would ensure that Stillion got at the very best a serious beating, at worst he could lose his life. Wilkes' reputation was terrible and he wouldn't, couldn't, let Stillion get away with sleeping with his wife.

Marcus slipped back to the apartment. Thanks to his father, his life and his mother's life were restricted and miserable. Sydney used them as he wished, puppets on the stage of his own life. But Sydney couldn't control Stillion, so he had arranged for someone else to punish him badly. If it ever got out that Sydney had been involved his reputation would be ruined, or he might even face jail. Marcus knew that, for his own sake and for the sakes of his mother, Stillion and even his father, he must do something to help Stillion. He was not going to let his father wreck all their lives by this one rash action, inspired by an irrational hatred. He decided to talk to his mother, now, before his father came upstairs.

Marcus loved his frail, sickly, kind and gentle

mother, but knew that she was incapable of standing up to his father. Susan's mother, Alice, had come from a large Sheffield steel-making family, one of ten children. Alice had met John, Susan's father, on holiday at Scarborough in the late summer of 1928. Alice had become pregnant and, not uncommonly for the time, her family disowned her. She was forced to flee her home and ended up in the Midlands where John Richards did the right thing and married her. Alice had died in 1942, killed by a bomb that hit the local weapons factory where she was helping pull others from the wreckage of an earlier direct hit. Susan was only thirteen then. Alice hadn't talked to her family since Susan's birth, and John had no family, so Susan had had to look after the two of them. She was asthmatic, at a time when cures and drugs were few, and her frailness and her father's needs kept her away from other children and from school, so her education had been patchy. She was small, frail and naturally shy. She wasn't pretty, or ugly, just plain. She had had few friends and had never expected to marry. But then she met Sydney. They had married and had Marcus, a feat that nearly tore her wretched little being apart. She loved Marcus, and he in turn adored her. She was grateful to Sydney, but couldn't love him; he was hard on her and clearly held no affection for her. But he had married her, and had given her her beloved Marcus. He had managed the business, had managed it well and secured their future. And he had managed her so well that she had become accustomed to leaving all the decisions to him, a state of affairs which suited Sydney fine.

The experiences of Susan's life and her ill health gave her an appearance of age beyond her years. She was twelve years younger than Sydney but could easily have passed for the same age. She was very thin; Marcus had sucked her breasts away, while her father and Sydney took the fat, and asthma stole what was left. Her kind, shy, insecure, darting eyes were surrounded by wrinkles, and her dark, unstyled hair had more than a little touch of grey. Her pale face often looked sad but could brighten into a smile, and when she smiled she looked neither plain, tired or ill. The thought, sight or sound of her beloved son made her smile. Marcus was her life, the one big pleasure in a numbed servant's life, the one thing that made any sense out of her existence.

Marcus found her in the kitchen, a long thin room with modern units and concealed lighting down either side, preparing dinner. As usual she was dressed in dreary, colourless woollies and wore no make-up. 'Mum,' he began, 'I must talk to you, now.'

'Of course, dear,' replied Susan. She stopped peeling potatoes, wiped her hands on her apron and turned to face the boy, bestowing on him a gentle smile.

'Mum, Dad and I had a dreadful row last night, about me coming into the business. I told him I couldn't. He told me to change my mind by Monday or get out.'

'Oh dear, we must talk to him darling,' interrupted Susan with a calm that hid her panic. She had noticed that the two hadn't spoken at breakfast and now her worst fears were being realised. She knew that Sydney would rather carry out his threat than lose face, and that she would be powerless to stop him. She couldn't bear the thought of Marcus leaving her to a life of waiting hand and foot upon the loveless Sydney.

'Mum, you must help me. You must tell him he can't do this to us.'

'Nobody tells your father anything, dear. You know he insists on being in control of this house, and the business. We'll have to ask him to listen to a compromise. Perhaps you could come into the business after university and give it a go for a couple of years. Yes?'

'No,' replied Marcus with a firmness that he, like everyone else, found easy to deliver to his mother. 'No, I won't. Look, this is your life, your business too. It was your father's business. You must stand up for me. He won't even give me the ten thousand pounds that Grandpa left with him for me when I was eighteen. We can't just go on being his slaves.'

'Look dear, I know your father can be difficult. He's strict, and expects to get his own way, but you know he loves both of us in his way and has worked hard to give us both a good life. He's an honest and loyal man.'

'Mother, he is neither honest, loyal nor good. This week there've been lots of strange things happening over at Sloanes and here. I don't know what's going on, but I suspect that Father is involved. I do know that he's told Harry Wilkes that Stillion is having an affair with his wife and I do know – and I hate to tell you this mother, but it's time we faced up to many things in this house – I do know that good old Dad has been having an affair with Joyce Higgins, for years. I don't call any of this honest, good or loyal. He's duped you, certainly throughout my lifetime, and now Stillion may even get killed.'

'Your father? An affair? Don't be ridiculous,' laughed his mother, who was secretly worried that things were clearly getting out of hand.

'It's not ridiculous. I bloody well heard him talking to her about it and about having Stillion beaten up,' shouted Marcus, with the courage that desperation brings. Susan turned away and looked at her reflection in the window at the end of the kitchen. She had put up with a lot in order to keep this secure apartment and family around her. At this moment she despised who she was, not because of what she had just heard from Marcus, but because he, her treasured only child, now pitied her. She turned back towards Marcus, who was breathing heavily with the emotion of the moment. She sat down quietly on a kitchen stool. 'I'm sorry you had to find out about Joyce, dear. Truly sorry.'

'Had to find out?' repeated Marcus. 'You mean you already knew? Mum, you knew. When did you know? For how long have you known?'

'I don't know, just years I suppose. He never told

me. I never caught them. I just knew or thought I knew, but I didn't want to know. So I never asked and he never told me. He did marry me. He did give me you. He may never have loved me but he did give me you, ran the business and didn't come home drunk to beat me.'

'Mother, you don't have to live with a loveless marriage, a slave for a man who's unfaithful to you for years with a friend of yours, just so you don't get beaten up. Look, you can stay and see me kicked out on Monday but unless things change I promise I will never come back. Never. And are you prepared for Stillion to be kicked within an inch of his life as well? I know Dad, Grandpa and perhaps you don't like the Sloanes but can you see him beaten up just because Dad wants it? And what if he dies? What if there's an investigation? What if Dad gets implicated?'

'No. No, you're right. You must find young Mr Sloane and warn him now.'

'What about the rest of it, Mum?'

'Later. We'll sort the rest out later. Now you'd better be off.'

'Promise?'

'Yes I promise,' said Susan with unusual conviction.

Marcus left the apartment. He passed his father on the stairs. They didn't speak; Marcus was galloping down, off to rescue Stillion, his father was trudging up to take the frustrations of the worst day of his business life out on the mouse he called his wife. It was twenty past six.

As Marcus went out of the front door a very angry Mr Razek Singh rang the bell. Marcus smiled as he said his father was in and would be delighted to attend to his every need.

* * *

On arriving in the hall Joyce waited while the old man showed a bereaved family out of the front door. Then she stepped forward, her hand held out and smiling as she greeted Stillion.

'Hello, young man, thanks for coming over to see me. I hope it hasn't caused you any inconvenience.'

Stillion was taken aback. Joyce's body language, eyes and voice all exuded friendliness. He hadn't expected her to be rude, but on the other hand it had taken James Steele a lot of hard chasing of her solicitors to get the appointment. He'd always thought that she would only sell to him if her head took over the rule of her heart, and if his offer was the highest, but now she was standing before him, eyes flashing, mouth smiling, delightfully scented and dressed in a neat double-breasted, pin-striped dark skirt suit with dark stockings, black shoes and apparently no blouse beneath the buttoned jacket. Once he had overcome the initial shock of her *bonhomie* Stillion found himself becoming rather intoxicated by this woman, eighteen years his senior, whom he had never found remotely attractive before.

Joyce was a bit younger than Susan and years ago

they had travelled to the same school on the bus, when Susan was well enough to attend. Joyce as a girl had looked up to Susan. They were both motherless – Joyce had lost her mother to cancer in 1943 – and the two girls became quite close. Their fathers were friends and fishing companions. However, as the teen years turned into twenties, the age gap narrowed and the younger girl outgrew her shy older friend in size and character. Susan preferred to remain at home, whereas Joyce learned to drive, went to parties, stayed out late and had boyfriends. Lots of them. Some time in 1952 she managed to persuade Susan to come to a party with her, and it was here that Susan had met Sydney. Sydney had chosen Susan and initially Joyce was amused, even pleased, by this. Then on the night of Susan and Sydney's engagement party Joyce had decided it might be fun to flirt with Sydney. It didn't work. She was too young to understand that Sydney had set his heart on the Richards' business rather than Susan. All she could see was that she had attempted to win Sydney, if only as a game, and had lost. She had lost to that dull, quiet and unfashionable thing. She could think of nothing else. She found herself longing for Sydney, unattractive, unfashionable and impoverished Sydney, simply because Susan had him and she, Joyce, didn't. She determined to seduce Sydney and take him from Susan. She succeeded first time, and Sydney, flattered and excited by Joyce's aggressive sexual manner, began to visit her regularly. But, easily as she may have taken Sydney from Susan, Joyce could hardly expect to take him from Richards & Sons and his new-found respectability. Susan and the firm were far too tightly wrapped together for Joyce to have any chance. So Joyce had spent her twenties, thirties and most of her forties fighting a campaign that she couldn't win. Sydney saw their relationship as a source of weekly sex and an iron in the fire for future business expansion, while Joyce looked for something better. She had often found better sex, but had never found a better relationship. When her father died she realised how the months had turned into years and her life had been slipping by with only snatched moments with a man she didn't love, who didn't love her and who she found increasingly dull sexually. Soon she would be fifty, and maybe it was already too late. On the other hand she now understood the game and for the first time had an important card in her hand, the sale of her late father's business.

'Let's go upstairs,' said Joyce. That didn't surprise Stillion, as he knew that the offices were upstairs, but he was surprised when she led on up to the second floor to her private apartment.

'Go through to the sitting room and take a seat,' said Joyce over her shoulder as she unlocked the door. Stillion walked through the small but well appointed hall and silently sat on the sofa. Stillion was taken aback by how tastefully the room was decorated; the blue carpet, magnolia walls, the oil paintings underneath individual wall lights and antique furniture were a striking contrast to the dull and dimly-lit chapels and the old fashioned and scruffy offices below. A few minutes passed before Joyce returned, with a bottle of Chablis and two large wine glasses in her hands. It was half past six.

* * *

At the same moment the gravel of Harry Wilkes' drive crunched under the wheels of his Rolls-Royce as he arrived home. He operated the remote-controlled electric door to the garage, drove in and parked next to Lottie's Mercedes. He walked out of the garage and across the drive towards the house. He usually paused on the front doorstep to admire the view of his front garden and paddock and beyond, off down the long lamppost-lit drive to the Lickey hills on the left and the Malvern hills in the far distance to the right. But not tonight. He opened the front door without looking back and entered the new mock Jacobean mansion, complete with leaded windows. He tossed his car keys down on the hall table and wandered through the house looking for his wife. His two teenage children were upstairs, getting ready for a Friday night out at the Midland Art Centre disco with their friends. He could hear his daughter's Wings' album competing with his son's Police tape. Lottie wasn't in the snug, drawing room or kitchen, so he walked through the conservatory and into the pool area. There she was, swimming slowly up and down to Frank Sinatra singing 'Strangers in the Night'. She turned at the far end and, seeing him, started to swim back. He walked down the side of the pool and she swam to that side. 'Hi darling,' she smiled. She was not surprised to see him, because although he spent almost every week night out without her he often came home to change before going out. He squatted on his haunches.

'Where were you on Wednesday night?' he asked calmly and perhaps a little coldly. Immediately Lottie was fearful, partly because she remembered exactly where she had been on Wednesday night and partly because, after all these years with him, she recognised the tone of voice. He had beaten her occasionally during their years together, usually when he was drunk and never with any good reason. But she'd never been unfaithful to him before, and she began to fear that she may be about to experience the violence of a man intoxicated by sober anger.

'Why?' she said, with a slight quaver in her voice.

''Cos I'm asking, babe,' he replied, more softly.

She took a little heart from the altered tone. 'I was out for dinner with a girlfriend.'

'Where?'

'At the new Spanish place in Broad Street.'

Harry didn't need to hear anymore. Following Sydney Gridley's call he had called the Plough pretending to have been there on Wednesday night. He told the receptionist he had met a couple there, lost their names and addresses, which was a problem as they had lent him a Webster's dictionary and he wanted to return it. He had described Lottie and the receptionist remembered her instantly. She couldn't, she regretted, give him Mrs Hopwood's address, but if he left his name and address with them they would pass it on. That was enough for Harry.

'You lying bitch Mrs fucking Hopwood,' he spat as he grabbed her by the hair and, without regard for his expensive mohair suit, hand-made shirt and Rolex watch, submerged her head at least a foot below the water's surface. With his right hand on her left shoulder and his left full of her black hair, he held her there. Seconds passed. Then, when she began to contemplate the final countdown, he released his right hand and dragged her head above the surface with his left. She spluttered and gasped for breath, her eyes wide open in shock at the speed of the attack.

'Now, I know you were at the Plough with Stillion Sloane 'cos you was seen there,' he shot into her frightened face. 'Admit it.'

'It's not tr . . .' Down she went again. She waved her arms in surrender. He pulled her again. 'Okay, it's true.'

'I knew it. You bitch. Make a laughing stock of me would you?' He pulled her from the water by her arm and her hair. She stood, dripping wet in her bikini, facing him. He was panting half from exertion and half from rage. His dark brown suit was mottled with water splashes and soaked on each arm to above the elbows.

'Fancied a bit with the upper class did you? You whore!' The back of his right hand arrived from nowhere, smacking her right cheek with enough force to send her to the pool room floor, before following through in true tennis pro style. She tried to scramble free. He grabbed the centre front piece of her bikini bra and pulled her to her feet with such strength that the clasp at the back broke and he was left with the bra in his hand as she fell back to the floor. He threw the bra into the pool and hauled her to her feet by her left arm. 'So, the public schoolboy's been having an eyeful of these has he?' he ranted, pointing at her exposed breasts, which were much whiter than the rest of her as he had always forbidden her to sunbathe topless, even on a beach full of topless women. 'Get in there,' he pushed her towards the door that led from the pool room back into the kitchen. 'You ungrateful whore! You fucking evil tart! How dare you do this to me. Yes, me. You ungrateful whoring little bitch!'

Now she was standing in the kitchen, shoulders hunched and arms trying to cover her breasts, like a little naked child pulled from the bath for peeing in the water, which she had been once. Here, now, there was the same fear, the same guilt. Their two children, having heard all the screaming, now arrived downstairs. They stood and stared. Their mother was crying, eye make-up running down her face, her semi-clad body exhibiting all the signs of fear and humiliation. Their father was standing behind their mother, red faced, eyes wild with rage and dripping almost as much water on the white-tiled floor as she was.

'What's going on, Mum? What's going on, Dad? What on earth's the matter?' said Charlotte, looking from one parent's face to the other and back again. 'What's happening Dad?' said David. Sure their parents often argued but neither could remember a scene which rivalled this for its potential danger. Violence was in the air.

'I'm sorry to have to tell you both that this bitch you call "Mummy" is little more than a whore. She's been having an affair with that toffee-nosed slime bag Stillion Sloane. Haven't you, bitch?' He cracked a left hand slap across the back of her head.

'Dad stop it,' yelled David.

'Shut it, boy, if you know what's good for you. Your mother is a slag and she'll get what's coming and if you don't want to join her, I'd pipe down if I were you.'

'Is any of this true, Mum?' said David who despised violence but was old enough to know that his father would lose even more control if provoked at this moment. And if it was true, he was enough of his father's son to understand why he was so angry.

'Tell them, bitch,' taunted Harry, cracking her across the back of the head again.

'Stop it, now, Dad or you'll have to fight Davey and

me 'cos whatever Mum's done does not give you the right to beat her and humiliate her in front of us like this,' shouted Charlotte.

'Humiliate! Humiliate! I'm the one who's been bloody humiliated, you stupid child. What about me? I bet half the bloody city knows about this already and the other half will within the week. They will all be laughing at me.'

'Dad, it takes two to tango,' said David, hoping to deflect attention away from his mother.

'Don't worry about the pretty Mr Sloane. He'll have an acid scarred face by the time any of you see him again. That is, if you do see him again.' laughed Harry.

'No, Harry,' cried Lottie.

'You bitch,' Harry pushed her to the floor.

'No, Harry, for your sake. Damage Stillion and everyone will know you did it.'

'You should've thought about that before you opened your legs for the bastard.'

'Dad!' exclaimed Charlotte.

'Well it's true, isn't it? Get dressed you cow. I'll deal with you later. Oh, and don't think of going anywhere. I'm going to immobilise your car.'

Harry picked up the telephone and dialled. 'Hello, Alf. Get four of the boys together and bring them round here. We'll leave Frankie here to look after Lottie while you, me and the other three go out on a little job. Now be quick about it or they'll be out on the piss. I want you here within half an hour, okay?'

He slammed down the phone. 'Right, you two get out of here and we won't speak of this again, to anyone. I won't. You won't. Now go or you'll be late for the disco.' The kids did as they were told. They didn't like violence but at least it now seemed to be directed towards Stillion rather than their mother. And as far as David was concerned, Stillion deserved it. After all, he'd been a guest in his father's house on several occasions and seducing the old man's wife, his mother, was no way to repay that hospitality.

Harry sat at the kitchen table and poured himself a tumbler of brandy. Lottie went upstairs. She considered trying to warn Stillion but she didn't know where he was and if Harry caught her on the phone she would almost certainly cop it a lot worse than she had already. Okay, she had seduced Stillion. Okay, it was all her idea. But he was a man after all and he could have said no. No, better keep out of it now. Better leave it to the men. She got dressed, did her best to cover up her bruised right cheek-bone with make-up, redid her swollen red eyes and brushed her hair before returning downstairs to explain to Harry how Stillion had phoned her persistently. It would, after all, be his word against hers. And Stillion was a gentleman so he would probably take the blame anyway. As she arrived in the kitchen 'Strangers in the Night' had come round again on the loop. It was twenty past seven.

* * *

Back at Joyce Higgins' flat, Joyce had poured two glasses of wine and had sat next to Stillion on the sofa. She crossed her shapely legs, smiled, batted her eyelashes and said nothing. Stillion, realising that this was his cue to start his sales pitch as to why she should sell to him, began. He didn't get very far. Joyce stopped him. 'What's the price, dear boy?' she enquired politely.

'Eh, a hundred and fifty thousand,' answered Stillion.

'Oh, I don't think so,' said Joyce.

'It's a fair price,' countered Stillion.

'That's as may be, but Mr Gridley has offered me two hundred thousand pounds. You can perhaps buy my business if you offer me two hundred and thirty thousand pounds.'

'You do three hundred funerals a year?' Stillion asked.

'I do.'

'And the property is freehold? And neither it nor the fleet have charges against them?'

'It is and they don't.'

'Okay then, subject to all of that being checked out, I will offer you two hundred and thirty thousand pounds.'

'Can I have that in writing?'

'Sure, I'll get a letter off to you first thing on Monday morning.'

'No, Stillion, now.'

'Now?'

'Yes, now. Handwritten will do.'

Stillion asked for a piece of paper and took out his fountain pen. At the top of the paper he wrote 'Subject to Contract and Without Prejudice', and followed it with a brief letter which adequately reflected the deal they had just made.

'Thank you,' Joyce smiled as he passed it to her. 'This will receive my urgent attention tomorrow and I will let you know my decision soon.'

'I thought you said if I offered you two hundred and thirty thousand I could buy the business,' said Stillion.

'No, I said perhaps,' she smiled, leaning forward, showing an exciting amount of cleavage, to pour both of them a second glass of wine, a clear indication that the meeting was not at an end.

Joyce kicked her shoes off and pulled her legs up underneath her on the sofa before saying, 'You don't mind paying for things you want, do you Stillion?'

'You mean two hundred and thirty thousand pounds?'

'No, I mean Monday afternoon.'

'Monday afternoon?' said Stillion, who could hardly remember Monday afternoon, such had been the events of the week.

'Yes, Stillion, Monday afternoon, when you paid with your body to secure the Martin funeral.'

Stillion was horrified.

'Shush, before you say another word you should

know that Gillian has no secrets from me. We had lunch on Wednesday and I had, shall we say, a blow by blow account of your afternoon together. You left our mutual friend a very happy woman. But it's a pity you screwed the funeral up so badly. My father would . . .'

'Turn in his grave at the thought of such a shambles. Mine too. But . . .'

'Well,' Joyce interrupted back, 'of course, the good name of Higgins & Co. and who will own it in the future are naturally important to me and will have to play a part in my decision.'

Stillion chose not to point out just then that his principal rival had also screwed up a major funeral this week. He wanted the Higgins' business and, although he would never forgive Sydney for destroying his two high-profile funerals, the one thing that he and Sydney would probably agree on at this moment was that the least that was said about all three funerals, and how they came to fall apart, the better. He knew somehow that he could rely on Sydney not to talk about it to anyone. Neither of them could have accused the other without fear of counter accusation, and to do so might trigger a scandal that would inflict lasting damage on their separate reputations and only benefit the Co-op or any of the other private local funeral firms.

'However, young man, I will weigh all of that up later. Right now the best thing you can do to convince me of the merits of your case is to do as you are told.' Joyce rose and, not bothering to put her shoes on, walked over to the tape deck, selected a tape and put it on. It was surprisingly modern, with a reggae beat that Stillion associated with Rastafarians bombing through Handsworth in their battered Escorts with a beat booming out that came up through your feet when they stopped by you at the traffic lights. Not really what he would have expected from Joyce Higgins or this room at all. Joyce walked towards Stillion, took his neck tie in her right hand and tugged on it gently, indicating that he should stand. Perhaps she wanted to dance, he thought to himself as she led him towards the centre of the room. She let go of his tie and cupped his cheeks in her hand. She was quite a bit smaller than Stillion without her shoes on. They both moved slightly to the music. 'Can you do as you are told?' she asked. Stillion nodded. 'Good, because we're going to play the same sort of game that you and Gillian did,' said Joyce, looking up at him. Stillion had had a growing suspicion that something like this might be on the cards, ever since Gillian's name had been mentioned and mentioned without disapproval.

'Except I like my games to be a little different,' continued Joyce.

'A little different?' Stillion repeated, looking down into her slightly flushed face and watching her darting eyes going from his left to his right and back again.

'Yes, we will play the game my way. You had Gillian. I will have you.' She removed her hands from his face, returned to the sofa and assumed her earlier position, her legs tucked up beneath her. Stillion stayed where he was but turned to face her fully.

'Strip,' she commanded.

'What?' A few moments ago Stillion had begun to suspect that sex might be about to become a negotiating tool, but the thought that Joyce wanted to be sexually dominating took him completely by surprise. His body shivered with excitement mixed with fear of the unusual.

'You heard,' said Joyce. 'Are you frightened? Well, who would have thought it?' she teased. 'Stillion Sloane falls at the first hurdle through fear of taking his clothes off.' She knew this would hit two chords; Stillion would not like being called a wet and he would not want to lose her business.

'I'm not frightened,' said Stillion.

'Good. Well, show me then,' said Joyce, picking up her wine glass and looking fixedly at his groin. 'Strip to the music. I chose it yesterday, especially for you.'

'Oh, thanks,' said Stillion, attempting, as he removed his jacket, to appear composed. 'How far should I go, Ma'am?' he added, in an attempt to play her game more convincingly.

'Until I tell you to stop. Oh, and leave your tie on, please.'

Stillion danced with small, unexaggerated movements. He found it tricky removing his shoes and socks in time to the beat but he managed. He loosened his tie and left it on as Joyce had commanded. Slowly and quite deftly he undid first his cufflinks and then his shirt buttons, before pulling the shirt tails out of his trousers. Then he pulled the shirt back over his shoulders and down to his elbows as he danced slowly around in a circle. He was feeling a lot more relaxed and was getting more and more confident, even cheeky. 'I wonder how brave he'll feel in a few moments,' Joyce thought to herself as she watched Stillion slowly undoing the front of his suit trousers with an action clearly intended to be seductive. The trousers fell to the floor and he stepped out of them. He was now dancing to the music in just his tie and boxer shorts. Joyce, keen to re-establish her control, got up from the sofa. As she walked towards Stillion she commanded him to stop. She grasped the end of his tie and without a further word she led him back into the hall and off to the right, into her bedroom. Joyce was completely dressed except for her shoes. Stillion was completely naked except for his boxers and tie. Joyce was playing this game the way that Stillion had played with Gillian, and he was feeling unsure of his role this time, being the man in a woman's control. Used to being the hunter, he was now the hunted, and whether it was sexual excitement or the thrill of danger, or both, he was aware that, despite a latent sense of shame, he was enjoying it.

'Get on to the bed, lie on your back, put your arms above your head and grip the bedhead with your hands,' Joyce instructed. Stillion, not wanting her to call him wet again, obeyed. She opened a drawer in her dresser and took out two silk scarves. She came back to the bed and knelt by him, reaching across his head and exposing the inviting cleavage once more. 'Just keep still. This won't hurt and it won't take long,' she said, nurse-like. And Stillion did feel that he was about to undergo an operation.

She tied his left hand to the brass bedhead with one of the silks. 'Not too tight?' she asked. 'No,' said Stillion, as confidently as possible. Half of him – the upper-middle-class English public schoolboy, God for England and St George half – was determined to show just how cool he could be. The other half kept telling him that once his right hand was secured he would be completely at the mercy of a woman he hardly knew and who could easily turn out to be a sadistic torturer, or worse. The God for England and St George half won, and he remained silent as she tied his right hand to the bedhead. She stood up from her task and looked down on her victim. 'Good,' she said with a smile, 'I've got you where I want you. You are completely in my power. Now, what shall I do first?'

'Get undressed,' suggested Stillion.

'Good Lord, no. Little boys like you don't get to see my naughty bits unless I say so. On the other hand I get to explore all of yours at my leisure.' She sat on the side of the bed and, facing him, ran the fingernails of her right hand lightly up his right foot, over the ankle, along the shin, over the knee and up the inner thigh. As her fingers moved slowly up, Stillion swallowed hard. His mouth felt dry. Powerful sensations, like charges of electricity, were running from his chest, down both thighs and onto the soles of his feet. His toes curled under and his penis had become, as a result of her touch and the novelty of being told what to do, so large that he feared it would explode. Her fingers reached the bottom hem of his boxers, within a few inches of his balls. She stopped there, prolonging the moment, teasing him, extending every second of every stage of her power. 'What have we here?' She looked at Stillion's face and pointed to the erection throbbing obviously beneath his pink shorts. 'I think it's time I took a look in here,' she said, her manner nurse like again. Very slowly she placed the fingers of both her hands just beneath the elastic top of the boxers. The muscles of Stillion's bottom contracted, drawing his flat stomach in lower than his hip bones. His rib cage moved up and down with his heavy breathing. She held the position for several seconds, relishing her own excitement, her position of supreme power and the delicious expectation of what she was about to uncover.

Joyce was living her favourite sexual fantasy and didn't want to miss one second of it. She moved her fingers gently across his tummy, deliberately just avoiding his helmet. The torment was almost too much for Stillion, who was breathing more heavily still. Joyce began to pull his shorts down. 'So, what have we got?' she said finally, easing them over his bursting penis. She drew the shorts off his legs and threw them aside, looking down on Stillion's exposed and captive, charmingly boyish body. Her elation was complete. She was fully dressed in a smart business suit, her victim completely helpless and open to her every fancy. 'Hmmm, not too bad at all,' she said smugly, almost as though she were looking at a horse she might buy. His body was pretty, to match his pretty face. His skin was smooth and clean and unusually fragrant for a man. Hair grew in all the right places, but not too much, and, as Gillian had told her, his pubic hair confirmed that he was a natural blond. Gillian had also said that Stillion was well-endowed. Joyce hadn't believed her, or thought she must be exaggerating, safe in the assumption that Joyce would never be in a position to find out for herself. But Gillian had not been exaggerating; Stillion, despite small hands and feet, had perhaps the largest penis Joyce had ever seen. To her sadness she hadn't seen that many, not so many as she would have liked. She was surprised and impressed. But she wasn't going to tell him that. Stillion was her prisoner, to be tormented, humiliated and teased, and for the next hour or so she would be the boss.

'Hmmm, not too bad at all,' she repeated, 'but I'm sure you can do better. Let's measure it.' She got up and fetched a tape measure from the dresser. 'Right, let's see now,' she held the tape measure with her left hand at the base of his penis and brought it up with her right hand to the top of his helmet. 'Dear me, only seven inches. Yes, I'm sure you can do better.' She wet the thumb and forefinger of her left hand with her tongue and started to lubricate his helmet, while the fingertips of her right hand teased his balls. His body throbbed and he was near to fainting from the lack of blood anywhere except for his penis. Involuntarily his knees folded up and outwards and he opened his legs as a woman might who was about to be entered in the missionary position. She noticed this and stopped her tormenting. 'Oh, I nearly forgot,' she said, and climbing off the bed and returning to the dresser, she produced two more silks and proceeded to strap each ankle to the foot of the bed, as far apart as possible. Her victim was now bound hand and foot in a star shape. She stood and admired her work and his helpless state.

Now that she was confident he couldn't move she felt it was time to show him some of her toys. From the dresser she produced a selection, brought them back to the bed and hopped over his captured right leg so she was on her knees between his legs. 'Look what we're going to play with,' she said. Stillion raised his head from the pillow as she held them up, one at a time. 'Handcuffs; they can be a bit distracting if too tight, so I don't think so at the moment. Two vibrators, one standard and one that looks a bit like your willy. They both work.' She turned both on and then off. 'A neck collar with lead; I may put you in this later and take you for a walk. A crop, in case you are naughty or don't satisfy me. A razor. I might amuse myself by shaving you. That would take a bit of explaining when you get home,' she laughed. She put the toys on the far side of the bed. 'But first I think a little satisfaction for me while your stem is so strong. Sensual pleasure first. Sexual pleasure next.'

Stillion didn't understand what that meant, but was too busy thinking about the razor and the problems that might cause to care. That remark of hers had begun to bring him to his senses. She sensed it too and set about her two-handed tormenting of his genitals again. 'We must beat seven inches or maybe I'll have to use the crop.' Even the razor remark hadn't made him shrink much, and with her new round of tormenting he was quickly back to bursting point.

Joyce moved up his body and in one easy motion sat astride him and slipped his penis up her skirt and deep into her warm and wet self. She placed her hands on his shoulders. She looked him straight in the eyes. He noticed her eyes were wild, with a look like that you might expect to see in the face of an insane person, a drunk or a druggie. She was there, yet somehow far away.

'You're my prisoner,' she said, breathing heavily, 'prisoner, prisoner, schoolboy, prisoner, schoolboy,' she repeated time and again in rhythm to her movements. She moved more quickly, and yet more quickly, and then her panting left the words behind just before she erupted into a long cry.

She'd come very quickly. He had tried very hard not

to as he didn't know what she would do next, so he'd spent most of her orgasm contemplating the Aston Villa squad to avoid coming with her. He was soon to be particularly grateful for this decision because, after only a few seconds rest, she burst again into a five minute frenzy during which she came no fewer than four times. During the last of these, and despite trying extremely hard to restrain himself, Stillion exploded as well, with a huge orgasm that sent him dizzy and light-headed to the point of passing out. He had experienced orgasms of love with Stephanie, he had experienced orgasms of lust with scores of girls before his marriage, and with two that he shouldn't have had earlier this week, but he had never had an orgasm of masochistic pleasure before. He was ashamed to admit to himself that it might have been the best he'd ever had.

Joyce dismounted. She was still fully dressed, except for her shoes, and no one would have guessed to look at her that she had just ridden one hell of a race. Apart from the flush on her face, the damp hair around her forehead and her breathlessness, she looked exactly as she had just an hour ago in the sitting room. Not so Stillion. But at least he had survived the course, or so he thought. He lay patiently on the bed, awaiting his release. In fact he was quite pleased with himself. 'She came five times and I didn't get off my back once,' he thought to himself. Soon he would be away, back to the office for a minute and then home to Steppie and, he hoped, the end of this nightmare week. He wondered what the time was but he couldn't see his watch because of the position of his left wrist. 'What's the time?' he asked. 'Time for sexual pleasure,' replied Joyce. 'Okay, so are you going to strip off and untie me for some sex?' asked Stillion, confident that he still had enough energy to perform, and feeling also that it was a little unfair that he hadn't seen or touched any part of her. 'You don't understand for a minute, do you little one?' Joyce said, as if speaking to a child. 'Sensual pleasure was my conventional orgasm. Sexual pleasure is my rape and humiliation of you. It's a different orgasm from a different place.'

She sat astride his right leg, her right knee on the bed and her left foot standing on the floor. She rested her clitoris against his knee and took his penis in her left hand, holding it still and pointing it towards his head. She then took the more penis-like vibrator in her right hand, turned it on and inserted it between his buttocks and beyond. She moved gently up and down on his knee. His body was engulfed in all sorts of sensations he had never felt before and within seconds, and despite his orgasm of only minutes ago and the fact that she was applying no friction to his stem, he ejaculated with such a violence that the semen shot from his helmet, above his stomach and chest before landing, some on the pillow and some on his face. He was panting for breath. He was suddenly aware of a pain in his bottom and his penis felt sore. He was also aware that his right knee was soaked from her bodily juices. She didn't stop. Instead she moved the vibrator further into him and soon his pain gave way to the exquisite pleasure of yet another orgasm. There was less semen than before and it flew less far but the sensation was even more pleasurable than the earlier two. Still she didn't stop. She wanted to take her victim to the limit. As he was shaken by his fourth orgasm since being strapped to the bed an hour before, she developed cramp in her right leg. At last she stopped.

She disappeared and then reappeared from the bathroom with damp tissues. She sat on the side of the bed and wiped away the sperm from his face and body.

'Who's the boss?' she asked.

'You are,' he replied.

'Good,' she smiled and then continued 'Before I release you I want to say something to you. I have enjoyed sex with you. I have had the best sex game ever. My domination and your humiliation were complete. And I have to admit that you were very brave, too. But I'm not going to sell the business to you. This is not because of the Martin funeral, not because Sydney will bid higher, which he will, but because you and me are not meant to be and because my father, although he would want me to get the best price, would want that price to come from his old friend John Richards' firm. You have given me a written offer, which Sydney will have to beat by twenty grand as he has promised to. And the sex? Well, I used you just like men like you use women. You will walk out of here without having seen even a glimpse of bosom, while I have had total power over you and now know your body better than your own mother did at birth. We will never speak of this again. If you wish to complain about what happened then all you have to do is think of the consequences for you. And I don't think anybody would believe you if you told them I had you. They would surely believe my version, that you raped me. But if you enjoyed being abused as much as I enjoyed abusing you, then we can do this again in the future as many times as you like. But don't try and change my mind about the business. It's made up.' With this speech over Joyce untied Stillion's wrists and ankles and released him.

Stillion was very angry with her, but was more angry with himself. However, he knew that it was useless to argue, and beneath his dignity to plead or otherwise display emotion. He found his clothes and dressed in silence before taking his leave of her with a polite kiss on the cheek, the only form of kiss they had experienced together. She showed him to the front door. As he walked to his car he looked at his watch; it was almost half past eight. As he trudged across the frozen car park, hands in pockets, shoulders slumped, he reflected dejectedly upon the past week, his collar turned up against the cold and his life. When would this nightmare end? Just last Friday night he and Steppie had gone to an Italian restaurant in St Chad's Square in Edgbaston with Winston Wylde and his wife. It had been such a happy night. They had talked about the future. It had been good, cosy and morally upright, and he had felt confident about the way he was building his future. Now, just one week later, he had cajoled his friend to get an important funeral; he had seduced a middle-aged matron to get another; both funerals had been conducted disastrously; he had started an affair with his wife's best friend, whose husband ran the local mafia; he had allowed Elton Field to sabotage a Richards & Gridley funeral, which made him no better than Sydney; and now he had been outsmarted, used and abused by a woman whom he had allowed to humiliate him to her satisfaction in the hope that she would sell him her business when all the time she had no intention whatsoever of so doing. 'Where now the bright Thatcher corporate future for me?' he thought as he turned the key in the ignition and drove wearily out of the Higgins car park for what he suspected may be the last time.

* * *

At approximately seven-forty that evening Alf and the boys had arrived at Harry's to find Harry hot, bothered and wild for revenge. In order to save herself, Lottie had used the twenty-five minutes she had with Harry, on her own, trying to deflect attention away from her and onto Stillion. He had chased her, she told Harry. Harry hadn't been paying her enough attention.

Stillion had wanted her. She had felt lonely. She had only ever really wanted Harry, but Harry was never there for her. She had been depressed and then at this, her low point of mid-life crisis, Stillion had arrived to take advantage of her. He had phoned her incessantly. He had sent her flowers. She had felt flattered. He had seduced her. She was sorry. It was only the once. It would never happen again. She only loved Harry. Harry was the only one for her. Harry should give Stillion lessons in love-making. He was just a clumsy boy. Even if Harry was going to cast her aside she would have no desire to see Stillion again. She lied in the confidence that Stillion wouldn't get a chance to put his side of the story; trying to tell his story in the middle of a five-to-one beating wouldn't be easy. But she was even more sure that it would never come to that; Stillion, by background and upbringing, would find it impossible to blame Lottie for their actions. Stillion's father, a Royal Naval Captain during the war, had brought his son up with a strict code of honour.

Harry believed her. Harry wanted to believe. It was much easier for him to hate Stillion than his wife. Their circle of friends didn't know about the affair, and he would make sure they never knew. Only the boys and the kids need know and they – or anyone else who found out – would remember what he was about to do to Stillion. Harry wanted Stillion to get it, but he also needed Stillion to get it to keep face. That was what happened when you messed with Harry Wilkes. That must be the clear message.

'Come on, Alf, we'll take your car. Frankie, you look after Lottie here until we get back, okay?' said Harry, putting on a bomber jacket and then twirling a baseball bat round the fingers of his right hand. 'The bastard has already hit her, just look at her face,' he said.

'The lousy bastard,' said Alf, and the others nodded in agreement. They could see she'd just been hit and they suspected it was Harry who'd hit her, but they just agreed with him. Nobody disagreed with Harry. And Frankie knew that he had better not let Lottie out of his sight, as he was really her jailer rather than her protector.

The posse left via the front door and poured into Alf's car for the fifteen-minute trip to Stillion's house. Alf was at the wheel of his rather battered 1960 Mark Ten Jaguar, Harry in the front seat and the other three wedged into the back bench seat. It was now ten to eight.

* * *

Marcus had left home at twenty past six and arrived at Sloane House ten minutes later, having taken longer than usual due to heavy evening traffic. He had rung the bell, and been received by the evening staff. He had waited in the splendid Regency hall, admiring the style of the place and admitting to himself that it was a far grander establishment than he had been led to believe. Eventually Victoria Thomas, Stillion's secretary, had descended the magnificent staircase which swept down around the far wall. He couldn't help noticing her pretty legs and trim figure. They had never met before although they had often spoken on the telephone. He didn't for a moment think she would be interested in him; she must be at least two years older.

'I'm so sorry, Mr Sloane isn't in at the moment,' she said, charmingly.

'Damn. You see, I really must get hold of him, now,' answered Marcus. 'Do you know where he is?'

'Actually, no,' she lied. Of course she knew that he had gone to see Joyce Higgins to discuss his buying of the company, but that was top secret and she wasn't going to tell Sydney Gridley's son about it. 'I'm sorry.'

'Thanks anyway. Look, if he contacts you, please remember to tell him I must see him urgently,' said Marcus earnestly. He returned to his car. 'Where to now?' he thought as he started the engine. It occurred to him that Stillion may have gone to the cricket club for a drink, but thought that it may be prudent to phone Stillion's home first. It was Friday night after all, and he knew that Stillion and Stephanie often went out to dinner with friends on Fridays and Saturdays. Marcus stopped at several public phone boxes along the way before finding one that worked. If Stillion was there he must arrange a meeting away from the house.

If he was out and he only got to speak to Stephanie then he must try to establish where Stillion was without alarming her or making her suspicious.

He dialled Stillion's number. Stephanie answered and greeted Marcus warmly; they had met on several occasions, mainly at those cricket matches when she had come along to support Stillion. Marcus liked her, and hoped one day to marry a girl like her. She was warm, kind, intelligent and positively the best-looking girl – yes girl, for she was closer to Marcus' age than Stillion's – in Birmingham, if not in the Midlands. Marcus couldn't understand how Stillion came to be unfaithful to her, if indeed he had been. Marcus knew that he himself could never have been.

'Is Stillion in?' he asked, once the friendly banter was over.

'No, darling, I expect he's stopped off for a drink at the club or somewhere on the way home. We're eating in tonight.' She lied too; she knew that Stillion may well be late back because of his meeting with Joyce Higgins. She knew how confidential it was and, although she knew that Stillion liked his cricket chum Marcus, she didn't forget that Marcus was Sydney's son, and that dangerous talk could cost acquisitions.

'Thanks Stephanie. Be seeing you soon, I hope. Take care. Bye.'

Marcus jumped back into the car and made for the cricket club, getting there at quarter to eight. He looked round the bar. Considering that it was the middle of December the place was pretty full. There were so many players, social members and wives already there filling the noisy and smoky pavilion bar that the large French windows running the length of the wall opposite the bar were clouded with condensation.

'Hi Marcus.' 'Hello, young man.' 'All right Marcus?' His progress across the room was slow. Marcus was one of the club's more successful and popular batsmen and had beaten Stillion to the top spot in last season's averages. He asked everyone he spoke to if they had seen Stillion but nobody had. Finally he asked at the bar. 'No,' said the barman, 'but there's a committee meeting later and I know that the committee want to speak to him. I think, between you and me,' he said, leaning across the bar and lowering his voice, 'between you and me, they want to convince him to stand for club captain now that Burt Goodrich is going to live in London. I heard two of the committee members saying they'd see him after the committee meeting, which should be over by half past eight.' The barman spoke the truth, but he failed to add that it all depended on whether Stillion came in or not. This omission made Stillion's beating inevitable. Marcus decided to put his search on hold and wait for Stillion there, so he ordered a pint of Brew XI and sat down to talk to some of his cricketing friends.

At five past eight the battered powder blue Mark Ten Jag pulled up outside Stillion's well-appointed house in Edgbaston. 'You lot wait here,' commanded Harry, leaping out of the front seat and slamming shut the car door. He strode determinedly across the drive and rang the front doorbell. Stephanie answered.

'Hi, Harry,' she smiled.

'Hello. Is Stillion in?' said Harry abruptly.

'No, not yet,' answered an unsmiling Stephanie, shocked by the abrupt response and the angry look in his eyes.

'Where is he?' Harry demanded.

'At work,' replied Stephanie. 'Look, what's all this about?'

'What's all this about? What's all this about? I'll tell you what all this is about. It's about your bloody, snotty high and mighty public schoolboy prat having my wife. That's what all of this is about, young lady.'

'I don't believe you. We're a happy couple. Stillion loves me. Lottie is my friend. They wouldn't . . ."

'Oh, wouldn't they?' he interrupted. 'Right, bloody listen to this.' He pushed past her and into the house. He picked up her kitchen phone and dialled his own number. 'Hi, Frankie, put Lottie on the phone. Hello Lottie, I have Stephanie here and if you know what's good for you, you had better explain to her everything you explained to me earlier.' Harry passed the receiver to Stephanie. So Lottie was forced to tell Stephanie the same version of events that she had explained to Harry earlier. She added some hysterical crying and insisted that Stillion had become so completely infatuated with her that she had felt like a stalked woman. She had wanted to warn both Harry and Stephanie but was fearful to do so because of the trouble it might cause. 'Then I agreed to meet Stillion on Wednesday night. I was going to explain that he must stop following me around, that he had a beautiful wife and I had a great friend. But he got me drunk and it just happened. I am so sorry, Stephanie darling, please understand. Please forgive me.' Lottie finished in between huge sobs.

Stephanie didn't want to understand, forgive or believe. She put the phone down in silence and brushed a tear quickly from her pretty cheek. She didn't understand. She wouldn't forgive. But she did believe.

Stephanie was only twenty-one. When she had married Stillion at nineteen she had achieved a long-held ambition. She had turned down the opportunity to read history at Nottingham University in order to marry Stillion, whom she had known and loved since she was a little girl. Her parents had been unhappy that she was wasting an expensive education, but their resistance was only token; Stephanie's family had been friends of the Sloanes for generations. Indeed, their fathers had been to school together and had served together in the Navy during the Second World War, even managing to serve on the same ship. Both families were happy with this match and Stephanie's education had to be the sacrifice.

Once married she had slipped quickly and easily into

a happy, if somewhat undemanding, life of coffee mornings with either her friends, her mother or her mother-in-law, and of playing tennis, working out in the gym and shopping in Birmingham and London. She had devoted herself to Stillion and the Sloane family. She had exchanged the chance of a University degree for an apprenticeship with Mary Sloane, from whom she hoped to learn how to be a matriarch of this crusty and self-confident family.

Now, in the twinkling of an eye, all could be destroyed. She stood in shock, her fair hair tumbling down and her blue eyes distant. She felt crushed. She had nowhere to go, nowhere to hide. She felt undone. The emotional pain was immense.

Harry said something. She hardly heard him.

'I said where is he?' he repeated.

'I have no idea,' answered Stephanie vacantly, as if her mind was a million miles away.

'He's at work. You already told me. If you see him before me, tell him he can't hide forever,' Harry called over his shoulder, leaving the front door open in his hurry to leave. Stephanie followed him through the hall slowly, as if in a trance, and closed the large oak door behind him. It was twenty past eight and the Jaguar squealed out of her drive, off to find Stillion before he did a runner.

Stephanie pulled herself together. She hurt, and she hated Stillion for what he had done, but she didn't want him beaten up. She ran back to the kitchen and phoned Sloane House. One of the night staff answered. She asked for Mr Stillion. The reply came back that he was not there but that Victoria Thomas was still in her office, working late.

'Put me through please . . . Hi, Vicky, it's Stephanie. Do you expect Stillion back tonight after the Higgins meeting?'

'Hello Stephanie. Yes I do. I've got several letters for him to sign and he said that he would pop in on his way home. I expect him any minute now. His meeting was at six o'clock, as you know, so he shouldn't be long,' said Victoria, efficient as always.

'Listen to me, Vicky,' said Stephanie with urgency in her voice. 'Don't let Mr Wilkes in if he comes to Sloane House. He may arrive in an old light-blue Jag and I think with other men. Don't let any of them in. Call the police if necessary. If Stillion arrives first tell him to avoid Harry Wilkes. If he asks why, tell him he should know. If they arrive first and don't leave, call the police. Have you got that straight, Vicky?'

'Yes I have, and yes I will do exactly what you say,' replied Victoria who could sense crisis but would not panic. She put down the phone and walked into Stillion's office from where she could see all of the front forecourt and a little of the side drive leading round the back of the funeral home towards the garages, mortuary, fitting shop and coffin store. She could see no one. Stillion's XJS wasn't there, and nor was there any sign of a battered old Jaguar. She wondered what this was all about. She didn't think it could be business. Stillion had always been squeaky clean. He was only interested in building Sloane & Sons. He wouldn't deal in scrap metal. She knew that Stillion and Stephanie had been seeing a lot of Harry Wilkes and his wife. She had booked several restaurants for them over the last few months and she had been aware of the increasing number of calls that Mrs Wilkes had been making to the office in the last few weeks. She also knew that Stillion could be a terrible flirt, although he didn't really flirt with her, which was just as well because she didn't think she'd have been able to hide her embarrassment if he had. She hoped her suspicions of a liaison between Stillion and Lottie were wrong, partly for Stephanie's sake but mainly for Stillion's; he might not survive an encounter with Harry Wilkes' gang if they got hold of him.

Back in her office Victoria started to worry, and she took to going into Stillion's office every few minutes to look out of the window. The concentration needed for her work had deserted her. Imagination is the worst enemy of a waiting woman.

By half past eight the Mark Ten had found its way onto the Soho Road. The car slowed down to avoid drawing attention to itself as it slithered past Sloanes, casing the joint. Harry saw that Stillion's car was not in the drive but that lights were on in his office. He also saw a figure at the window. It was a girl, probably Stillion's secretary.

Victoria saw the car. She couldn't tell what colour it was because of the effect of the orange street lighting. She didn't think it could be the right car, because it drove on up the hill towards the Albion ground.

'Drive up towards the New Inns. Turn round there and come back down towards the funeral place,' commanded Harry. 'Stop a hundred yards up the hill from Sloanes, on the same side.' Alf did as he was told. 'Let's go,' Harry ordered the others. All five got out.

'What are we doing now?' enquired one.

'We're gonna wait in the grounds of the funeral home,' answered Harry.

'I ain't fucking going into any funeral place, boss. Fuck me, we'd be mad to do that. Bloody 'ell boss.'

Harry turned and stared. He said nothing, but his man changed his mind all the same. 'Okay, boss.'

All five strolled down the street with their hands in their pockets, as if on the way home from the pub on this bleak December night. Harry and Alf held baseball bats inside their jackets. They sneaked up the main drive and hid in the shadows of the side drive, next to the large old brick wall that divided Sloane House from the Asian wholesale clothes warehouse next door. It was twenty-five to nine.

'Now, everyone, shut it,' whispered Harry. 'Either he's in and he's comin' out or he's out and will come in. We'll soon know.'

'How do you know that Harry?' asked Alf.

'Because the lights are on in his office. His secretary

is up there and his wife said he was at work. And because we have to start somewhere, don't we,' answered Harry, proud of his logical deductions.

'True,' reflected Alf.

Four minutes later Victoria looked out of the window. Nothing. She returned to her office to tidy her desk for the night. Just one minute later Stillion's car pulled onto the Sloane House forecourt. He got out and locked it, and walked towards the night entrance. A quiet Birmingham voice that he didn't recognise addressed him to his left.

'Oh Mr Sloane, thank goodness it's you. I've been ringing and ringing the night bell.'

Stillion turned to his left in the direction of the voice. He saw nobody.

'I'm here, trying to find the back door Mr Sloane,' said the voice. Stillion advanced into the black. Crack, a violent pain struck him across the back of the head. His head spun, his knees buckled. As he fell to the ground he was aware of thinking that it was true, you do see stars.

It had been Alf's voice and Harry's strike. 'Pick the little fucker up,' said Harry in a loud whisper. They obeyed. One had Stillion in a full Nelson, the other two had an arm each to hold him up. 'Wake up. Wake up,' snapped Harry, slapping Stillion around the face. 'Wake up and listen. I'm going to teach you a lesson you'll never forget, if you manage to wake up after it. I'm going to burn that pretty face away with fucking acid and I'm going to cut your fuckin' cock off and feed it to my dog. Got it? Bastard. Fucking got it, I said?' And with that he smashed his baseball bat up between Stillion's legs, cracking his balls with such force that the semi-conscious Stillion thought they may shoot out of his ears.

'So you thought you could meddle with what's mine, did you boy?' asked Harry. He decided to take pleasure in beating Stillion with his fists and put the bat down. Of course the story around the town tomorrow would be that Harry did all the damage with his fists alone and without the help of four others and certainly with no mention of sneaking up in the dark and attacking from behind. Harry, unofficial king of Brum, had no need of such help and the pleasure the ex-boxer got from maiming with his own knuckles, especially when there was no fear of being hit back, was hugely pleasurable to him. The blows rained in on Stillion's face.

A voice cried out from the forecourt 'Stillion is that you? The police are on their way.' It was Victoria's voice.

Just after Stillion had driven up onto the forecourt Victoria had completed tidying her desk and had returned to her lookout position. She had seen Stillion's car on the front immediately, with no lights on and nobody in it. Yet he hadn't arrived upstairs. She instinctively knew something was wrong, and also knew that if her imagination was getting the better of her then he would be coming up the main staircase to meet her. She ran downstairs and outside. She could see nothing but coming from the black she could hear the sounds of violence above the mutterings of a man's voice which she believed to be that of Harry Wilkes.

She spoke out. The magic word 'police' did the trick. None of them wanted to get involved with the police, Harry least of all. Harry had the most to lose, and knew that the cops would just love a good reason to do him. His growing mafia-like reputation did nothing to enhance theirs. All five took off down the drive, but Harry, in his panic, forgot his discarded baseball bat lying on the dark tarmac. Victoria advanced into the dark, where she found Stillion's bleeding form attempting pathetically to get up from the drive, like a finished boxer from the canvas or a horse with a broken leg.

'Steady, steady,' she said gently, 'perhaps you'd better keep still for a minute.'

'I'll bloody freeze to death if I do, old girl,' said Stillion. Their attention was at that moment drawn down the drive by the noise of the Jaguar speeding past down the Soho Road before skidding hard right into Booth Street, burning rubber as it did so.

'Victoria, you probably saved my life. Thank you very much,' said Stillion, still badly dazed.

'Let's get you inside.' She helped him to his feet and with his left arm around her shoulder and her right arm round his waist they managed to negotiate the main staircase without bumping into the night staff and made it all the way to Stillion's office. Stillion slumped into his executive chair. Blood was running from the back of his head, a cut above his right eye, his nose and the left side of his mouth. He didn't think his balls were bleeding but it was all too painful to find out. Victoria fetched water and disinfectant and started to clean her patient up. Secretly she was never happier than when mothering.

'The police are taking their time,' said Stillion.

'I didn't call them,' answered Victoria. 'There was no time. I just knew they were down there waiting for you when I saw your car on the forecourt and no sign of you.'

'That was very brave of you, but what made you think they'd be waiting there at all?'

'Because Stephanie phoned here to warn you,' replied Victoria in a matter of fact sort of way.

'Oh shit, oh bloody hell,' moaned Stillion. On Thursday night he had thought that life couldn't get worse, but it had, and then just an hour ago, as he left Higgins & Co., he had thought it couldn't get worse still. But now, not only had Harry Wilkes found out about him and Lottie, but he had obviously told Steppie too. What a bloody mess.

'Stillion, you know, I know – we both know – I adore working for you. In fact, we both know I adore you so please don't get cross with me but I've just got to say something to you. You're a fool. No, you're a bloody fool.' This was strong language for the normally reticent, calm, quiet and polite Victoria. 'You have it all, a beautiful wife who loves you to pieces, a great business, a loyal staff, and a super mum. You've had a great education and you could look forward to a great career. Most people like you and we all love you. So, why oh why have you suddenly started to do your level best to ruin it all? I know you're hurting over the two messed up funerals but that was no reason to send Elton over there for revenge. Mr Gridley was wrong, so was Elton, but so too were you and John Palin.'

'You know about that? Who told you? I'll bloody kill John.'

'No, it wasn't John. I could hear it all from my office last night when you had Elton up here. Now let me finish before I lose courage. You only bring yourself down to Mr Gridley's level or worse. People could have been killed at Witton today.'

'No, no, I had nothing to do with that I promise you. That was Elton, for whatever reason, acting on his own.'

'Okay, but it was wrong to get involved at all.'

'Yes it was,' agreed Stillion.

'You seduced Gillian Weston to get the Martin funeral and probably Joyce Higgins so you could buy her business.'

'Well if I did, it didn't work. She's selling to Sydney,' Stillion interrupted dejectedly.

She ignored this comment and continued, 'I guess

this punch-up tonight has something to do with Lottie Wilkes? If you like I'll just give you some matches, because you might as well burn this place down now if you are determined to wreck everything and turn from a good guy into a Wilkes or a Gridley. You're much too good for that and anyway you're not very good at being like them. Look how you've got on this week. Think about it. I think you should phone Stephanie right now.'

Victoria shut up, her emotional speech at an end. Stillion looked up. The green-shaded desk light, the only one on in the room, was shining in her face. Her neck had come out in a nervous rash and her eyes were blinking rapidly to keep the tears from falling.

'Thanks Vic Vesta,' Stillion touched her hand.

Stillion picked up the phone and dialled his home number. It rang. It kept on ringing. Steppie must either be not answering the phone, or she had gone. He put the phone down. His heart ached badly. He suddenly felt an inkling of what it might be like to lose Steppie. The other pains disappeared, blinded by this one. He must find her, now. He must see her. He must explain. She mustn't stop loving him. If God would give him but one chance he would grab it and love her faithfully for evermore. 'She's not there,' he told Victoria. 'I must find her. You don't think Harry Wilkes would have kidnapped her? No, he would've done that already if he was going to. Anyway, kidnap would land him in prison.' He answered his own question. 'No, she's gone away from me. It's what I deserve. I must find her.'

'Later. First we've got to get you to Casualty. I've stopped the cuts on your face from bleeding but the one on the back of your head is serious; I think it'll need stitching.'

They got up to go. The front door rang. They looked at each other. 'Go to your office and lock the door in case it's them,' Stillion ordered Victoria.

'I'm staying with you,' she said.

'No, you're not. It's not your fight and, what's more, you can always call the police from there unnoticed.'

There was a tap on his office door.

'Come in,' commanded Stillion.

It was a member of the night staff. 'There's a Mr Marcus Gridley for you downstairs sir.

'Show him up please Jones,' smiled Stillion.

Jones diplomatically left without appearing to notice the state of Stillion.

'Marcus came earlier,' said Victoria. 'He said he needed to see you urgently. I'm sorry, with all the commotion going on I forgot to tell you.'

'That's okay. How the hell did you know about Gillian Weston and Joyce Higgins?' asked Stillion.

'I didn't,' replied Victoria. 'I just know you and what you wanted. And I know them and what they wanted. You all wanted what you wanted badly enough to do deals. And I guessed what their deals would be and that in your current frame of mind you would comply.'

At that moment Marcus arrived at Stillion's office door. 'Come in, old man,' said Stillion. Marcus approached Stillion's desk and looked down at the bowl of bloody water. 'Shit, I'm too late,' he exclaimed.

Marcus had waited at the cricket club for the end of the committee meeting. He'd been enjoying a few pints with some fellow members of the first eleven when he had suddenly noticed that it was already a quarter past nine and Stillion still hadn't arrived. Marcus had phoned Stephanie again but this time got no reply. Perhaps Stillion and she had gone out to dinner after all. Probably. On his way home he had thought to pass Sloane House, just to be on the safe side. He had seen Stillion's car and stopped. Now he was devastated because it occurred to him that if he hadn't stayed and gossiped at the club he could have warned Stillion or at least helped him defend himself against Harry Wilkes.

'I'm so sorry. If I'd been here we could have sorted out Harry Wilkes,' he told Stillion.

'No, old man, you couldn't have. I was attacked in the dark from behind, by four, five or even six of them. I couldn't see how many it was because it was so dark and it all happened in a flash. You'd only have got hurt too. I was saved by Vic Vesta here. She was brilliant.'

'I bet,' said Marcus, who didn't attempt to conceal his admiration of her.

'But Marcus, how the hell did you know about Harry Wilkes wanting to beat me up in the first place? It seems the whole bloody city seems to know.'

'I'm afraid I overheard my father telling Joyce Higgins that he'd told Harry Wilkes about you and Lottie, so mother and I decided I should warn you and I came here, phoned you at home and went on to find you at the cricket club. The barman there told me you were coming in later,' said Marcus.

'Wait a minute. You mean that I have your old man to thank for the fact that I've been beaten up, my wife has probably left me and that half the city will now know of this affair?'

'Well, thanks to Mr Gridley and yourself. He couldn't have achieved all that without your help,' interjected Victoria.

'Thank you. One lecture from you is quite sufficient for a lifetime,' said Stillion lightly.

'But you're right, I'm afraid my old man started the ball rolling. How he knew or why he did it I don't know,' said Marcus.

Stillion didn't want to get back onto the subject of who wrecked whose funerals. The least said by anyone on that subject the better. 'I must find Steppie,' he said. 'You didn't let anything slip out when you phoned her did you?' he asked of Marcus.

'Do me a favour, Stillion. I was trying to help you, and anyway, when I phoned she seemed very happy and looking forward to you going home.'

'Mr Wilkes must have gone to your house first, because when I spoke to Stephanie she knew he was in that old Jag and she thought he had several men with him,' added Victoria.

'I must find her now,' insisted Stillion, attempting to stand.

'You must have that head stitched now Stillion,' demanded Victoria. The towel she had put round his shoulders was soaked in blood and his fair hair at the back of his head was matted and clotted dark red. Marcus took a look. 'She's right, old boy. That was a bigger smack than Holding gave Amiss a couple of years ago.' Stillion remembered the mess Michael Holding had made of Dennis Amiss' head at the start of the '76 season and admitted that Victoria and Marcus were probably both right. 'Okay, I'll go, but just a couple of calls to find Stephanie first.' He picked up the phone with the intention of phoning her family first but found that prospect too daunting so he dialled his mother instead.

Mary Sloane was fifty-three years old. She was an attractive, strong-featured woman, matriarchal and firm of purpose. She often fell out with her eldest son, proclaiming him to be pompous and self-opinionated; she failed to see that he had inherited many of these characteristics from her. But she adored her son, although she always appeared to find fault with him and was continually telling Stephanie that she was wasted on the boy.

Mary was small, and trim for her age. She had been trained as a secretary and bookkeeper and, after her marriage to Arthur Sloane, in 1947, she had kept the company books full-time until her children were born. Stillion had arrived in 1950 and Paul in 1954. Paul, Stillion's younger brother, was in the Navy and only came home rarely. Now that she was a widow she spent her days with friends, or travelling, and watching her elder son raise the family profile. She referred to Streetly, the North Birmingham suburb where she lived, as 'gin and Jag country', and she continued to drive her late husband's Jaguar XJ12. She had been born into a middle-class family, which her husband's father tended, without saying as much, to look down upon. This had secretly always annoyed her and so she now revelled in her role as matriarch of the Sloane clan.

'Hello, mother, it's Stillion.'

'Hello Stillion. Why do you always have to phone just as *News at Ten* is starting? You know how much I enjoy *News at Ten*.'

'Yes, yes, I'm sorry about that mother, but I was wondering if Steppie was over at your place.'

'Yes, she is,' came the reply down the line. The feeling of relief was enormous.

'Thank God. Can I talk to her?'

'No, you can't. She doesn't want to talk to you and nor do I especially while *News at Ten* is on.'

'Just tell her I love her.'

'I shall do no such thing because you obviously don't.'

'Now listen to me mother ...'

'No, you listen to me young man. Your behaviour towards Stephanie has been disgraceful and I am not prepared to talk to you about it now other than to say that I would just keep out of Mr Wilkes' way if I was you.'

'Well, you're not me.'

'No, thank God. Goodnight.'

'Thanks a lot,' finished Stillion sarcastically. The phone call was at an end.

Mary Sloane turned back to the television set just in time to catch the opening headlines. When they were over, she spoke to Stephanie without turning her gaze from the screen.

'That was Stillion.'

'So I gathered,' said Stephanie. 'Is he okay?'

'It appears that way,' answered Mary. She continued to look at the screen, partly because she was interested and partly because her daughter-in-law's tearful state was making her feel extremely uncomfortable.

'Mother, please talk to me.' Stephanie had taken to calling Mary 'mother' after her marriage to Stillion. They both felt comfortable with it, Mary because she had never had a daughter and Stephanie because she felt she could confide in Mary. They were close. Stephanie had run to Mary for help tonight rather than to her own family, because she knew that her own family, who held Stillion on a pedestal, would never forgive him for hurting her so badly. Mary loved Stephanie too, but, despite her harsh words to him, would forgive her beloved boy in the end.

'Talk to me. It hurts so much I think I'm going to die,' pleaded Stephanie.

'Dear girl,' Mary turned away from the television screen, 'Sloane men have always been the same. Stillion's father was not perfect and his grandfather was known as the Stallion of Handsworth. Perhaps I should have called Stillion Stallion instead.' This last remark upset Stephanie even more. So Mary dealt with the situation the only way she knew how. 'Now look here, young lady, we've got to fight this. Do you still love him?' Stephanie nodded. 'Do you want him back?' Stephanie nodded. 'But back as a good and loyal man who won't ever do this again?'

'Yes, that's it,' said Stephanie.

'Well then, understand this. Stillion is a Sloane. He can't help that. Sloane men marry ladies but fuck tarts.' Stephanie was shocked by Mary's language and Mary noticed. 'That's the plain truth of it. They marry ladies but fuck tarts,' she repeated. 'Now, if we're going to break Stillion of the habit he is going to have to learn a big lesson. He is going to have to miss you so badly that he hurts as much as you do now and if he doesn't, well he's not worth having back, is he?' Stephanie nodded. 'Now, dry those eyes, I'll pour us a stiff gin and tonic and tell Josey to put the heating on in your bedroom.'

Stephanie still felt dreadful but was comforted by Mary taking control.

Meanwhile Stillion, Victoria and Marcus were leaving Sloane House for the hospital. It had been decided that Stillion was in no state to drive, what with that bump on his head, so his car was to be put in the garage at the rear and he was to go in Victoria's car with Marcus following in his car to keep an eye on them.

Stillion, with the bloody towel still on his shoulders and blood seeping from his wound, climbed carefully into his car for fear of getting blood on the leather seats. As he took the car down the side drive his headlights caught a wooden object on the tarmac. He stopped, and got out to take a look. He called out to the others. 'Well, well, look what I've found'.

Marcus and Victoria came round from the forecourt to join him and all three looked at the bloodied baseball bat. 'Brilliant,' said Stillion. 'Nobody touch it,' he commanded. 'Vicky, go and ask Jones for the keys to the mortuary.' She obeyed, returning a couple of minutes later with the keys. Stillion took them and walked down the side drive, across the back yard. The other two saw the mortuary lights go on for a minute and then off again. Stillion returned with a transparent plastic body bag. He gave the keys back to Victoria who in turn returned them to Jones. Stillion placed the body bag next to the baseball bat with the zip open. Then, by putting one finger on each end only, he gently lifted the bat up and lowered it into the bag before closing the zip. 'Okay, let's go.' He put his car in the garage with the hearses and limousines for the night, picked up the body bag and got into Victoria's car. They set off for the hospital.

'I'm sorry about the mess in here,' said Victoria, seeing Stillion notice the old sweet wrappings, leaflets and dry cleaning slips strewn around.

'I should think you are,' he responded dryly.

'Oh, you're getting better,' she smiled.

'And you're getting cheeky,' he replied.

'No offence meant,' she apologised.

'None taken,' he said, more gently.

They arrived at the hospital at about half past ten. Stillion registered and, while Victoria and Marcus settled in for the usual wait, Stillion found a payphone. He returned to them saying, 'Vicky, have you got your phone book?'

'I have.'

'Good. Give me the Wilkes' home number.'

'I don't think you should . . .'

'Vicky, the number,' interrupted Stillion.

She flicked quickly through the pages to find it. 'Er, it's, er it's Bromsgrove 347500,' she said, and then added, 'here, you'll need this,' pushing change into his hand. She knew he hated carrying change in his trouser pockets.

'Thanks.' In his haste to make the call he moved off quickly.

'Don't you think you should stay still with that gash pumping out blood, old man?' asked Marcus.

'I won't be a minute,' came the reply over Stillion's shoulder. Once at the payphone he dialled the number. Harry answered. Stillion stuffed in a pile of change.

'Good evening, Harry, and how are you? Well, I trust. And how am I? Well, I'm fine too. No thanks to you, of course. You fat, finished old coward. It takes a group of you to attack from behind in the dark, does it?'

'I don't know what you're talking about. The boys and me have had a night in playing cards. Lottie, Alf, Frankie, Dennis, John, Phil and me. A quiet evening playin' poker. But when I get my hands on you shitbag I wouldn't be in your shoes . . .'

'I don't think so Harry. I'll meet you anytime for a one-to-one old man. In fact, after tonight I hope you'll take me up on the offer. But you and your thugs will never approach me, Steppie or any of my family again. Is that quite clear?'

'Listen, you bastard. You're in no position to dictate to me you little . . .'

Again, Stillion interrupted aggressively to cut Harry off in mid sentence. 'Oh yes I am.'

'Fuck off, bastard.'

'I would listen if I were you and then laugh at me if you like. You see, you were in such a hurry to run away from a twenty-year-old girl that you scarpered without your baseball bat. Now the said bat is in my possession, hidden very safely with your fingerprints and my blood on it. A letter describing the events of tonight, including the reason for your cowardly attack, is lodged with my solicitor already, along with the instruction that should I or my family ever be bothered by you or any of your pathetic retards again, then the letter is to be released to both the police and the press. Okay? Now, I'm sorry about Lottie and me. It was a mistake and it won't happen again but that's the end of the matter,' said Stillion, slowly and firmly.

'You've got a fuckin' cheek. I call this blackmail,' raged Harry, who had forgotten all about the baseball bat. He hadn't even missed it. He would have killed one of the boys for such an amateur mistake.

'I call it self-preservation. I'll be bidding you good-night now Harry. Oh, one last thing Harry. If you want to go round cutting cocks off, I'd start with yours. I mean what's the point of having a cock when you've got no balls?' He slammed down the receiver and returned to the other two. 'We won't be hearing from him again,' he told them. 'That bloody bat is our insurance.'

It was midnight before they left the hospital. Marcus offered to drop Stillion off at his house in Edgbaston as it was on his way home. The faithful Victoria, who had waited until the end to ensure her employer was properly stitched up, lived over on the other side of town, in Solihull. Stillion, with eight stitches in the back of his head and two above his right eye for good measure, followed her to her car to collect their 'insurance' from the boot. He was a mess; he had a plaster over his right eyebrow, a black eye was forming around his left eye, his face was bruised, his nose was sore, his bottom lip fat. He didn't look so pretty any more. He didn't look at all like a funeral director. He picked up the body bag and turned to Victoria. 'Goodnight Vic Vesta,' he said. 'Thanks for everything, you gorgeous thing.' He kissed her on the cheek.

'That's okay. Goodnight.' Victoria watched him walk back to Marcus' car and thought to herself with a smile that he didn't even know when he was flirting. She drove home thinking, with some guilt, that she had really enjoyed the evening. It had been so very exciting, not unlike a 1930s black and white gangster film.

Marcus drove Stillion the short journey from the hospital to his house in Edgbaston. As they went he said, 'Look, Stillion. I am truly sorry for what's happened. I don't know why this feud has developed between Dad and you and I don't want to know. I won't do the old man down because he's my father after all. But I can't agree with what he did. He is just so unreasonable at the moment. He's determined to buy Higgins & Co.'

'Well, there's your answer about the feud chum. Perhaps he'll be a happy old man now that Joyce Higgins is going to sell to him,' said Stillion.

'Is that true?' asked Marcus.

'That's what she told me. She told me this evening that she'd decided on Richards & Gridley. I made her a fabulous offer but apparently whatever I bid your Dad will better. They seem to get on well.'

'You don't realise how well,' said Marcus.

'What?' asked Stillion.

'Oh, nothing,' answered Marcus, 'but if Dad gets Higgins & Co. then he'll never change his mind about me.'

'About you?'

'Yup. The old man says I can go to university, and he even agrees, albeit reluctantly, that I can have a year out first and travel, but after that I must come into the business.'

'And you don't want to?' was Stillion's next question.

'No. I hate funerals. I hate dead bodies and I hate grieving families. I want to be an architect. But Father says if I don't give him an undertaking to join him immediately after university, then he'll kick me out now without a penny. Not even the ten thousand pounds Grandpa left with him for me.'

'Why didn't your Grandfather leave it in trust to you?' Stillion asked.

'Undeclared cash from the old days. You know, one in the book and one on the back of a fag packet.' Stillion didn't know, because his father had never done such a thing. 'Anyway,' continued Marcus, 'if I don't give in, I'm out on Monday. Unless Mum helps me that is. But she won't. She never stands up to Dad. The old man runs the family like the business – exactly how he likes – even though she owns more shares than Dad and me put together. She's frightened of the old man. It's just become a habit really. Anyway, that's enough of my problems old boy. You've enough of your own.'

'That I have,' confessed Stillion as the car pulled up in his drive. 'Thanks for the lift Marcus. You've been a good friend tonight. I hope you get it sorted with the old bugger. If you need a roof over your head come Monday, I'm here. I'll probably be glad of the company.'

Stillion opened the large oak door and ventured inside. He turned the lights on room by room. It seemed so empty. The heating was on yet it seemed so cold. He couldn't remember this mansion without Stephanie. He couldn't believe she wasn't here, or worse she may never come back. He went into the kitchen to get a drink to take to bed. There was a scrap of paper on the kitchen table. It simply read 'Stillion. How could you?' It was her writing. He traced the words with his fingers. She had touched the paper but may never touch him again. He felt lonely. He felt guilty. But above all he felt regret. If only he could turn the clock back. If only it could be last Friday again. They had sat on the kitchen table, dangling their legs down and chatting after getting home from dinner with the Wyldes, just one week ago. Why, oh why, had he been such a fool? 'Oh good old Stillion. What a boy. Fucks who he wants.' He spoke out loud. Then after a pause added, 'Yeah, especially himself.' He was so sorry and so guilty that he vowed such events should never possibly occur again. He hoped he could do that. He hoped he was feeling guilty for all the right reasons. He really wanted to be. But then he knew his failings, and even in this state of perfect misery couldn't be certain that he wouldn't succumb again. He turned the light off and went upstairs to bed. It was one in the morning and it had been one hell of a long day. He didn't sleep. He lay in bed, on his back, in the dark, his eyes wide open. Eight miles away, at Mary Sloane's house, there was a young lady doing exactly the same.

6

Saturday

Stillion woke and, having momentarily forgotten the events of yesterday, moved to cuddle Steppie. His hand came to rest on a cold, empty pillow and he remembered. He looked at his watch. It was half past six. He had an idea. His old buzzard of a mother would be fast asleep and she refused to have a phone in her room. If he phoned now Josey would already be up and would answer. Josey had been with the Sloanes since Stillion was a small boy and had brought up both Stillion and his brother. She had cooked for them, bathed them, helped with their homework and cuddled them when they were upset. She adored them both. She would put Stephanie on the phone, he knew. Good thinking. He leaned across the bed, picked up the phone and dialled his mother's number. 'Hi, Josey, it's me.'

'Hello me. I hear you've been a very bad boy.' That was Josey.

'Look, Josey. You must help me. I have got to speak to Steppie,' he said with urgency.

'She may not wish to speak to you,' was the reply.

'Well please ask her, at least,' Stillion pleaded.

Josey was much softer than Stillion's mother and after only a little more persuasion she agreed to wake Stephanie. 'There's a phone call for you Stephanie. You can take it in the hall if you like.'

'But it's so early. And nobody knows I'm here,' said Stephanie. 'Who is it?'

'They didn't say,' Josey fibbed for Stillion without even having been asked.

Stephanie, intrigued, walked along the broad landing and down the large main staircase of the mock Tudor mansion. She picked up the phone in the hall. 'Hello.'

'Hello, Steppie, it's me.'

'I don't want to talk to you. Not now. Not tomorrow. Not ever. It's over Stillion.'

'Steppie, please darling, I'm so sorry. I promise I'm sorry. I really miss you. I love you.'

'Love! What a joke. You don't know the meaning of the word. Love is just a word for you, something to do with cricket, Aston Villa, Paul McCartney and Maggie Thatcher. And making love is what you do when you've got a hard on and apparently even with my ex-best friend who you chased all over the city until you seduced her.'

'Who said that?' asked Stillion.

'She did, actually Stillion. She bloody did. Do you imagine how humiliating it was to be told by my friend that you wanted her instead of me and that you needed her so badly that you bombarded her with flowers and phone calls all day long.'

'That's just not true. Ask Vicky,' demanded Stillion.

'Ask Vicky? Why the hell should I ask Vicky?'

'Because she can tell you that Lottie bombarded me with phone calls,' was Stillion's reply.

'Oh she can, can she? She would swear black was white for you, and anyway if it was true does that make it any better? It makes it okay if she was chasing you? Oh I see, I should feel sorry for you should I? Poor little Stillion, seduced against his will was he? Get lost Stillion.'

'No, please hold on. I'm not making excuses. It was wrong. I was wrong. I am sorry. Please let me see you. We must talk. It's no good me coming over without you agreeing. The old girl won't let me in unless you agree.'

'Well, okay, you can come here at midday.'

She put the phone down. Stillion was happy. Stephanie was not. Talking to Stillion hadn't helped. Yesterday she'd hurt badly and needed Stillion back. In the cold light of this new morning she was angry, and not so sure she wanted him back. Perhaps she should just get away from everybody and take her time to sort out how she really felt. It may be that this outrageous act of betrayal had ruined their relationship forever. She had loved him so dearly since she was a little girl, and he had remained her hero while becoming her lover and then her husband. She could never see a fault in him, so blind had been her devotion. But after last night, although she still thought he was beautiful on the outside, she knew he was badly flawed on the inside. The boy she had loved and the man she had married wouldn't, couldn't, have slept with Lottie, whatever the temptation. But the man she found herself married to this morning had, and that changed everything. She decided to take a hot bath. As she soaked she tried to put the case for Stillion but it just wouldn't come. Every time she tried she could only imagine his naked body entwined with Lottie's, writhing on a bed in a passionate embrace. She felt so angry at the deception and so hurt by the act that she felt sick.

* * *

Sydney rose early for a Saturday. He couldn't linger in bed; he couldn't wait for it to be a respectable hour to phone Joyce Higgins. He waited until eight o'clock, still early for a weekend but he could wait no longer. He went down to his office and dialled the private line in her flat. As the phone rang he fidgeted nervously. In just a few minutes he would know his fate. Joyce answered.

'Hello. Sydney here.'

'Yes, Sydney. What can I do for you today? I hope you realise that you've got me out of the shower,' said

Joyce, loudly and with a hint of annoyance in her voice. She was standing, dripping wet, in her sitting room, wearing only a shower cap, exposing everything that she had kept so well hidden from Stillion yesterday.

'Look, don't torment me. You promised me a decision today following your meeting with Sloane last night.'

'Oh, that.' Joyce was doing her best to provoke him. 'And here was I thinking there was about to be an IRA bomb attack. Sydney, I am not prepared to conduct a business conversation standing in my sitting room, stark naked and dripping wet. Please ring me back.'

'When?'

'At, say, ten o'clock. Yes, ten o'clock will do,' replied Joyce, relishing her hold over him. 'And don't be late because I've got to go the hairdressers at eleven.'

Sydney trudged back upstairs. His nervous system was in a mess. When would this bloody woman make up her mind? He could tell she was enjoying playing with him over this deal and he must be careful not to lose his temper with her at this late stage. He could get his revenge when the deal was done. But he was cross. If he'd had a dog he would've kicked it. He didn't have a dog, but he did have Susan. He walked into the kitchen.

'Good morning dear,' said Susan.

'What's good about it?' snapped Sydney.

Still trying to be bright and cheerful, Susan brushed off Sydney's acid remark. 'What would you like for breakfast Sydney?' She smiled at him nervously.

'Some bloody peace and quiet and a rest from your constant empty-headed babbling.' Sydney picked up the newspaper and pretended to read while his brain tried to assess his conversation with Joyce. Susan busied herself with pretending to work in the kitchen, trying all the while to pluck up enough courage for another attempt at conversation. She wanted to bring up the subject of Marcus, but after several minutes of pregnant silence she decided that Sydney wasn't going to be drawn. She knew she would have to be direct and, however daunting, she must go straight to the heart of the matter.

'Sydney, I know you're upset about the Lyons funeral and worried about the damage to the fleet. And I know you're desperate to win the race to buy Higgins & Co., we all hope you do, but you must . . .'

'Must!' Sydney interrupted. 'Must! Did you say must? I must do what? Nobody says "must" to me in this house.'

'I'm sorry, Sydney. I have no wish to aggravate you, but we simply must talk about Marcus,' Susan pleaded.

'Marcus? What about Marcus? The lazy lout is still fast asleep, I'll be bound,' said Sydney.

'Well, it is Saturday and he is only a boy.'

'No, he's not. He's eighteen years old and a sad disappointment to me. He's so ungrateful for all I've done for him, the education I've given him, the car, the cricket coaching. Everything. He doesn't care about the business, or all the work I've done, standing out in cemeteries in all weathers, on call twenty-four hours a day all year and never taking holidays. This business has given your son everything a young man could wish for. And how does he repay all this kindness? I'll tell you how. By becoming a bloody architect and leaving me to run the business on my own. This is a family business and as such that boy should take his place in it. I kept your father and I've kept you and Marcus. And now it's his turn to look after me. I don't want to be standing at bloody Witton Cemetery in ten years' time, fending off offers from that bloody public schoolboy twit because I've no one to run the business when I retire. This is a family business. I said this is a family business.' By the time he'd finished this speech Sydney, far from the quiet, thin-lipped, monotonous manner in which he usually spoke, was in a high state of emotion.

'We could always employ a manager,' suggested Susan.

'Oh, for Christ's sake, you don't bloody listen to a thing, do you woman? Why are you so thick? I've just told you, this is a family business. The public expects it to be run by the owning family. If they got a manager they might just as well go to the Co-op, you bloody stupid woman.'

Susan was used to this. Sydney had called her thick,

stupid, useless and much more, every day for as long as she could remember. But she knew that Marcus' leaving on Monday would be so much harder for her to bear than Sydney's insults. 'I can see your point of view dear, but I don't think it's right to give Marcus an ultimatum that he either undertakes to join the business or leaves here penniless on Monday,' she said, with as much resolution as she could muster.

'Oh, you don't?'

'No, I don't. I would miss him terribly.'

'In that case why don't you bloody join him? You're replaceable. A live-in housekeeper wouldn't cost me much and she'd probably do a better job than you. But without me you'd both be lost. I'm the one who brings in the money, puts the clothes on your backs and the food in your mouths. You and that ungrateful son of yours, who would rather play cricket with bloody Sloane than work with me, can sod off if you like. I don't need you but you bloody well need me. He does it my way or he goes on Monday, and you can always join him if you wish,' Sydney challenged.

'But, Sydney, this is my home,' replied Susan.

'No. This is the family home and I run the family.' With that Sydney threw down the newspaper and left the kitchen for the quiet of his office. He flopped into his chair. That had been an unusually long exchange for the two of them. What a week. He had experienced the biggest funeral nightmare of his career, his mistress was playing ducks and drakes about selling her business, his son refused to join his business and now his wife dared to oppose him.

At ten o'clock Sydney rang Joyce again. She knew it would be Sydney and let the phone ring for a long time before answering. Eventually she picked up the receiver and cheekily said 'Hello Sydney' before he had a chance to speak. Sydney ignored the taunt.

'You promised me a deal,' he spat out.

'Yes I did.'

'Well, what's the price?'

'Just calm down. You can buy Higgins & Co. for a quarter of a million pounds.' There was a pause.

'What did you say? Two hundred and fifty thousand pounds? You must be joking. Blunts in Wolverhampton was sold to the Co-op last year for that and they do a thousand funerals a year. I can't afford that.'

'Okay, goodbye. I must phone Mr Sloane to say I've changed my mind.'

'Wait. Just a minute. Are you telling me that bloody Stillion Sloane has offered you that? I don't bloody believe you.'

'Okay, then you can hear it from the cemetery staff in a few weeks' time when the deal is closed. Goodbye Sydney.'

'No, wait. I'm sorry. Just tell me what happened,' said Sydney, trying to hide his indignation, and to appear calm.

'He offered me one hundred and fifty thousand. I told him you had offered me two hundred.'

'But I hadn't' interjected Sydney.

'No, but he didn't know that, and then I told him that perhaps he could buy at two hundred and thirty thousand if he put it in writing there and then, which he did. Now, as I recall, you promised me twenty thousand more than whatever Stillion offered. You, who always hold everyone to their promises with your famous claim that "my word is as good as my bond". Well, Stillion offered me two hundred and thirty thousand pounds. I have the letter here. I can read it out to you if you like. You, therefore have to offer me two hundred and fifty to keep your side of the deal and I have to sell to you at that price to keep mine. So make up your mind, Mr JP. Do we have a deal or should I phone Stillion back and say I've changed my mind? I'm easy either way. He is rather dishy and his offer shows quite clearly that he is more confident of the future than you.' Joyce's last comment was intended to twist the knife and provoke Sydney's envy and jealousy.

'That bloody boy is going to have your business over my dead body,' Sydney raged.

'If you don't calm down he may just do that. Now, your answer please. I've given you my decision, what is yours?'

'It's a deal. It's too much bloody money but it's a deal. You can have a confirming letter by hand today. I will draw up heads of agreement with my solicitor over the weekend. Bring your solicitor to my office at ten o'clock on Monday morning. I want the heads of agreement signed off then, before you start any more Dutch auctions going. Now listen to me. I have proved that my word is my bond, even though you tricked me. I want your word that this is it and that you will sign heads of agreement allowing Richards & Gridley six months to complete the transaction without fear of you talking to any other parties, including that bloody public schoolboy twit.'

'Why do you want that?' questioned Joyce.

'Because I have no intention of letting you hold any more guns to my head. Deal?'

'Yes, darling. Deal. And we can celebrate with some horny sex.'

'Please. Not over the phone.'

'Okay, get the letter round and a copy of your heads of whatever and if I don't see you before, see you on Monday at your place. I'll look forward to that. I haven't seen Susan for years. Byeeee.'

She replaced the receiver and smiled. She had done well. She had doubled the market price of her business by playing on the determination of Sydney and Stillion to win, while still selling the business to the company her father would have wanted her to. It was also where she'd wanted it to go, as long as the price was right.

Stillion's humiliation yesterday evening had been fun, but dishy twenty-nine-year-old married men didn't have long term relationships with forty-seven-year-old women. No, it had been a great one-off experience but he wasn't going to get into her life, even if he'd wanted to, which she rather doubted. She was no fool. With two hundred and fifty thousand pounds coming in and Sydney, perhaps, going out – although he mustn't know that yet – life could well be about to begin at forty-seven.

She must go or she would be late for her eleven o'clock wash, set and flirt with Carlo the Italian hairdresser in Erdington High Street. It was twenty to eleven as she left the flat, with thoughts of holidays in the South of France buzzing round in her head. Saturday, like all the days of this week before it, was a bleak and freezing day but Joyce didn't feel the cold this morning. The elation of the last twenty-four hours had placed her beyond all that.

* * *

John Palin had arrived at Sloane House early as usual and had set methodically about his duties. He was a reliable man.

John was tall, thin and resembled the French President, Valerie Giscard d'Estang, so just as one might expect a funeral director to look. He had met Stillion Sloane at the local Conservative club in the early seventies and had joined the business at Stillion's request following the death of Arthur Sloane. He was an excellent funeral arranger and a wizard administrator but had never learned to drive, and his lack of understanding of the time it took to drive from one place to another occasionally drove Stillion berserk. John hated dead bodies and avoided the mortuary. Everybody was the same dead. He even had little genuine sympathy for their living relatives. Years of watching the grief of others had immuned him like most funeral workers. It was simply the climate in which he worked. But his own grief, when eventually hit by personal bereavement, would be as overwhelming as those he witnessed every day; familiarity, however long, does nothing to insulate us from our own grief.

John liked the West Indians; they were polite, grateful, amusing and spent a lot on their funerals. Asians, he found, tended to be rude and ungrateful, and did their funerals on the cheap. But most of all he couldn't abide bossy middle-class women; they chose the cheapest coffins, saying, 'It's only going to be burnt, isn't it?' but then rang every fifteen minutes for the next two days, wanting to make lots of non-standard changes to the arrangements, and odd requests, as if they were organising a daughter's wedding. Naturally they didn't expect to pay a penny extra for any of it. John was famous at Sloanes for spotting these women even as they got out of their cars on the forecourt for the first time, and all knew what he meant when they heard him say, 'here comes an Upton Oak and three days of "Now, Mr Palin, I . . ."'

John had arranged such a funeral on Friday, and now

the telephone had started to ring. 'Right, madam. Absolutely madam. Don't worry, madam. Leave it to me, madam.' His head was getting closer and closer to the telephone on his desk.' I have got it all under control madam. Rest assured it will all be dealt with, madam. Thank you, madam.' He put the receiver down. 'Fucking cow.'

* * *

Stillion had dropped off to sleep again, comforted by his conversation with Stephanie. Eventually, at nine o'clock, he got up and had a bath. At a quarter to eleven, having shaved and dressed, he phoned John Palin to make sure all was well at Sloane House. It was; four funerals had come in already that morning. 'One's a West Indian casket job, big money,' John told Stillion, 'one a family from Edgbaston, the usual cheap job. "Well, it's only going to be burned isn't it?"' he continued in a la-di-dah voice. 'All kippers and curtains those bloody Edgbaston lot. Then there's a Catholic one from Father O'Rourke – now there's a turn up for the books. And a headdress job.'

'You mean a Sikh funeral, John,' said Stillion, sternly.

'Yes a Sikh funeral,' John repeated dutifully but unrepentant.

'Yes, a Sikh funeral. Their money is as good as the next man's and if we take it they are the client and entitled to the same respect as anyone else.'

John waited for this oft-heard speech of Stillion's to finish before he continued. 'So that's forty-eight funerals for the week. Bloody great ain't it?' John knew that Sloanes did eight hundred funerals a year, on average sixteen a week, so forty-eight a week must mean that business was booming. But Stillion always remembered what his father taught him: what you don't get today, you'll get tomorrow, and what you do have today, you can't have again. People only die once but they all die eventually. So you don't have to wish death upon anyone. The only thing a funeral director need worry about was that when someone died their families chose his services and not anyone else's. Stillion knew that this week's impressive figures were probably due to the winter death rate, and that the coming summer would be quieter than usual as a result. But he was nevertheless very pleased that Sloanes wasn't being bypassed as a result of Thursday's cock-ups. It may be that these families hadn't heard about what had happened and that anyone who had wouldn't use Sloane & Sons. He couldn't tell. It was too early for that and he wasn't going to worry about it now, he had a marriage to save.

'Better go. See you on Monday,' he said to John.

'Okay, have a nice weekend,' replied John, adding, 'Jones tells me there was some commotion here last night and that you were bleeding and that Vicky and Marcus Gridley were here late with you. Is everything okay?'

'Yeah, Yeah. It was another little piece of Sydney Gridley business. I'll tell you all about it on Monday. Oh, yes, and can you leave a note on Vicky's desk asking her to find out the maximum size of the personal boxes at the Midland Bank in Hockley?'

'Sure, what have you got in mind?'

'A body bag with a baseball bat in it. Got to dash. Oh, by the way,' Stillion's voice dropped, 'it looks as though that little shit Gridley has got Higgins & Co..'

'Couldn't we offer more?'

'I offered top price at last night's meeting and she said he'd beat it and that her father had always wanted it to go to John Richards.'

'Yes, but John Richards is dead and old man Higgins would never have wanted his business to go to Sydney if he knew the sort of tricks he got up to. Couldn't you have told her about Thursday?' John asked.

'What, and then gone on to tell her about us and Friday, because if I hadn't Sydney would have. None of us should ever mention any of that to anyone,' said Stillion firmly.

'Well, okay, but couldn't you just have given her one?'

'Really. John, what an imagination you have mate. I must go.'

'Will you think about giving her one? Everybody knows she's up for it.'

'I'm a married man and I'm late. See you Monday.'

Stillion put down the phone and then remembered

he hadn't got his car. It was still in the garage at Sloane House. He called the local cab firm and got a car back to the office, where he rescued the XJS from the fleet garage. He raced out towards Sutton Park and on to his mother's house in Streetly. He had to speed to make up time. He didn't want to be late. Stephanie had said midday and truly sorry people trying to make an impression weren't late. He mused that with his luck this week he was bound to be stopped for speeding. But he wasn't and the midday news was just starting on the car radio as he pulled into his mother's long drive.

He rang the front doorbell. Unusually it was his mother who answered.

'Oh, it's you. You had better come in.' Stillion stepped into the large oak-panelled hall of his childhood. It never changed. He always missed his father particularly during the first few seconds after he stepped inside the hall. Indeed it had been in this room he had penned his despairing lament 'White Swans and Silver Geese' following his father's death and on the morning of his funeral.

'I've got a dinner party tonight, so I can't give you long,' said Mary abruptly, leading him into the dining room.

'That's okay, it's Steppie I've come to see.'

'You're too late. She's gone.'

'Gone! Gone where? When? She told me to come here at midday.'

'Well, she obviously changed her mind. A bit like

you changing your mind about your marriage vows, I suppose. Funny, isn't it, that you, the great, good Stillion Sloane can change your mind like your clothes and we should all understand but Stephanie fails to keep an appointment and I should be sorry for you because you've driven all the way out here.'

'No, I'm not saying that. I am saying I'm sorry. I'm saying it won't happen again and I'm asking you to tell me where she is.'

'I don't know,' replied Mary.

'Don't give me that shit. She would have told you where she was going.'

'Don't bring your gutter language into this house. And what's more, say I do know, I'm not telling you. Now, if you'll excuse me, I've got a table to lay, food to prepare and flowers to arrange. Goodbye.'

'Mother, I'm your son, not the man from the census office. For God's sake, where is she?'

'Goodbye,' Mary repeated. Then, raising her voice so that Josey could hear her, she continued, 'Josey, see Stillion out please, he's going now. And Stillion, try not to phone me when *News at Ten* is on in the future, there's a good boy.'

'I'll see myself out mother. You should see a doctor; you're stark, staring, raving mad. Goodbye.'

As Josey opened the door to let him out she whispered, 'Twelve thirty-eight London train from Birmingham International. First class is at the front of the train. Hurry or you'll miss her.'

Stillion kissed Josey on the cheek. 'Thanks Josey,' he whispered back and sprinted for the car. The XJS squealed out of the drive. Mary wandered back into the hall just in time to see Stillion's car disappear out of sight. 'You told him, didn't you?' she challenged Josey.

'That I did,' replied Joey defiantly.

'I knew you would,' said Mary, pleased, 'I knew you couldn't resist.'

Josey shut the front door. Mary returned to the dining room leaving Josey to ask herself why her employer couldn't have told Stillion herself, as she had so obviously wanted him to know.

Stillion was driving the XJS hard over the speed bumps along the private road beyond his mother's drive. Fierce acceleration followed by desperate braking meant that the poor car bottomed every time it landed on the far side of each bump. The road seemed to go on for ever. He was going to have to take risks if he was to get to the train. There were two routes to choose between: the quiet but less direct country route, by the Belfry golf course and through the NEC, would take half an hour; the more direct, busier route through Sutton Coldfield and Erdington, which picked up the fast collector dual carriageway that ran down the side of the M6 and on to the station, would take anything between twenty and forty minutes, depending on the traffic. There was really no choice, he had to take the direct route.

He turned right out of the private road and blazed over the traffic lights, up the hill past the pub, the shops, over kindly green lights by Mere Green church and down the hill towards Sutton Coldfield. It started to rain. It would. He turned on the wipers.

Traffic was tailing back from the roundabout at the bottom of the hill. Stillion had to slow. He knew he couldn't afford this queue. In a split second he made a decision. He pulled the automatic lever down from 'D' to '1', hit the right pedal hard, turned on the headlights to full beam, dragged the wheel to the right and propelled the car down the wrong side of the road and straight at the oncoming traffic. Cars braked. Cars stopped. Cars pulled up on to the pavement. Horns sounded. Men swore and gesticulated fingers as he made the island and took it on the wrong side. He was through. He was going to make it because he needed to. It was a matter of life and death and nobody, he decided, not even a policeman, was going to stop him. He headed for Sutton Coldfield, weaving in and out of the traffic. He overtook. He undertook. He even used the pavement. As the car screamed round the one-way circuit through Sutton Coldfield and up the main road towards Erdington Stillion put on the hazard flashers and sounded his horn when necessary, which was often.

Out the other side of Erdington he approached the lights at Yenton. There was very little traffic. The lights were green. Please God, stay green. Yes, please

God, let the lights stay green. He was just three hundred yards short when they changed to red. There was a garage on the left corner with exits to both roads. Instantly and instinctively Stillion knew what to do. He hit the brakes, spun the steering wheel left, pulled up the handbrake and entered the garage forecourt in a four wheel drift. He released the handbrake, corrected the car's position and hit the accelerator, steering straight through the one vacant line of pumps to the wide-eyed astonishment of motorists refuelling their vehicles on the other lines. It was exactly half past twelve as he shot out from the other side of the garage, pulling up the handbrake again, spinning the wheel left and joining the two lanes of traffic which were enjoying the green light advantage until a midnight-blue XJS leaped out of the garage without pausing and drifted with all four wheels locked sideways through the inside lane and across into the outside. Cars in both lanes were forced to hit their brakes hard on the wet road. Stillion released all brakes, hit the right pedal again and the car sped away from the danger zone, apparently unaware of the chaos left behind in his wake. One man filling his car at the garage was so spellbound by the five seconds of madness he had just witnessed that he failed to notice that he was now pumping petrol over his feet.

Stillion made the island at the start of the collector road by twelve thirty-three. He had five minutes. With his right foot on the boards the car hit the road's bump and dip combination at its beginning and flew through the air before landing hard enough to send sparks flying as the chassis smacked the tarmac. A hundred. A hundred and twenty. A hundred and forty. Off the clock. The collector road was empty which was just as well because Stillion would have taken the XJS to the limit whether he'd had company or not.

At the end of the collector he span round the island, down the hill and turned left at the next island before powering up the drag through Chelmsley Wood and turning right onto the single carriageway that led to the station. He had about a mile to go and two minutes to get there, park and run for the train. Please God let bloody British Rail be as late as usual. He overtook a transit van and just got back to his side, out of the path of an oncoming car, with inches to spare. He roared over the bridge and, looking down and to the left, saw the London train pulling into the station. He had one minute. He skidded left into the station, right around the small roundabout and roared up to the main entrance.

He grabbed the ignition keys and the body bag and left the car on the taxi rank with the hazard and headlights still blazing. He dashed up the escalator three steps at a time. He skidded hard right on the slippery stone floor. He was at full speed as he burst through the ticket barrier. 'Hey! Where do you think you're going? Come back,' cried the fat ticket inspector. 'Come back. I said come back.' The inspector left his seat to give chase. Stillion bounded down six steps at a time in the dash to make the platform, to the sounds of a Spencer Davis song playing in the railway cafe off to right. 'Keep on Running'. 'You. I said come back,' yelled the fat ticket inspector, his breasts wobbling as he bounced down just one step at a time. Stillion peeled off to the right and was on the platform. He turned left to face the front section of the train, and just caught sight of Stephanie getting into the second coach, a small overnight bag in her hand. 'Steppie,' he yelled, 'Steppie, wait!' He ran flat out. She turned and saw him but got on and shut the door. She didn't want to, but she couldn't help pulling down the window and looking back. The train started to pull out. Stillion was up by her. He pleaded, 'Steppie, don't go. Please don't go. I love you.'

'Go away Stillion,' she replied. The train speed picked up. Stillion was about to run out of platform. He had not come this far to lose. He leaped at the train just before the platform finished beneath his feet, baseball bat and body bag still in his left hand. His feet landed on the wooden footplate. With his free right hand he grabbed at the open window, managing to get a grip at the second attempt. He may never have been granted a second attempt if Steppie hadn't grabbed his flying jacket front as the first attempt failed and he began to fall backwards.

The inspector had made it to the platform and had seen Stillion leap against the train. He screamed to the guard as the guard's van passed him, 'Stop the train. Stop the train, there's a man clinging onto the outside.' The brakes squealed and the train stopped slowly.

Stillion looked at Stephanie. 'Steppie, don't leave me. I can't make it without you. I love you.'

'Do you, darling?' She threw her arms round his neck. He had risked his life for her and in that split second the possibility of him being taken away from her forever by death had flashed through her mind, and she knew that even if it was against the logic of her head, her heart wanted this man, her lover, back in her arms. They kissed. The first-class carriage applauded. Stillion opened the door and helped Stephanie down just as the fat inspector, followed by the West Indian guard, came jogging along the track side.

'What the hell do you think you're up to son?' asked the ticket inspector. Before Stillion could reply he continued, 'It's an offence to travel without a ticket. It's an offence to board a moving train. And what's more, you've caused an InterCity train to be stopped. You're in trouble.'

'Yes, I suppose I am, but at least I've got my wife back,' smiled Stillion.

'This is not a joking matter. You'd better come with me,' commanded the inspector.

'Look, I'm really sorry. I'm not going to ride. I just wanted to stop my wife from riding and she had a ticket to ride,' Stillion explained.

A passenger poked her head out of the train window

and said to the inspector, 'Look, can't you tell they're in love. Haven't you ever been in love?'

'That's not the point,' said the ticket man.

'Okay, man, I'm leaving them to you,' said the guard to the ticket inspector, returning to his van. The train began to pull out for the second time. The ticket inspector escorted Stillion and Stephanie back to the platform and up the escalator to his box. It was Saturday and he couldn't find a policeman anywhere. He explained the matter to a senior colleague who seemed to be more concerned that the inspector wasn't checking tickets. He suggested it might be a sensible idea to take the couple's address and then get on with his job. Turning to the Sloanes he warned them that Stillion may well be contacted and even prosecuted by the police following submission of the ticket inspector's report. Stillion nodded his understanding and gave their address. They were released.

They walked hand in hand back towards the escalator that took them down to the road. 'Oh my God,' exclaimed Stillion as he remembered the car. He ran down the escalator and out of the doors, pulling Stephanie with him. Outside the station they turned immediately right to find a gaggle of taxi drivers around the XJS, bemoaning its presence on their rank. Stillion, with Steppie in one hand, the baseball bat and her overnight bag in the other, squeezed through the small crowd and offered profuse, polite apologies, explaining that he was most sorry but that it had been a matter of life or death. As he spoke Stillion put Steppie's bag and his body bag in the boot and locked it, then opened the passenger door for his woman. Then, before the group of taxi drivers could recover from the distraction of Steppie's long and lovely legs to demand a proper explanation, Stillion climbed into the driver's seat and, with a wave and a smile, drove off.

They retraced his earlier route down the collector road, much more slowly than Stillion had driven it twenty minutes earlier.

'What happened to your face?' Stephanie asked, looking at the damage of the previous evening. 'Did Harry do that?'

'No, it was Harry plus friends. They decided to give me a lesson in baseball. I deserved it, I suppose.'

'Is that why you're carrying a baseball bat in a body bag around with you?' she asked.

'You mean to hit him back with?' he replied.

'Yes, because if it is I don't think it is a very . . .'

'Good idea,' he finished for her. 'No, nor do I. It's not for that. Harry and I won't be talking about Wednesday again. Listen, I know it's going to be hard to forgive me, but please try, even if it takes time. I don't underestimate what I've done or the pain it has caused you but try to believe that I never want to feel like I have in the last twelve hours ever again. Please try to believe how very much I do love you,' he said quietly, with great feeling.

'Stillion. I have loved you, and when you were

falling from the train just now I knew that however hurt I was, I still loved you. But whether we can ever be the same only time will tell. Until now, if you've been working late or out at the cricket club, I've never worried. Now I know I'll fear my imagination. We'll have to re-create trust,' said Stephanie, thoughtfully.

'Would it help if you got even?' Stillion asked.

'Would it help you with the guilt?' she asked back.

'No it wouldn't help me but...'

'But nothing,' she interrupted. 'Two wrongs don't make a right. I hurt right now because I love you, not because I was dumped for a night in favour of Lottie. I'll give it a try, which is more than you deserve. You know something, you look more like a gangster than a funeral director this morning. Lunch?'

'Gino's?'

'Yep. Followed by some serious retail therapy which you can pay for. You can also come and help me choose so don't even think about going to Villa Park.' Stephanie knew that, although Stillion had destroyed her trust and maybe damaged their relationship for ever, if they were to stand a chance then she would have to try as much as him to turn the clock back.

'Talking of clothes,' said Stillion, 'how the hell could you have survived in London with only an overnight bag?'

'That was my survival plan. A brand new wardrobe on your Harvey Nichols' and Harrods' accounts to be worn at endless dinners at the Ritz, the Caprice and San Lorenzo's on the joint credit card and sleep taken in between such fun at the Dorchester on the company account that your father opened years ago and that you have never closed in case we needed it.'

'You wicked girl!' exclaimed Stillion. They laughed. Instinctively they each reached for the other's hand. He was so grateful to have her back. She was his best friend. He enjoyed her company. She, although still shocked, hurt and unsure of him, couldn't help but be dazzled and impressed by his act of brave love at the station. She was going to try to make her marriage work, despite his stupid lapse, because she had never found another man remotely as interesting as Stillion, and had no desire to.

Half of him wanted to make a clean break and confess to his sessions with Gillian and Joyce too, but the other half told him that this would be madness and that it might destroy Steppie. And who could blame her? Three different women in a week. All three acts just motivated by sex and greed. Not a nice picture. Not a man to be trusted ever again. And with three in a week who would believe that it stopped there? No, put the other two to the back of his mind and just hope and pray neither of them did or said anything to put his marriage in jeopardy. They may be two swords of Damocles hanging over his head, but there was no alternative and he only had himself to blame.

An intimate and happy lunch at Gino's was followed

by much laughing and spending of money in Rackhams for Charles Jordan shoes, in Just Imagine for clothes and at Johnson's for a beautiful and very expensive three-colour gold ring adorned by a large solitaire diamond. Then they headed home, where they crashed on the floor of the snug, all the shopping bags around them, and celebrated an Aston Villa win by tugging each other's clothes off and making a kind of love that Stillion hadn't experienced that week. He'd been a willing prostitute for the likeable Gillian, he'd foolishly given in to Lottie's excited lust and he'd allowed himself to be humiliated by the sadistic Joyce for the sake of ambition. But this was a demonstration of love and they both came in a crescendo of desire and relief.

* * *

Mary finished her week entertaining her friends with the wonderful food, wine, flowers and chat that made her dinner parties so good. Josey, as usual, served dinner and cleared it away.

John Palin was at home watching *Match of the Day*, having spent the afternoon Christmas shopping with his wife.

Elton Field was at home with an angry wife, little money and even less hope.

Rolley Brown spent the afternoon in his flat, watching the horseracing on *Grandstand*. He didn't plan on moving until he learned that West Bromwich Albion had lost. After that he didn't fancy staying in for *Match of the Day*.

Lawrence Kemp and Walter Warburton had gone drinking over in Dudley. Lawrence fancied the drink, Walter only decided to go when he heard the Albion result.

Victoria Thomas was having dinner with her boyfriend in the Warwickshire village of Knowle.

Gillian Weston had gone with Joyce Higgins to the Dudley Road Hospital ward sisters' and staff nurses' Christmas Party. They both hoped to get laid.

Father O'Rourke put his feet up in front of the presbytery fire, with a large drop of the hard stuff in his hand. He was still in a mild state of shock from his ride in Sydney's limo, but whiskey, Irish folk songs on the gramophone and warm feet seemed to bring him comfort.

Reverend Price was alone in the huge, cold vicarage, save for the dog asleep at his feet. He read the *Telegraph* and half listened to the Saturday night play on Radio 4. He tried not to think of the Martin funeral.

Winston Wylde was out with his wife and family, leading the choir on a mammoth candlelit carol-singing procession around Handsworth and Lozells. He'd forgotten about the Griffiths funeral already; it wasn't his fault and he was just too busy to dwell on such matters.

Harry and Lottie Wilkes were out to Saturday night

dinner as usual. The same old restaurant with the same old people, but for the first time in years Lottie was making an effort and was grateful for what she'd got. Harry appeared to be happy in public. Privately, he was angry, depressed and unable to forgive or forget.

Sydney Gridley was having dinner with his solicitor at the Midland Hotel in Birmingham city centre. They were drawing up the heads of agreement as planned. Repairs to his smashed fleet were underway, and he'd been able to hire a temporary fleet until they were completed. The funerals kept coming in, and he had secured the acquisition of Higgins & Co. Even better, Sloane had suffered two equally public setbacks, not got the Higgins deal and with any luck had been beaten to a pulp last night. Sydney didn't spare a thought for his wife and son. He'd no need to. They always did as they were told and would continue to do so.

Whatever the damage that had been done over the last few days to Stillion and Stephanie Sloane, Elton Field, Rolley Brown, Victoria Thomas, Marcus Gridley, the priesthood, the mourners, the cemetery staff or even Sydney Gridley, who had invented most of it, none was greater than the damage done to Susan Gridley. Marcus had forced her to look in the mirror and admit the truth about her existence. He might lose his home and inheritance on Monday, but if he left without her she would lose her very reason for living. To be bullied by Sydney for the rest of her life and not to be able to see her baby was a prospect too unbelievably bleak for even Susan to bear. She was desperate.

Marcus saw this and, to his credit, cancelled his night out at a Christmas party for old Solihullians to be with his mother. They had little more than twenty-four hours to solve their problems.

7

The End

At ten to ten on Monday morning Joyce Higgins walked confidently into Richards & Gridley's reception, accompanied by her solicitor. She was met by Susan Gridley. As they embraced Joyce thought that Susan looked rather less dreary than she remembered her during the years of their friendship. She didn't dwell on this observation because Sydney arrived, dressed smartly in a blue suit, white shirt, red polka-dot tie and matching pocket handkerchief. He had arranged for Rolley Brown to conduct the morning's funerals while he concluded the business at hand. He also noticed that his wife appeared very smart but like Joyce had little time to consider it. As Susan showed Joyce and her solicitor into Sydney's office he wondered vaguely whether she was planning to leave today after all. But no, she wouldn't do that. Whatever, he would deal with her later, once the acquisition of his mistress's business was put finally beyond the grasp of Stillion Sloane.

Sydney's solicitor was already waiting in Sydney's

office. The meeting was just about to begin when Marcus put his head around the door.

'Goodbye, Father,' he said.

'What?' Sydney was annoyed by the interruption.

'It's Monday. I'm just saying goodbye.'

Sydney didn't want Marcus to leave without knowing where he was going. Indeed, Sydney didn't want him to leave at all, but he had given the boy an ultimatum and intended to see it through. Marcus must learn not to defy his father. And now here he was embarrassing him in front of Joyce and his solicitor. Susan would have a forwarding address for him; Marcus wouldn't leave without telling her where he was going.

'Goodbye then,' said Sydney, turning away from Marcus and back to the meeting.

At a quarter past ten the reception bell rang. Sydney heard it, and when it didn't ring twice relaxed in the knowledge that Susan or one of the staff would have answered it. Of course, that must be the reason why Susan was looking so smart today – one of the arrangement staff must be ill and she was standing in for her.

By half past ten the heads of agreement had been signed and Sydney was as near to happy as was possible for him. Realising that he had been remiss in not offering his guests refreshment, he telephoned through to the general office. 'Come to my office please,' he asked the arranger who answered. There was a knock at the door. 'Enter,' called Sydney. The door opened and in came Susan. 'Yes?' said Sydney. 'What do you want? I asked for one of the arrangers to come in. Our guests should have had tea half an hour ago.'

'Would you like tea now?' Susan politely asked the assembly. Before any of them could answer Sydney blurted, 'No, they wouldn't like tea. Why the bloody hell would they want tea now, you stupid woman. They want champagne now.'

'Champagne?' said Susan.

'Yes, yes, champagne woman. Bloody champagne. We have just signed heads of agreement that give the company of Richards & Gridley the irrevocable right, provided we meet the terms and the timetable, to buy Higgins & Co.. We have won. And that bloody Sloane man has lost. So hurry up with the champagne.'

'Sydney, I have no intention of fetching champagne for you and your mistress. I'm going to Barbados with Marcus and we will be there for Christmas.' There was a general intake of breath in the room. Those who knew Susan had never heard her speak so confidently and those who didn't know her knew that this was no ordinary speech. Sydney and Joyce looked nervous. Susan continued, 'Sydney, you have always been in control of this business and have made all our domestic decisions. You have often told Marcus and I how grateful we should be to you. For fear of displeasing you Marcus has spent his entire young life doing what you wanted him to, with little thought for himself. I have washed, cleaned, cooked and scrubbed. I've been talked at, bawled at and generally treated like a skivvy, and I put up with it because I knew I wasn't attractive.'

'This is not the place,' Sydney interrupted her.

'Oh, yes, it bloody well is,' said Susan with venom. Sydney was taken aback. He'd never heard her swear before. 'Oh yes, it bloody well is,' she repeated. 'I have wasted the best years of my life being grateful to a man for marrying me. A man who didn't love me and who only wanted to marry the business. And he has treated me little better than a dog turd caught on the bottom of his shoe, while having an affair with my childhood friend behind my back. And in case you two don't know who that is,' she said, turning to the solicitors, 'then perhaps Joyce should tell you.'

'Sydney, I'm not staying here to listen to this,' said Joyce, unable to look at Susan as she stood up.

'Sit down, whore. For nearly half my life I have suffered in silence over your affair with my husband. Then, when Sydney threatened to throw Marcus out on his ear because he didn't want to join the business, I learned that Marcus, my only child, knew about your shameful affair. He didn't think I knew and when he found out that I'd turned a blind eye to it, I wanted to die. But Marcus made me realise that neither of you are worth it. So we're off to Heathrow for the three o'clock flight to Bridgetown for the best Christmas we've ever had.'

'Don't be idiotic you stupid woman, you haven't any money,' growled Sydney, who was seething with rage and embarrassment at his wife's behaviour.

'You're wrong there, Sydney dear. I have three things in common with your whore. Firstly, you. Secondly, both of our fathers left us funeral directing businesses. Thirdly, we have both sold out.'

There was a brief silence as the implications of what Susan had just said sank in. Then there was a general gasp. Sydney, white and shaken, whispered, 'What?' Then his bottom jaw fell slack in shock, and fear.

'I've sold my seventy per cent stake and, as sole signing trustee, Marcus' ten per cent stake. Between us we raised three hundred thousand pounds. So, Sydney, Marcus and I will easily be able to afford Christmas, this year and for many years to come. The new owner has said they will allow me to stay on in the flat, so I would be pleased if you could move out while we're away. Perhaps you could move in with Joyce?'

Joyce had no intention of letting Sydney move in with her, but her main concern at this moment was her deal. Three hundred thousand for eighty per cent of Richards & Gridley was a good sale, but then they did conduct five hundred funerals a year. That made the two hundred and fifty thousand that she had negotiated a particularly spectacular price for a company that only did three hundred funerals a year. It couldn't be jeopardised.

'What about my deal with Richards & Gridley?' asked Joyce, looking up to Susan for the first time since childhood.

'What about it?' retorted Susan.

'Well, will the new owner of Richard's & Gridley honour my deal?'

'Oh, I believe he has to and probably wants to. But the best thing to do is to ask him yourself. He arrived about fifteen minutes ago with the banker's draft for us. Perhaps you heard the bell go.' She opened the office door into the reception. 'Would you like to come in?'

Stillion Sloane walked through the door. 'Good morning, Sydney,' he said, his smiling face still battered.

* * *

The reception bell rang. It was Mr Razek Singh.